A Deadly Confession

A Lipton St Faith Mystery

A Deadly Confession

KEITH FINNEY

LUME BOOKS

LUME BOOKS

Published in 2021 by Lume Books
30 Great Guildford Street,
Borough, SE1 0HS

ISBN 978-1-83901-223-5

Typeset using Atomik ePublisher from Easypress Technologies

www.lumebooks.co.uk

For Joan

Chapter 1: Night Walk

Witton Wood looked and sounded idyllic as vicar's daughter, Anna Grix, and American army lieutenant, Eddie Elsner, took advantage of a late September Indian summer's evening. A light breeze blew lazily through a maze of tree branches, causing a million leaves to dance in unison.

For forty-five minutes, the two companions breathed in an intoxicating mix of damp tree ferns, tall grasses and delicate forest flowers as they picked their way through one overgrown trail after another.

'What time did you say we arrived?'

Eddie looked at his watch. 'Well, it's 9.45 pm now and we've been walking about three-quarters of an hour, so that would make it 9.00 pm.'

Anna raised her arm and pulled back her light cardigan sleeve to reveal a small wristwatch given to her five years ago by her parents to mark her twenty-first birthday. 'You didn't by any chance set your watch to the clock in the church steeple, did you? I thought it odd you wanted to take a run-out so late in the evening.' The few seconds of silence that followed confirmed her deduction. 'The villagers agreed they should set the clock one hour slow to confuse the enemy, would you believe? Didn't it strike you as a little odd that we were losing the light?'

Eddie looked at the Radium dial of his military issue watch and shook his wrist, before looking at the glowing dial again. 'You mean to tell me, as well as turning all the road signs around, you lot have also set up your own time zone?'

He shook his head as his companion offered a confident smile. 'Well, it caught you out, didn't it? And if we assume the Nazis are stupid, they don't stand a chance, so we'll all be safe.'

'You believe that nonsense?' replied Eddie as he kicked a short length of broken branch out of the way.

'Not for a minute, but if it makes the locals feel one ounce less anxious, it's worth it. I'd have thought the Germans are far too clever to fall for that old trick. Of course, as for you Americans, well, that's quite another matter.'

You walked straight into that one, fella.

The light-hearted exchange ended as a dreadful scream chilled the evening air. Rebounding from one gnarled tree trunk to the next, the unsettling sound caused a menagerie of colourful birds to flit about in panic amongst the dense canopy.

'What the…' Anna froze, unable to finish her sentence, instead looking around to pinpoint from where the woman's distress call had originated. 'She could be anywhere. I think we should go this way.' Anna pointed to a tree-clad embankment to her left.

'It's as good a guess as any. Come on, we'd better get a move on,' replied Eddie as he scrambled up the gentle incline, his steps cushioned by a thick bed of compressed leaf mould.

As they struggled to clear a path through a patchwork of low spindly branches, a sharp crack pierced the air. Instinctively, they ducked.

'Gunshot?'

'Difficult to tell. It doesn't sound like an American rifle, nor the Lee Enfield you lot use, but we should presume the worst. Come on, we may still be in time to help her.'

'Look, there, I see something.' Anna rushed forward with little regard for her own safety as she tore through the untidy undergrowth and down the far side of the embankment. Almost tripping over a surface tree root disguised among the organic litter, Anna managed to stay on her feet as she neared a figure lying face down in a patch of brambles and mixed grasses.

'Have you found something?' shouted Eddie as he struggled to catch up with his companion.

She didn't answer. Instead, Anna stood silently, staring down at the still figure of a young woman.

'Is she breathing?'

Eddie's question shocked her into action. Kneeling to one side of the prone figure, she felt for a pulse. 'I think she's gone, poor soul.'

No one deserves this.

Anna couldn't help contrasting their beautiful surroundings, its aroma and sounds, with the sad scene at her feet.

'You stay here and keep your wits about you. I'll take a quick look around to see if the culprit is still in the area.'

Practical as ever.

Eddie's warning put Anna on edge.

How far can he have gone in the few minutes since she screamed?

Minutes later, the lieutenant returned. 'No sign of him, I'm afraid. He could be anywhere by now. Are you OK here if I shoot off to call the police?'

Anna didn't answer; instead, she focussed on the woman's still frame.

'Did you hear what I—'

'She's dressed for a good ramble; you know, hiking boots and

3

backpack. What I don't understand is, there's no blood, nor can I see any trace of a bullet wound.'

Eddie came nearer and knelt over the dead woman. 'That's not quite the case – see here? a small trickle of blood.'

His companion struggled to see. 'Not really, no.'

The American retrieved his handkerchief from a trouser pocket and wrapped one corner around two fingers. Next, he gently parted a section of the woman's hair. 'See it? She's been hit with something hard. It's not caused too much damage to the skin, so I'd say a lump of wood or a metal pipe was used – but nothing with a sharp edge, nor more than two inches wide by my reckoning.'

This time Anna had a clear view. 'Yes, I get what you're saying.'

'It's probably safe to say she was waiting for someone, perhaps even the person who did this to her. Perhaps they intended to camp out somewhere. To confirm what actually killed her, my guess aside, we'll have to wait until the police get here because she may have injuries to her front. We'd better get a move on and make the call.'

Nodding, Anna slowly paced around the petite corpse. 'Shouldn't we at least look in her rucksack? It may give us a clue what she was really up to in the middle of a secluded wood.'

He shook his head. 'Let's not upset the inspector. If we open the bag, it won't change what's happened, but it might alter what the inspector lets us get up to... Hang on, be careful. There's something in front of your right foot.'

Anna froze before looking down to see what he'd seen. 'A coin?'

'Let's see what we have here.' Eddie crouched down, took out a pen from an inside pocket of his army jacket and used it to pull away several strands of grass that cradled the metal disc.

Moving his head nearer the object to get a better view, he flipped

4

the coin over with the end of his pen. 'It's an Italian fifty centesimi piece minted in 1939.'

Anna bent forward. 'Do you think it's been there long?'

He shrugged his shoulders. 'There's no way of saying for sure. It could be something and nothing. Anyway, let's get the police up here.'

'I'll go. You stay with her; I need to clear my head.' Anna moved off before her companion responded.

This place makes me feel uneasy.

After retracing her steps to the entrance of Witton Wood, Anna arrived at the main road and looked to her left to see the reassuring sight of a public telephone box.

Please don't be broken.

Having covered the fifty yards in double quick time, she opened the door and gave a sigh of relief to find all as it should be.

'Yes… that's correct, Witton Wood… I'll wait here to guide you in. Please come as quickly as you can.'

The next twenty minutes felt like a lifetime as she waited for the police to arrive. Eventually, Anna heard the reassuring sound of a bell ringing as a black car approached from her right.

Thank heavens they're here.

She could see her long-time friend Constable Tom Bradshaw at the wheel as he brought the squad car to a screeching halt across the gravel entrance to Witton Wood, causing small stones to spray forward as a cloud of dust enveloped the front of the vehicle. The familiar figure of Detective Inspector Spillers sat in the passenger seat, his eyes fixed on Anna as he opened the car door.

'What are you doing out here so late?'

His question threw her for a few seconds. 'Without putting too fine a point on it, Inspector, it's as well we were.'

Tom Bradshaw silenced the piercing trill of the police bell, unfolded his tall frame from the car and strolled around the vehicle to join his superior. 'Is the lieutenant with the body?'

Anna nodded. 'It's about a five-minute walk.' She turned to begin the short return journey without checking if Tom and the inspector were following. The occasional grunt and 'damn' signalled to her that her companions were having their own battle with the vengeful undergrowth and insidious brambles as they attempted to make headway.

'I thought I'd lost you.' Eddie's calm tone settled Anna, even though she was back in the presence of the dead woman.

'Hilarious, I don't think,' responded Anna.

Detective Inspector Spillers' concentration remained on the body and the immediate area surrounding the tragic scene. 'What can you tell me?'

Eddie recounted the events of the evening as Spillers continued to take in every visual detail available to him. 'You think they shot this unfortunate lady?'

'I said we heard what sounded like a rifle shot. As you can see, there are no obvious signs of a bullet wound. The only injury we found is a small cut to the back of her head.'

Spillers crouched next to the body. 'Are you taking notes, Constable?'

Tom wet the tip of his pencil on his tongue and nodded.

'Much though it goes against the grain, we must turn her over. Are you willing to lend a hand? I know it's unpleasant. However, it's necessary.'

Anna froze momentarily at the thought of touching the body.

Pull yourself together. It's not the first time you've done this.

The sergeant continued to record the scene as the other three positioned themselves equally along the young woman's torso.

'We'd better take her rucksack off before we do anything.' The inspector spoke in a low, gentle voice to the victim as he delicately slid the straps from the woman's shoulders and lifted the canvas bag clear of her body. 'There, we're all done.'

Spillers loosened the white pull chord at the neck of the rucksack and peered into its interior. 'She was going camping all right, except there's not enough equipment for a comfortable night. She must have intended to meet someone here who had the rest of the stuff.'

A few seconds later, the inspector pulled out a folded card from deep within the grey bag. 'It's her ID card.' Spillers opened the document so the others could read the details. 'Well, we have a name: Ruth Cotton.' After handing her ID to the constable, Spillers turned his attention back to the body. 'OK, we'll roll on my count – one, two, gently now.'

Moving the body as one, they completed the upsetting manoeuvre without disturbing the crime scene.

'A bullet didn't kill this woman. There're no other obvious signs of injury apart from this.' The inspector pointed to a small cut above Ruth's left eye. 'Probably from when she hit the ground, but it wasn't enough to kill. That leaves the damage to the back of the victim's head as the most likely cause of death.'

'We also came across this, Inspector.' Eddie pointed to a spot four feet away from the body.

Spillers stood and walked the short distance with deliberately delicate steps, checking every inch of ground as he did so. 'Isn't there a camp for Italian prisoners of war near here?'

'It's about a mile west of here, Inspector,' replied the constable while making a note of his superior's observation.

'OK, I think we know where our investigation must begin.

'My dear, we thought something dreadful had happened to you. Where have you been until this time?'

Anna looked at the large round clock on the kitchen wall as she and the lieutenant fell into their chairs and leant on the white scrubbed surface of the pine dining table. 'Is it really 1.00 am?'

The vicar and his wife, Helen, looked on in concern as Anna told them what had happened.

'Do the police know who the unfortunate woman is? If so, I must visit her next of kin later this morning. They'll be devastated.' The deep baritone sound of her father's voice lent extra gravity to the situation.

'Detective Inspector Spillers gave her bag a quick search before the light failed. He found an identity card for someone called Ruth Cotton. It's not a name I recognise, so assume she's not from around here.'

Anna's mother brought a saucepan of milk to temperature on the AGA before filling two white enamel mugs with the steaming liquid and carrying them over to the table. 'This will help. Come on, both of you, drink up.'

They needed no second invitation, and each took a sip of the calming balm.

'Thank you, ma'am,' said Eddie as he blew over the top of his hot drink.

'I know it's only milk, Mum, but I can't make it taste the way you do.'

Helen smiled. 'Made with a mother's love, my darling.'

'Cotton, you say?'

Her father's question threw Anna for a second as she concentrated on her soothing milk. 'Yes, I'm sure that's what the inspector said.' She looked to Eddie for confirmation.

'Erm, yes. Cotton. That's right. This is superb, ma'am.'

Anna raised an eyebrow at his inattention to her question as he drank his milk.

The vicar's wife smiled while frowning. 'Don't you think it's time you called me Helen? After all, you've been drinking my tea in this kitchen for a couple of months now.'

8

The American blushed. 'Well, err, if you say so, ma... I mean... Helen.'

The other three burst out laughing at his awkward response.

'By the way, that goes for me, too, Eddie.'

'Are you sure, Dad?'

Her father gave Anna a confused look before catching on. 'Oh, yes, very good, darling. I mean, call me Charles... not Helen, obviously.'

This time it was the vicar's turn to be the object of the others' entertainment.

After a short while, Anna returned to her father's question about the victim's name. 'You know the family?'

Her father shook his head. 'Not really. I stood in for the vicar at St Ann's in Silby Magna last year. I buried a chap called George Cotton. Lovely set of people. He was the grandfather and his granddaughter attended. I'm sure her name was Ruth. What did she look like?'

Helen reacted with horror. 'My darling, what sort of question is that?'

The vicar frowned. 'What do you... Oh, no, I don't mean her injuries. I apologise, Anna. I simply wish to help.'

His daughter finished the last of her hot milk before returning the enamel mug to the tabletop. 'It's OK, Dad. Well, she had short brown hair that I thought a bit masculine for a young woman. I'd say she was about 5'2" with a slim build. Her ID card said she was twenty-five.'

The clergyman's shoulders dropped as the realisation sank in. 'I'm afraid to say we are talking about the same young lady. What a tragedy. Once I've confirmed with the police we are talking about the same person, I'll call on the poor girl's parents after Evensong.'

Helen collected the enamel mugs from the table and carried them over to a sizeable Belfast sink, where she ran each one under cold water and used a small stiff brush to scour the insides, before placing each upside down on the scrubbed beech draining board.

After a few hours of much-needed sleep, the Grix family were up and about early to prepare for a busy day of church services and socialising amongst the parishioners.

The vicar emerged at speed from his office, his vestments flowing behind him as he sped down the vestibule towards the front door of the vicarage, clutching his sermon as if it were a pot of gold.

In the kitchen, Helen and Anna finished tidying the breakfast things away before rushing upstairs to change into their Sunday best.

'You look nice.' Eddie's attempt to offer a compliment failed dismally as both Anna and her mother glared at the American. Realising his mistake, he quickly regrouped. 'Both of you, yes, I mean both of you, naturally.'

The two women smiled at one another before letting the lieutenant off the hook and wishing him good morning.

'I didn't expect to see you until after lunch. I assumed Three-Mile-Bottom would be a stronger draw for you since you keep telling me how good Hilda Crossman's breakfasts are.' Anna delighted in watching Eddie squirm as she caught sight of Helen's disapproving look.

'Well, that's to say, present company excepted.' He gave Helen a pleading look.

'Good to see you're thinking on your feet so early on this sunny Sunday, Lieutenant. The church bell has stopped ringing, so if we don't get in now, Anna's father will be most displeased.'

A hundred heads turned in unison as the three latecomers tiptoed down the aisle, the noise from the shoe heels reverberating around the silent building, before taking their usual front row pew less than six feet from an impressive medieval pulpit, with its sizeable oak carved eagle emerging menacingly from the top of the ornate structure.

'You think anyone noticed?' whispered Eddie into Anna's ear as they sat down.

'Bravo, your interpretation of British irony is getting better.'

Within seconds, her father appeared from the vestry as he processed first to the altar, before turning 180 degrees and walking along the short chancel, stopping at the rood screen to welcome the congregation.

The next forty-five minutes followed a pattern set centuries earlier. As with every week, children fidgeted as mothers tried to keep them occupied; several parishioners competed with one another in who could sing the loudest, if not necessarily in tune; and young adults engaged in covertly consulting their wristwatches to calculate when they would be free.

At last, Charles Grix blessed the congregation, which provided the signal for the organist to strike up with an uplifting postlude. It was also the signal for the weekly race to exit the church before the vicar made his way from the vestry and along the outside of the church, back around to the main entrance to bid his parishioners farewell.

Learning from years of practice, Anna placed a restraining hand on Eddie's arm and leant into him. 'It's best to hang back, remember, or you risk life and limb in the scramble to get out.'

Eddie raised his eyebrows. 'I'd forgotten about that. If only the world knew that you so-called reserved Brits act like stampeding heifers after church, folks might take a different view of you lot.'

Helen shook her head and smiled, before turning to respond to Alice Stanmore's tap on the shoulder. 'Hello, Alice, is anything wrong?'

'No, no, and I'm sorry to disturb you, but I wanted to let you know I'll be late for my shift in the thrift shop tomorrow. My mother's bunion is playing up again, and she's driving me to distraction. The only way to put a stop to it is to yank her along to see Doctor Brabham. I should be in by half past ten, though. Is that OK?'

11

Helen chuckled. 'Of course it is, and your mother has my sympathy. Bunions are terribly uncomfortable things.'

'Not half as terrible as her moaning, I can tell you. Anyway, I'll leave you in peace and see you tomorrow.' Alice offered a cheery wave as she turned and made her way up the now empty nave aisle.

'Come on, you two, the coast is clear now. I expect my husband will need a calming cup of tea. I'll come back later and tidy everything up.'

'Ah, there you are, my dears, and welcome, Eddie. It was good to see you in church today. I was having a word with Sandra.'

The vicar took hold of Sandra's hand and gently patted it in a show of sympathy.

Anna smiled at Sandra, whose sadness confirmed her father had broken the sad news to his parishioner. 'I'm so sorry. Did you know Ruth well?'

The young woman slowly shook her head as she toyed with the straps of a small over the shoulder handbag. 'Not really. We worked in the same place but had little to do with one another. So many people work there and we each have our job to do; it's difficult to make friends with anyone.'

Meanwhile, the vicar became distracted as another parishioner demanded his time. He released his grip on Sandra's hand, smiled a kind smile, and left the four of them to continue their difficult conversation.

Eddie placed both hands in his uniform trouser pockets and spoke to Sandra in a quiet voice. 'This has been a terrible shock for us all, and as a stranger around these parts, I can't begin to understand the way the local community must feel. I don't know whether the vicar told you that it was Anna and I who found Ruth. For that reason, we want to uncover what really happened late last night. Do you think you might help us?'

You have a way with words.

Sandra stopped fiddling with the straps of her handbag and gave Eddie an intense look. 'If I can help, I shall, but I'm not sure what you want from me. I didn't know her very well. Ruth was always immaculately turned out. Crazy when you think about the dirty jobs we all have to do. I know she always liked to keep her hair short so she didn't have to wear one of those horrible nets around the machines. Some of them are death traps, I tell you.'

'She was always careful about her appearance?'

Sandra nodded. 'Ruth liked the boys, and she knew how to keep their interest. Don't think I'm talking out of turn; I mean nothing bad by that. It's simply a fact. All the men found her attractive, and she knew that. Ruth was so confident.' Sandra's voice tailed off. 'And look where it got her.'

Anna looked around to see only Sandra, Eddie and she remained. She hadn't noticed her mother slip away and assumed she'd done so to finish her preparations for Sunday lunch. 'Why do you say that, Sandra?' She found Eddie's hand gently touching her elbow.

He thinks I'm going too far.

'I'm sorry, Sandra, I didn't mean to be so forward. I'm sure this is an upsetting time for you.'

The woman shook her head. 'I'm sad, of course, but it's not as if she was a close friend or anything like that. But you can't tell me that flirting with men like she did ends well. After all, she has… or had a steady boyfriend. What must he think?'

Anna looked up at the church steeple to read the large round clock, added an hour onto the reading and calculated they were going to be late for lunch.

Better get a move on with this.

'Do you know him?'

Sandra shook her head. 'No, but I've heard about his reputation.

13

He's the jealous sort, which is why I always found it strange that Ruth led the men along so much.'

I wonder how far I can push this.

'I know what you mean. After all, if she had a jealous boyfriend, why would she risk him finding out? That's if there was anything to find out. Or was there someone who held a torch for Ruth at the boatyard?'

Sandra appeared deep in thought for a moment. 'I don't think so; she seemed to flirt with all the men… although…'

'Although…' responded Anna.

'There's this one lad. Geoffrey Lenox is his name. A strange one, if ever I saw. Anyway, I've noticed him leering at Ruth, but now as I think about it, he was the one bloke she totally ignored. I've never thought too much about it before, but I suppose it was a bit strange.'

A car horn interrupted the conversation.

What the heck…

The trio turned to see Detective Inspector Spillers in his police car, leaning across to the passenger side and winding down the window. Before Anna had time to stop her, Sandra had slipped away, much to Anna's frustration.

'Time to catch our killer,' shouted Spillers through the open window. 'I'm off to the prisoner of war camp to track down the Italian. Up to you whether you come, but I'd rather have you with me than prancing about the place doing your amateur sleuth thing. We have a killer to find. Perhaps today will be our lucky day.'

Chapter 2: Prisoners

The journey from Lipton St Faith to the prisoner of war camp took less than thirty minutes, aided by the inspector's habit of ignoring the speed limit along Norfolk's narrow roads.

And I thought Eddie's driving was reckless.

Anna hung on for dear life as the police vehicle's constant lurching from side to side made her slide along the shiny leather rear seat of the car.

Why is it the woman must always sit in the back seat? I've yet to see a sign that says 'Reserved for men only' on the front one.

'Nearly there,' announced the inspector as he gave the steering wheel one last yank to the right, allowing the car to leave the main Norwich to Cromer road and ride the bumps and troughs of a dusty track that led to the entrance of the camp.

I wonder if he ever uses the brakes.

To Anna's astonishment, the police vehicle glided to a controlled stop a few feet away from a red and white painted metal pole that barred the way into the camp compound.

Inspector Spillers wound down his window and leaned out to greet an approaching army guard. A second guard sauntered to Anna's side of the car, bent slightly and peered through the glass to give Eddie and Anna the once over.

'And your business, sir?' The burley six-foot-something military police officer poked his head through the open driver side window, forcing Spillers to lean sideways and out of his way.

That military policeman is quite dashing, even if his revolver is a bit intimidating.

The guard stepped away from the driver's window, allowing Inspector Spillers to resume an upright position. 'I'd have thought the big bell on the roof and the sign that says "Police" speaks for itself?'

The man pulled himself to his full height and spoke over the roof of the police car to his colleague. 'We got a clever one here, Arthur.'

'It seems we 'av, Reggie. What do you reckon we should do with them?' The second guard tapped his fingers to a tuneless beat on the black-painted steel top of the police car.

Frustrated at the lack of progress, Anna leant forward and addressed the military policeman directly. 'Are you always this obtuse? We have an appointment with the camp commander, something I'm sure you're aware of, so please, let's stop this nonsense and lift the barrier.'

That will either get us through or shot.

Mention of his superior did the trick. After giving Anna a dismissive smirk without bothering to answer her question, the disgruntled guard offered a sideways nod to his opposite number, immediately marched back to the guardhouse and lifted the barrier.

'I'll ring through to inform the major you have arrived. Good luck because you'll need it.'

Strange thing to say.

Spillers engaged the car's clutch, slid the gearstick into first gear and edged the police car forward as he followed the military police-man's pointing finger to show where he should park. As he eased

16

the vehicle to a stop with its front bumper inches from the army green-painted wood building, a soldier immediately approached the car from the right.

Holding a clipboard and pen, the short man in an untidy brown khaki uniform waited until all three occupants cleared the police car. 'May I check your names before we move off?'

I don't think there's any 'may' about it.

With the formalities completed, the young soldier snapped to attention, completed a smart about-turn and marched the few feet to a set of three concrete steps that led to the double door entrance of the administration block.

Without looking back to check whether his charges had followed him, the lance corporal knocked on a plain and unremarkable door and waited.

After a few seconds, a gruff sounding 'Enter' rang out.

He sounds like a right charmer, I don't think.

Turning the Bakelite doorknob to the right, the escort opened the door in one sharp action. Standing a little inside the room, he snapped to attention, faced his superior and gave a salute. 'Your visitors, sir.'

The stark interior of the camp commander's headquarters took Anna by surprise. The room measured approximately fifteen feet by eight feet, its only furniture being a desk, an old-fashioned wooden swivel chair, two chipped grey filing cabinets and four unmatched plain chairs. The wall behind the senior officer's desk carried a large line drawing displaying the outline of the camp, with each prisoner of war hut numbered and showing which nationality of detainees it held.

The commander raised his eyes from a document spread out in front of him on the desk. Placing his palms on the edge of the workstation, he slowly got to his feet. 'I'm Major Leonard-White, CGM, DCM.'

And modest with it.

Detective Inspector Spillers attempted to respond by introducing himself.

The major was having none of it. 'I know who you are, so there is no need for any of that nonsense. I have to say I'm perplexed as to why a vicar's daughter should favour us with her company, especially on a Sunday. Good morning, Lieutenant Elsner. I've heard a lot about you.'

Anna watched as the inspector's cheeks flushed.

I sense trouble brewing.

'That's kind of you to say, Major. However, our presence here is completely down to Detective Inspector Spillers. Miss Grix and I are in attendance purely because we found—'

'Ah yes, the unfortunate Miss Cotton.' The major turned his attention to Spillers. 'So you link the discovery of a single Italian coin to this camp and deduce one of my prisoners committed this heinous crime. What would we do without His Majesty's Constabulary to entertain us in these tough times?'

He's a right smarty-pants.

Inspector Spillers did well to contain his indignation and remain calm as he countered the major's sarcastic comment. 'Major, we each have our part to play in this war. You hold an important office, which I'm sure you're proud of and execute to the fullest extent within the bounds of both military and, of course, criminal law, which as you know informs my jurisdiction.'

Round one to you, Inspector.

The major let out a gruff cough as he tucked his undersized shirt into his trousers, the front waist of which sagged over his army issue belt to accommodate his extensive stomach. 'I'm in no need of a lecture on jurisdictions, Inspector. I have concluded this distasteful matter falls squarely within my sphere of operations. As a matter of courtesy, I will, of course, keep you informed of developments. As

18

far as investigating an allegation of murder by one of my prisoners, well, it's for me to decide how the investigation progresses. Do we understand one another?'

Anna looked across to Eddie without making it too obvious she wanted him to intervene. He read her intention immediately. 'Major, I know that the inspector will agree with me when I say how important it is that we all work together. Clearly, as suspicions currently point to a person under your – how shall I put it – duty of care, you will, of course, wish to take the lead. On the other hand, the woman Anna and I found last evening was a civilian. Therefore, it's the detective inspector's duty to investigate the death. I have a proposal. What say I act as a liaison between military and civilian authorities looking into this disturbing case?'

You are a clever American.

Lieutenant Elsner's proposal seemed to take the wind from both the major and Inspector Spillers' sails.

Anna drove Eddie's initiative on. 'And if we do this with intelligence, both parties will look like paragons of virtue by their respective superiors and, I would've thought, the community at large. What's to lose?'

Spillers, the major and Eddie exchanged serious looks as they considered her suggestion.

Why are men so stupid?

Anna took the exchanges of clearing throats and gazing at the floor as a tacit agreement for the plan to move forward. 'Does that mean, Major, that we can interview some Italian prisoners?'

Leonard-White plonked himself down in his chair, leant forward and opened a plain brown foolscap folder that was on his desk. Without raising his eyes, he barked his response. 'Out of the question.'

Eddie intervened to calm proceedings. 'You still have a work party at the farm, Major?'

The senior officer engaged Eddie with an unblinking stare. 'I can neither confirm nor deny that.'

'Does that mean—'

'Thank you, Major. We won't detain you further.' Eddie gave Anna a sharp look and surreptitiously pointed at the office door.

'I look forward to working with you, Major.' Spillers smiled at Eddie as he spoke.

What's going on here?

The ride back to the village took place largely in silence, which Anna couldn't quite understand.

Either I'm thick, or these two are up to something.

'OK, you're clearly going to make me ask what that was all about.'

Eddie turned his head so he could see Anna, who noted the inspector's smile as he once more threw his police car from side to side, racing along the meandering road. 'I suppose you could call it facing both ways.'

'What? You do talk nonsense sometimes.'

Eddie sighed. 'There you go again, not listening. As I was about to say, it means that the major has given us the green light to speak to his prisoners on the farm. Of course, should it all go wrong, he can say he did no such thing because he refused your direct request. So, any denial he gives, should it hit the fan, will sound more than plausible. Get it?'

Two smarty-pants in one morning.

Applying the handbrake after bringing his car to a stop outside the vicarage, Detective Inspector Spillers gave a serious look to both his passengers. 'Let's remember that I took you to the camp to stop you roaming about the place and ruining my investigation. Don't spoil things now by going off and doing your own thing. Are we agreed?'

'Sure thing, Inspector.'

Anna proved less forthcoming, which led to Spillers giving her a suspicious look followed by a raised finger that he moved from side to side. 'Are we agreed?'

This time she had no choice. 'Of course, Inspector.' She could see the detective was less than convinced as she offered a meek smile, opened the car door and walked the few feet to open the vicarage garden gate.

'It's only us,' said Anna cheerily as she opened the kitchen door to see her mother and father doing the washing up following Sunday lunch.

'We thought you'd got lost,' replied her mother as she placed a tea towel onto a small hook on a kitchen cupboard.

'I'm sorry we've been so long, Helen. Something came up about Ruth Cotton, which we needed to check.'

Anna's father dried his hands and rolled down the sleeves of his crisp white shirt. 'Would that have anything to do with being kidnapped by Inspector Spillers?'

'Word sure gets around fast,' said Eddie.

Anna gestured for her companion to take a seat at the table as she prepared to ask her mother a question that would determine whether they were to be fed. 'I really am sorry, Mum; I know we don't deserve it, but I don't suppose there's anything left of lunch?'

Helen at first gave her wayward daughter a stern look, which she couldn't keep up for long. Relaxing into a motherly smile, she pointed at the table for Anna to take her seat. 'You're lucky Sunday lunch isn't in the dog.'

'We haven't got a dog.'

'No, we haven't, but next door has.'

I don't think I'll win this one.

Anna gave her mother a deliberately long blink as a young child might give its parent when hearing something not necessarily to its advantage.

21

A burst of hot air shot from the oven as Helen opened the stove's enamelled door. Protecting her hands with a pair of oven gloves, she retrieved two large oval, glazed earthenware containers. One contained a mix of vegetables with the second about a third full of roasted and boiled potatoes.

'I don't suppose there's any gravy left, is there?'

Anna's mother gave her daughter a disapproving look. 'Don't push your luck, young lady.'

Eddie let out a brief burst of laughter.

'You can stop that, Eddie Elsner. It's your fault we missed lunch.'

The American returned the surprised look. 'Er, I don't remember you refusing the inspector's offer to have us tag along. Anyway, if it means I can still have some of your mother's wonderful cooking, I admit to anything.'

Helen beamed as Anna scowled.

It hasn't taken you long to work your way into my mother's affections.

'May I look at your paper, Charles?' asked Eddie as he attempted to read the Sunday paper headlines upside down.

'Yes, of course. Be my guest.'

A few seconds of silence followed as he scanned the broadsheet for anything of interest. 'Well, what do you know, it says here that South African scientists have discovered the flu germ and expect to create a vaccine, which they say, and I quote, "will be wholly successful".'

'Wouldn't that be marvellous? It's bad enough in normal years but thinking back to the epidemic at the end of the Great War, what a marvel that would be. Do they say how long they expect it will take to perfect?' asked the vicar.

Eddie skimmed the rest of the article. 'No, only that they're working hard to make it happen.'

'Well, I for one cannot wait,' said the vicar. 'There was so much suffering at the end of the war. Do you know it's said that the epidemic killed more people around the world than died in the war, as if that wasn't obscene enough.'

Anna poked Eddie's elbow as her mother looked to set their meals on the table.

'Oh, I'm sorry, I got caught up reading about the daylight raids the RAF are carrying out over Germany, France and Norway. As if flying a bomber isn't dangerous enough at night. Wow, to do it in daylight takes a special type of guy.' He quickly folded the paper and sat back in his chair as Helen reached over to deliver his lunch. 'This looks wonderful, Helen. Thank you so much.'

Crawler.

'You're right,' said Charles, 'I can't imagine the terror of being in a Lancaster with ack-ack anti-aircraft shrapnel coming at you at 30,000 feet in broad daylight. We owe those men so much.'

Helen chipped in. 'I don't diminish their heroism for one second, darling, but we're all trying to do our bit. Listening to a bomb whistle as it falls and wondering if this one has your name on it must be just as terrifying. Being killed is awful, but how much worse to be grievously injured and conclude life's not worth living yet be forced to by those who love you.'

Anna paused eating her lunch, such was her shock on hearing her mother's view. 'Do you mean to say that if you got severely injured – let's say you needed others to care for you – you'd rather die?' She looked at her father for moral support.

'It's no use looking at me like that, Anna. We are all grownups now, and these things require discussion. You know as I do things can change in a heartbeat and we must listen to what each other feels.'

She glanced at Eddie, who looked as though he was busy avoiding getting involved.

'But isn't that a sin in the eyes of the church?'

Anna's father bridled. 'Suicide is regarded as a sin, a doctrine I have no truck with since I regard such wretched people as needing our love and support. Deciding not to receive treatment is quite another matter. Who is to say how any of us might feel in such a situation as your mother describes? Can you honestly tell me now, Anna, that in all circumstances you'd wish to remain alive?'

Anna averted her gaze to look at the tabletop.

'Your hesitation tells me everything, and I don't condemn you for that. As you know, part of my job is to give succour to the dying. I tell you this, sometimes I see the most wonderfully peaceful deaths, awe-inspiring. But occasionally—'

'That's enough, Charles, I think we understand. Let's change the subject. How do you two intend to spend the rest of the day?'

Anna looked at Eddie. 'Wow, after that brief interlude, I think a trip to Wells-next-the-sea calls. I could do with the sea breeze blowing away my war cobwebs.'

Eddie nodded. 'So be it. I'd have liked to crack on with speaking to the Italian prisoners, but I guess even they get Sundays off, so yes, I'm up for a bit of sand and sea.'

The sound of men shouting in the street filled the vicarage kitchen.

'Oh no. It's the Home Guard practising Operation Repel,' said the vicar.

'Operation what?' replied Eddie.

'Well, it seems the local platoon commander, or should I say Mr Brightman, manager of Brightman's Men's Outfitters, has got it into his head that a Nazi invasion is imminent. Not only that, the enemy will use Winterton as a beachhead, preceded by paratroopers descending en masse across the local area. When I asked him why he thought such a thing, the extent of his military thinking amounted to two words: "Why not?". I don't know about you, but such a response does not fill me with confidence. And they make so much noise, not to mention the mess when they practise. After all, it is the Lord's day.'

Anna giggled. 'It sounds fun. Shall we watch?'

Her father shook his head and left for his study as she opened the kitchen door, leaving Eddie and her mother with mouths wide open.

'I'm not interested, but something tells me she expects you to play the part of a military observer, so off you go. I'll keep Charles company. He's got plenty to do if he's to be ready for Evensong.'

The American sauntered down the path between the vegetable patches in what had, before the war, been a pristine lawn. 'Be careful or else they'll think you're a German Stormtrooper.'

Anna looked over her shoulder, as she leaned on the low garden wall, to see Eddie approaching. 'If that's the case, what will they think about you?'

'With a bit of luck, they'll think I'm crazy and wearing a costume for some age-old village custom.' He grinned as he joined Anna.

'If you say so, but—'

A shattering bang interrupted her flow. 'What the...' She instinctively snuggled into Eddie for comfort as the uproar continued.

He's got his arm around me.

Her attention fell on one of the Home Guard volunteers taking part in the exercise. 'Look at that poor chap. He doesn't seem to be enjoying the experience.' The old man was cowered behind a picket fence opposite the vicarage. 'Well, all I can say is if the Nazis ever swarm around our village butter cross, that chap won't be much use.'

Eddie laughed. 'Thanks for planting such a crazy image in my brain. Listen, we'd better get a move on if we want to make good time to visit that well.'

Anna looked at Eddie with suspicion.

Is he taking the rise out of me?

'I assume you mean Wells-next-the sea and just for that, you're paying for afternoon tea.'

The town hall clock read 3.00 pm as they arrived at their destination, which was almost deserted except for a few men tending to the small fishing boats in the pretty harbour. Eddie parked the Jeep up in a safe spot on one of the many tiny roads that boarded the seafront.

'What a beautiful spot. You guys are so lucky to live in such a place.'

Anna looked around to take in what Eddie was seeing. 'And that's even more reason to make sure no one takes it away from us. You see why we're prepared to stick it out even though the rest of Europe has gone up in flames?'

'Yes, I understand, but hopefully you won't be on your own too much longer.'

Anna turned to her companion but thought better of pressing him on his oblique comment.

One of these days he'll tell me what he's up to.

'The beauty of this place makes what we saw last night even more disturbing, don't you think?'

His question set Anna thinking. 'I suppose the same thing is happening all over the country. We read in the paper about the rise in crime and it makes you consider what sort of mess we've all got ourselves into.'

The conversation tailed off into a comfortable silence as they took in a sight Anna mused hadn't changed in a hundred years.

She recognised the pungent aroma swirling around the harbour-front. 'Cockles!'

'I beg your pardon?' replied her surprised companion.

'You know, shellfish. Can you smell it? Isn't it lovely? Look, there's a chap selling them from a barrow over there.' Anna pointed to a spot twenty yards away.

Still trying to make sense of her sudden outburst, Eddie questioned her choice of snack. 'I thought you said you wanted a cream tea?'

Anna shook her head and smiled at the American. 'I'm a woman, my rules. It's a tub of shellfish and a toothpick.'

Before either made progress towards the shopkeeper's barrow, the sound of a man shouting caught their attention.

'He sounds angry. What do you reckon is going on?'

Eddie moved forward a few feet before turning back to Anna. 'She is much younger than him, so I guess he's her father. Whatever their relationship, I don't like what I'm hearing or seeing.'

Suddenly the man doing all the shouting caught sight of Anna and Eddie looking on. 'Can I help you?' he said roughly, his manner threatening.

Eddie took a further step forward. 'I thought perhaps the young lady might need some help. You normally speak to people like that?'

The angry man now totally ignored the young woman and squared up to Eddie.

'That's far enough, sir.' said Eddie. 'I suggest you don't come any nearer. After all, we don't want any unpleasantness, do we?'

'Don't threaten me.'

Eddie showed the man his open palms. 'I'm not threatening you, sir, but I'm not prepared to stand here and see a young woman spoken to like that. Do you know this lady?'

The young woman broke down. 'Please, don't get involved. This is my father. I can deal with it.'

Anna took matters into her own hands and made her way over to the distressed woman. 'Now, come close, you're safe now.' She put her arm round the stranger who, like the man, appeared smartly dressed and spoke like someone from an upper-middle-class home.

Well, you're not pulling away. That tells me a lot.

'She's my daughter. This is my responsibility, and not a matter for either of you to interfere in.'

For the first time, Eddie flashed a hint of anger. 'If she's your daughter, all the more reason not to talk like that. Now, you have two choices: calm down, or the police will deal with the matter. Which is it to be?'

The burly man laughed. 'You're not in America now, my man, military uniform or not. It's a domestic matter, and it's something the police rightly don't get involved in. We do things differently here.' He turned back to his daughter. 'Get in the car.'

The woman became hysterical.

'You stay here with us,' whispered Anna as she pulled the woman, who she thought to be around her own age, closer.

In an instant, she pulled away from Anna and made off into a maze of tangled streets and within seconds, was out of sight.

'Now look what you've done. That's what you get for interfering.'

Eddie was now standing within a few feet of the angry man. 'I'll tell you what you're going to do. Get into your car and drive back to wherever you came from. We'll deal with this now. If I see you again, I won't bother involving the police. Do I make myself clear, sir?'

For a second or two, Anna thought the man might attack Eddie. In the event, he backed down, slammed the driver's door closed as he gripped a leather-clad steering wheel, and sped off in a cloud of exhaust fumes.

Clambering back into the Jeep, Eddie looked across to Anna. 'Well, that went well.'

Anna had no choice but to laugh. 'You really are getting quite good at British parody. Anyway, better get a move on and see if we can find her.'

After a few frantic minutes of navigating the narrow, twisting streets in the Jeep, Anna pointed excitedly. 'There she is.'

The woman was crying her heart out as she leant against the flint-covered wall of the corner shop.

'Is there anyone we can contact for you? Your husband, or a boyfriend?' Anna's offer appeared to have the opposite effect to what she'd intended as the stranger's distress intensified. 'I'm sorry, I'm being clumsy. Is he away fighting?'

For the first time, the woman calmed. 'No… no, he's here. It's complicated, that's all.'

'Or we can give you a lift to a place you feel safe,' said Anna.

The young woman shook her head. 'I'll be fine; I live quite nearby and the walk will do me good. My father won't be at home. He'll have gone to his floozy's place, so it'll be Mum and me… as usual.'

With that, the young woman broke off the conversation and began to walk away.

Anna was keen to follow.

Eddie disagreed. 'Let's leave it. She's an adult, and we did all we could to make sure she was safe. If it's all right with you, I've rather gone off shellfish. Shall we head back? I've got a busy morning tomorrow. Why don't I pick you up after lunch and we'll head over to those Italians?'

Chapter 3: Rations

It hadn't taken long for word to get around the village that the butcher had received an extra allocation of scrag end. Regardless of whether the rumour was true, such news always resulted in a long queue outside Mr Leatherbarrow's shop.

This drizzly Monday morning proved the point since by 10.30 am, a dozen women stood patiently in line waiting for the proprietor, who most could see was already in the shop, to flip the sign that hung on the inside of the entrance door to 'Open'.

Queueing was something everybody was used to, whether it be for an expensive item or, as with today, a cheap cut of lamb.

I don't mind lining up, but I need the rain like a hole in the head.

They accepted that although inconvenient, the daily ritual of queueing for everyday items at least allowed for the sharing of news of the latest scandal and tittle-tattle in the shortest time.

One of the great joys of such gatherings was the opportunity for the women of the village to make fun of any male having reached his majority.

This morning it was the turn of Constable Tom Bradshaw.

'Go on, show us your whistle,' shouted one.

'Have you got your truncheon with you?' teased another.

The sergeant did his best to rise above the double entendres and maintain his dignity. 'Now, ladies. I'm an officer of the law and charged with maintaining His Majesty's peace.'

A collective giggle rippled through the line.

'He's got a lot of shiny buttons, hasn't he?'

Anna could see Tom wasn't sure how to handle things.

Poor man, he doesn't stand a chance.

'Never you mind this lot. I think you do a wonderful job in keeping us all safe.' A second round of giggling broke out. Anna concluded she'd made matters worse for the unfortunate constable.

'Not to worry, I'm quite used to it.' He smiled and pointed his finger playfully at a large-framed lady who was tucking straggly bits of hair back into her headscarf. 'We'll see whether you're quite so…' Tom stopped himself saying a word he knew he'd regret speaking, '…err, outspoken on Saturday night when it's chucking out time at the King's Head.'

This time the collective chuckle was more stifled, yet no less effective for that. 'He's got your number, Ethel,' shouted one of the crowd.

Ethel valiantly tried to ignore the attention by opening the clasp on her small leather purse to check she had enough coins for her intended purchase.

'And on that note, ladies, I shall leave you to your shopping and continue my beat. Good morning to you all.' He offered a quick salute by raising his right hand to the side of his bobby's helmet, placed his hands behind his back, open palms facing outwards as per regulation, and set off by immediately settling into the ubiquitous style of the British bobby.

As the women settled back into the more important business of exchanging the latest gossip, the woman immediately in front of Anna turned around. 'Hello, Anna, I thought I recognised your voice.'

'Good morning, Martha, how's Tilly doing?' Given Anna's

31

involvement with overseeing the welfare of child evacuees, mainly from London, she was even more interested to hear about Tilly Smith, who was staying with Martha.

'Oh, you know, up and down. She is a tough little girl and does her best to keep her spirits up, but losing her mother like that, well, it's going to take time, isn't it?'

The two women exchanged silent glances for a few seconds.

'It might sound a harsh thing to say, but Tilly will learn to live with the tragedy and make her way in life,' replied Anna.

Martha shrugged her shoulders. 'So many children damaged by this war. None of us know how it'll end, but I tell you this. It'll be stupid politicians who'll decide, like last time. Then they'll expect everyone to go back to normal as if nothing happened. Until the next time. And when will that be? 1960, 1970?'

What a dreadful prospect.

'Anyway, listen to me going on. I'm a right misery guts this morning. How is your WVS training going?'

Anna snapped back to the present and thought about Martha's question. 'Do you know, I didn't expect to enjoy it as much as I am? I know that may sound odd, but I wasn't sure how the youngsters would react to me.'

Martha smiled. 'Why ever not? One thing I've learnt is that yes, they're terribly homesick when they arrive, even though sometimes they're escaping a dangerous place. But all the children really want is someone to love them. Give them that and they'll get on with the rest of it.'

Anna reached around her friend's waist and gave her a friendly squeeze. 'That's a wonderful piece of advice, Martha, thank you.'

'Get away with you – from what I hear, the children idolise you. Now, enough of that soft soap.' Martha whispered into Anna's ear, 'What's this I hear about a girl found dead in Witton Wood?'

The question took Anna a little by surprise. 'You've heard? So sad, it was a girl around my age called Ruth Cotton. I—'

'That's what happens when a girl goes out at night on her own. You've got to ask yourself what type of woman she was, if you know what I mean,' interrupted local busybody Beatrice Flowers, who'd been listening while giving the impression of tying her bootlaces some feet away.

God forgive me, Beatrice, but you can be dreadful sometimes.

'And what type of girl would that be, Beatrice Flowers? If you have something to say, please tell us all.' Anna spoke loudly enough for everyone in the queue to hear.

Anna purposely looked at each of the women, which seemed to prompt a collective checking of headscarves to ensure hair in need of care remained tucked away from public view.

'You seem to be saying that had the unfortunate woman been a man, it would have been perfectly acceptable for them to be out late at night. Is that what you mean?'

Beatrice was having none of it. 'Vicar's daughter you may be, but it doesn't give you the right to twist my words. I have an opinion and am perfectly entitled to express it.'

'You do, Miss Flowers. But what it does not entitle you to do is disparage the dead and cast libellous slander concerning someone you don't know.'

Why are none of the others backing me up? I despair sometimes.

The spinster had had enough. 'I have no need for extra scrag end, unlike some greedy people I could mention. Good morning, ladies,' she said, before marching off, swinging her wicker shopping basket with furious intent.

One woman shouted after the spinster, 'That's because you've no one to cook for, except Monty.'

33

The old lady turned on her heels. 'You leave Monty out of this. I'd rather have a faithful cat than a philandering husband, Gertrude Shuttlecock.'

With that, Beatrice swivelled around to continue her journey as half a dozen of the women shouted, 'Meow,' sarcastically.

Gertrude attempted to defend her husband to the others. 'That old bag has a mind like a sewer. My Eustice is a good man. Anyway, he's too lazy to get up to that kind of nonsense. He knows he won't get a better shepherd's pie anywhere, nor anyone else to put up with his snoring and smelly socks. He's that bad that the military wouldn't have him. They said he'd alert the enemy to our lads being close by.' A roar of laughter broke out with Gertrude first among equals.

When things calmed down, Gertrude spoke to Anna in a quiet voice. 'I don't know if it helps, but I knew that poor girl, you know, Ruth.'

The revelation took Anna aback. She worked hard not to show it. 'Are you certain?'

'Yes,' replied Gertrude. 'I worked at the same boatyard as she did for a bit, but when the military took the Broads over, it was a pain to work there. I got to know Ruthy – that's what we called her – quite well.'

Having finally untangled herself from the melee in the butcher's shop, Anna plonked her precious cargo of scrag end wrapped neatly in brown greaseproof paper onto the counter of the thrift shop.

'You look exhausted, darling.' Anna's mother offered a maternal smile as her daughter took respite in an old chair set amongst piles of gifted clothes.

'Do you know, for a moment there, I thought I might never escape from Mr Leatherbarrow's place. The other ladies, although lovely, well, goodness me, can they talk? And when they thought the scrag end was about to run out – I thought there'd be a riot.'

Alice Stanmore, one of two volunteers who assisted Helen Grix at the thrift shop, stepped from a small storeroom. 'I told my mum there was no point going since I'm sure the butcher has his favourites.' Alice suddenly realised what she'd said. 'Oh, err… present company excepted, of course.'

Mother and daughter laughed. 'Don't worry, Alice, no offence taken. Now, why don't we make a start on sorting through all these clothes?'

The shop bell tinkled again to show someone had opened the door. 'Only one for you today, Helen. It looks official, though. I hope you've been behaving yourself?'

'We do our best,' replied Helen light-heartedly as she took the slim white envelope from the postman. The other two women crowded around Helen. 'Now girls, let me have a bit of air.'

She stepped over to the counter and took a brass letter opener from a drawer. After expertly slitting open the outer covering, she laid the intriguing document onto the countertop. Quiet followed as three pairs of eyes scanned its contents.

'It's from the War Office, isn't that nice of them,' said Helen.

'I should jolly well think so,' replied Anna. '£200 is a lot of money and it took a lot of collecting, although we've yet to match the £500 we collected last time, even if it was because that horrible Sir Reginald put so much in. Look, it says we now have our very own machine gun on a Spitfire.'

Alice chipped in. 'I hope ours is used to shoot down plenty of those horrible Messerschmitt fighters.'

Helen leant against Alice as a gesture of support. 'I know what you mean, but don't forget there's a young man in each one of those planes.'

Alice pondered the point before replying. 'I know, and you must think me horrible, but it doesn't detract from the fact that they keep trying to shoot our boys out of the sky, does it?'

She's got a point there.

Helen chose not to answer; instead, she turned her attention back to the greaseproof paper package. 'Did you pick anything else up from the butchers?'

Smart move, Mum.

Anna shook her head. 'That's the daft thing; there's money to buy things and the coupons to make it happen, but Leatherbarrow, like other shops, doesn't have the stock to sell. That said, I'm sure he gave us more than he should. To be honest, I felt a little guilty looking the other ladies in the eye. I'm sure they noticed.'

Her mother picked the packet up from the countertop. 'You have no need to, my darling. Your father will most likely give most of it away. You know what he's like.'

The women exchanged knowing looks.

A harassed-looking woman, entering the shop holding a small boy and girl by the hand, interrupted their conversation.

'Miss Broadbent, how nice to see you,' said Anna as she smiled at the two children, who were clearly in a foul mood.

The woman was Anna's WVS training supervisor. 'I'm so sorry to drop this on you at such short notice. I know you haven't fully completed your training yet, but I'm desperate. I've arranged for these two mites to stay with Len and Daisy Bancroft, but they've arrived early, and the Bancrofts aren't at home. Can you look after them for a couple of hours? This young man is Timmy, and his twin prefers Peggy, although her proper name is Margaret. They will be nine next month. Now, I think that's all there is to know for now. I'll be back by four o'clock to collect them, I promise.'

What am I supposed to say?

'Of course, that will be fine, Miss Broadbent.'

Anna's agreement spurred her supervisor to scarper at pace,

36

leaving the three women attempting to engage the young ones.

I've got an idea.

'Why don't I take you two to my house for some strawberries drenched in condensed milk? I'm sure I have a tin somewhere.' Anna knew she'd triumphed when the siblings exchanged suspicious looks before breaking out into broad smiles.

Over the course of the two minutes it took to walk back to the vicarage, Anna sensed the anticipation of strawberries and cream improving the little ones' moods. Inserting the key into the Yale lock of the front door, she stood to one side and informed the children the kitchen was the second door on the right.

Having followed the children in, Anna came to a halt as the siblings took in the Victorian splendour of the black and white tiled vestibule and ornate plaster mouldings to the ceiling. Suddenly, the sound of someone on the landing caused the young ones to cuddle into Anna as if their lives depended on it.

Poor little mites.

'Is this a church?' asked Timmy as Anna's father descended the open stairway that hugged one wall of the vestibule. The vicar's facial expression displayed a combination of curiosity and kindness.

'And who might you two be?'

The young girl released her grip on Anna and took half a step forward. 'My name is Margaret, well, really it's Peggy, but I want to be a princess like the one that lives in a big house in London.'

It didn't take you long to get your confidence back, madam.

His sister's forwardness encouraged the boy. 'My name is Timmy, and I'm the oldest by eleven minutes. That makes me in charge.'

Margaret gave her sibling a withering glance. 'But I'm cleverer than you.'

'No, you're—'

'Right, you two, no you're not in church and the vicar is my father. Let's get you into the kitchen and have those strawberries.'

'And the condensed milk, miss, you promised,' insisted Timmy.

As the two children followed Anna's pointing finger to the kitchen door and disappeared into its interior, she could see her father was waiting for an explanation. In the few seconds it took her to appraise him of the situation, an argument broke out between the siblings.

'All right, you two, that's enough. Now, sit yourselves down at the table or it'll be worm pie instead of strawberries.'

The children competed to see who could make the most gruesome face at the idea of eating worms.

'You're a natural, my darling,' said Charles, who had followed her into the kitchen.

Anna smiled as she opened the larder door and retrieved a handsome wicker basket of ruby red fruit. Pleased to note her father had found the precious tin of condensed milk, she watched his efforts to get at its contents with a dangerous-looking can opener on the draining board.

Contentment descended on the large space as the two young ones tucked into their treat. Anna and her father exchanged smiles before the moment passed and Eddie rushed into the room.

'We got a name for the chap at the camp, and he's up at the farm today.'

Anna gave the vicar one of those looks reserved between daughter and father.

'Go on, I can manage these two. Make sure you're not too late getting back, mind; I've Evensong to prepare for.

'You realise it's midday, and it looks as though I'm going to miss my lunch again, Eddie Elsner?'

The lieutenant ignored his companion's complaint as they raced towards Top Field Farm. 'How do you reckon we should play it?'

Talk about being in a world of your own.

'Do you think they feed prisoners of war?'

Eddie let out a sigh. 'OK, I get it, you're hungry and annoyed at missing your strawberries. Who were those two young ones, anyway?'

Anna held on for dear life as her driver threw the Jeep into one blind corner after another.

You've caught Inspector Spillers' bad habits.

Explaining what had happened, her relief was palpable on seeing a large hand-painted sign jutting out of an unkempt hedgerow.

Thank heavens for that.

'Turn right, Eddie, didn't you see the sign to Top Field Farm?'

She immediately regretted her prompt as her companion stamped on the brakes and spun the steering wheel to the right, causing Anna to slip violently to the left.

'Stupid man,' were the only words Anna thought worth saying.

'Sorry, missed it. Anyway, look over there by the hayrick.' He pointed to his right where, in the distance, a group of men and women huddled together.

Still rubbing the side of her head, Anna frowned at Eddie. 'So how did you come to find this place, let alone discover the man we're after works here?'

I'm talking to you.

Eddie's eyes remained fixed on a group of people in the distance as the Jeep made slow progress up the deeply-rutted soil trackway. 'What? Err, simple really; I looked at the map and this farm sits next to Witton Wood. I called in and met the owner, Joe Applemead. He's a great bloke. Anyway, he said he had a load of them working here and that they're a godsend given most of the local men are away fighting.'

Anna frowned. 'Interesting, I'm sure. You said you had a name?'

At first, Eddie failed to respond. It was only after his companion reached over to get to the Jeep's horn that he looked at her. 'Well, that's the thing. I don't exactly have a name, but the fact the farmer may allow us to talk to them is the next best thing, don't you think?'

Something's not adding up here.

'I, too, checked one or two things out, Lieutenant. Top Field is one of four farms that connect to Witton Wood. So why have you brought me to this one in particular? You seem to know the farmer very well. What is it you're not telling me?'

A deep rut in the trackway interrupted Anna's line of questioning.

'Look, there's Joe Applemead,' shouted Eddie as he navigated the last of the baked soil and drove the Jeep onto the concreted surface of the sizeable farmyard.

Sometimes, Eddie Elsner, I could pinch you on the nose.

'One thing, Mr Clever Clogs. Won't Inspector Spillers have been here already?'

'He has, but Joe reckons he didn't get far. That said, he won't let it rest. My guess is he'll catch them at the camp and have an interpreter with him. That gives us one chance to see if we can find anything out.'

'What makes you think the men can speak English?'

Eddie smiled. 'Because they're working cheek by jowl with Land Girls. You don't seriously think a group of hot-blooded young men will pass up the chance to flirt with a field full of English girls for the want of knowing a few words of the lingo, do you?'

'Nice to see you again, Eddie. Who's this you've got with you?' Joe Applemead, a jovial sort in his late sixties with a healthy waistline, ruddy cheeks and receding hairline, strolled over to the stationary Jeep. 'Are you Charles Grix's lass?'

Anna could feel herself blushing. 'I'm a big girl now, Mr Applemead.'

The farmer let out a roar of laughter as he tightened the string holding his baggy trousers in place. 'Bless me, so you are. And now you're hitched up with this handsome fella.'

Before Anna could correct Joe, the lieutenant interrupted. 'Strange times, Joe, strange times. Anyway, may we have a word with your Italians?'

The smiling farmer winked at Anna as he pointed across the field. 'Help yourself. They stopped for dinner and if you're quick, there'll be some bread and cheese left for you.'

You cheeky thing, Eddie Elsner. Now look what you've done.

Over the course of the few minutes it took to trudge across the dusty field, Anna tried twice to correct the impression Eddie had left on the farmer concerning their relationship. Yet somehow, she couldn't find the words.

As they neared the group of twenty or so young people, it soon became clear that Eddie had attracted the attention of several Land Girls.

'It looks like your lucky day, Lieutenant. Is it possible for a man to have too much female attention, or is that a silly question?' She knew her question would embarrass the American, and his flushed cheeks told her she'd succeeded.

'You talk rubbish sometimes, Anna Grix, and you a vicar's daughter.'

'Vicar's daughter or not, I know how women think. Men are something else, though, and it looks as though your uniform is upsetting those Italians.'

As Eddie's attention turned to the prisoners of war, one of them made a run for it and disappeared into Witton Wood.

As he fled, one of the Land Girls shouted after him, 'Enzo, come back.'

Eddie turned to Anna. 'At least we have a name. Come on, we need to get after him before the camp commander and the good inspector get their hands on our POW.'

Chapter 4: On the Land

Retracing the journey along the rough farm track, Eddie threw caution to the wind as he flung the Jeep into the ridges and furrows of the compacted surface, causing dust to swirl around the speeding vehicle. Within minutes, the impatient pair stood with Joe Applemead at one of several overgrown access points to Witton Wood.

'This is hopeless; he could be anywhere.'

'It's not like you to be so defeatist. Where's that British grit I keep reading about? Why don't we work our way through what we think is the shortest route from here to Top Field Farm? if I were Enzo, I'd be running in the straightest line possible to put as much distance between the open fields and the safety of the trees as I could.'

Joe Applemead breathed heavily, trying to keep up with the hectic pace Eddie had set as they walked towards the woods. 'Is he always like a bull in a china shop?'

Anna was having her own challenges maintaining the pace. 'Once he gets an idea into his head, there's no stopping him, which leaves the rest of us hanging onto his coattails. Come on, let's get a move on.'

A few minutes later, Eddie came to a halt and raised his hand as a silent sign the other two should follow. 'Do either of you hear anything?' he whispered.

'What, you mean other than my heart trying to escape through my gullet?' said Joe breathlessly.

All three took stock as they listened for anything out of the ordinary that might indicate Enzo's presence.

'I guess the thing that's puzzling me is why he ran in the first place. Why should the sight of my uniform spook him?'

Joe ruffled his thinning hair to dislodge the midges that had taken a liking to his liberal use of Brylcreem. 'My guess is he'd picked up that the authorities were looking for one of them from the girls gossiping. Don't believe all that rubbish about the POWs not understanding English. They can when they want to. I guess Enzo put two and two together and assumed you were there to arrest him.'

Anna shook her head. 'That makes no sense. Why should an Italian assume an American has anything to do with the camp, or the police?'

Eddie briefly removed his cap and dabbed his forehead with a handkerchief. 'Who knows what goes through the head of somebody who's a prisoner in an enemy country.'

Progress proved slow as the three comrades in arms struggled to move forward through a landscape of fallen trees, tangled undergrowth and ill-tempered bracken.

'I hear voices,' exclaimed Anna.

The other two halted and strained to pick up what their companion had detected.

'You're right, I can hear them. It's not English. Some of them must have come after Enzo,' replied Eddie.

'I imagine his oppos are trying to get him back. They know they'll all be in trouble if Enzo's not found. Believe you me, they'll know a lot more than they're letting on to Inspector Spillers.'

Within minutes, the two search parties met up.

'My name is Lieutenant Eddie Elsner. I have no attachment to the British army or the police force.' He turned to Anna. 'This is my friend, Miss Grix, who is the daughter of the vicar at Lipton St Faith. You have nothing to fear from us.'

The POWs maintained a safe distance, waving their arms around flamboyantly as they exchanged views.

Eddie took two steps forward, which silenced the Italians immediately. 'I know some, if not all of you, understand what I'm saying. Let me make something clear, gentlemen. You now have a choice to make. Either the soldiers or the police will find your friend, or you can help us get to him first. I ask you this: which do you think will be better for Enzo?'

Following several seconds of animated discussion with each other, one of their number stepped forward. 'We not know where he goes. Must find him before others. We help you.'

Eddie took a further step forward and shook the man's hand. The gesture did the trick in calming the others as Anna and Joe joined in their newfound fraternity.

Anna leant into the Italian spokesperson and whispered in his ear, '*You* know where he is.'

The man took a step back, shrugged his shoulders, simultaneously opening his eyes wide while holding his open palms towards Anna.

Joe Applemead intervened and addressed the prisoners. 'You must trust these people. It's not that you don't have a choice; I'm telling you they're good people. Do you understand?'

The POWs exchanged anxious looks before nodding at the man who spoke for them. 'Enzo like girl,' he said. 'Maybe he go there?'

Eddie briefly looked at his two companions before turning back to the Italian. 'Do you mean he's escaped before?'

To his astonishment, the Italians laughed.

'And what's so funny? Do you want to help your friend or not?'

Anna's stern words snapped the men out of their humorous mood.

'We… err… sorry. Not make joke at you. But it's easy to escape camp. British soldiers are good men. As long as we come back in time for roll call, they no worry.'

Anna turned to her companions and spoke so that the POWs couldn't hear. 'Let's hope the girl they mentioned isn't Ruth Cotton. If it is, we won't have any choice but to hand him over if we find him.'

Before either Eddie or Joe could respond, the familiar sound of a police alarm bell floated above the tree canopy. In seconds, the Italians had disappeared into the trees like spirits into the night.

'We'd better get back to the Jeep and make ourselves scarce,' said Eddie.

The others needed no second invitation to follow.

Eddie's plan came to no avail.

'I assume you have a sound reason to be scampering from Witton Wood?' Inspector Spillers gave Anna a weary look.

'I'm sorry, Inspector, but there wasn't time to tell you beforehand. It's—'

'Yes, Miss Grix? I'm waiting, and this had better be good.'

'What Anna is trying to say, Inspector,' began Eddie, 'is—'

'Enzo Conti – yes, you two, I know his name – is on the run for suspected murder. You see, Miss Grix, we don't sit around all day drinking tea, despite what many members of the public think.'

How did he get Enzo's name?

'Enzo Conti? Who's he?' asked Anna in the most feminine voice she could conjure up at short notice.

Her efforts had the desired effect. The inspector took his trilby off to scratch his forehead. 'If you say so, Anna, but please understand what we're dealing with. The camp commander is partially correct

45

when he says he has jurisdiction over the Italian. If we don't get to him first, it'll be out of my hands. Major Leonard-White will confine him to solitary confinement if he gets his way, and I'll be struggling to complete a murder case without having access to the prime suspect.'

Anna turned to Eddie. 'He's right. What do you think?'

The American sank both hands deep into his trouser pockets and swivelled on his heels to address the inspector. 'Before we go any further, Inspector Spillers, I want to be certain you believe we have no ill intent as far as your investigation goes.'

'I accept that, but we must get a move on. There's no time to lose. Is there anything that I should know?'

Anna turned on her little-girl-lost look again. 'I have an admission to make, Inspector. When I indicated before that I hadn't heard of Enzo, well… I wasn't being strictly accurate.'

'Now why doesn't that surprise me, Miss Grix?'

Now he's got me blushing. I must look stupid.

'You see, we went to speak to the Italians. The ones on the farm. When they saw us one of them ran away.'

Spillers shook his head. 'Let me guess – Conti bolted?'

'We think Enzo may be heading to a girlfriend. We don't know who she is or where she lives. May I ask a favour, Inspector? Please let Eddie and me speak to him first.'

Inspector Spillers once again took his trilby off, this time lifting his eyes to the heavens before concentrating on Anna's pleading eyes. 'Miss Grix, this isn't a game. I have a witness who swears they saw a man, answering to Enzo's description, talking to Ruth Cotton on the edge of Witton Wood the day you and the Lieutenant here found her body. The man you appear to have sympathy for may be a murderer and as I speak, no one knows where he is.'

The revelation rocked Anna. 'A witness?'

46

Inspector Spillers raised his eyebrows. 'You two are so wrapped up in your own world that you seem to forget I do this sort of thing day in and day out. Do you take us for fools?'

Eddie attempted to speak again without success as the inspector continued to press his position with force.

'We're in a race against time to catch a desperate man suspected of a heinous crime before the military get their hands on him and do heaven knows what to keep this thing quiet. I suggest you both get back to the village and leave this to the police. Do I make myself clear?'

After dropping a subdued Joe Applemead off at Top Field farm, Eddie steered his army Jeep towards Lipton St Faith. 'I think we can safely say we've had better days.'

Anna quietly clapped her hands and smiled at her companion. 'See, you really are getting the hang of this understatement thing. But you're right. Things have got a lot more complicated and we can't afford to get on the wrong side of the inspector.'

A scene of mayhem met the pair as they bustled into the vicarage kitchen, still mulling over recent events. Two flour-covered children squealed with delight, at play with an equally messy vicar.

It's 2.30 pm, the kitchen's covered in flour and Father's reverted to his childhood. I won't half be in trouble with Mum.

'Allow me to introduce you to Master Timmy and Miss Margaret, or "Peggy", Cooper of Clapham, London. Not so much pearly king and queen of that parish, but bakers of distinction.'

The twins looked at Anna pensively, waiting for her reaction. A broad smile soon put them at ease.

'I see you're baking. I'm sure those… err… will be lovely.'

The children giggled as they clapped their hands, sending a cloud of flour everywhere.

47

'We're making little current cakes,' said Margaret as she held up a ball of whitish-grey goo from a baking tray greased with margarine.

Anna tried to hide her surprise and not to come across as too negative. 'But we haven't any currents?'

Timmy was in like a shot. 'The vicar said God provides and if we close our eyes and remember what currents taste like when we eat our cake, then it'll be like they have currents in them.'

'You've got to admire your father's style,' whispered Eddie.

'That's one way of looking at things, I suppose.'

Anna moved over to stand between the two giggling children and placed an arm over the shoulder of each. 'Why don't I make us all a nice cup of tea and check to see whether there's any of my mum's special sponge cake with jam in the middle?'

The children cheered and celebrated by making flour palm prints on each other's back.

The vicar dusted himself down as Eddie stepped forward and picked up the baking tray, on which sat a dozen spherical dollops of cake mixture. 'Why don't I put these in the oven while we have our afternoon snack?'

A few minutes later, the children sat expectantly at the kitchen table and giggled excitedly as a cup of tea and a slice of cake materialised for each of them.

'There you are, you two. Only one rule in this house: we don't speak with our mouth full, OK?'

Timmy and Margaret smiled at one another as they each took a huge bite of their treat. Once it was devoured, the children turned expectantly to Anna.

'I know what you two are after. Well, if you're good and your baking turns out well, perhaps they'll be a supper treat. Now, what do you say to that?'

Their subdued response spurred Eddie into action. He searched his jacket pockets with exaggerated vigour while frowning and sticking his tongue out the side of his mouth as if concentrating on some fiendish task. 'Ah-ha!'

All became clear as he slowly withdrew a Hershey's chocolate bar from each pocket.

Anna thought the children would explode with excitement as they caught sight of Eddie's treasure.

'Are they real?' squealed Margaret.

'Why don't you find out?' Eddie held a chocolate bar in each hand.

Gently relieving the American of his country's famed confectionery, both looked on in wonder as they inspected every square inch of the brownish-red packaging and silver wording.

'I'd forgotten what chocolate smelt like, Peggy.'

'So had I, but today my name is Margaret, silly. Remember, I'm a princess.'

It's good to see them happy.

With the children lost in their own world as they delicately unwrapped their chocolate, Anna told her father about the run-in with Inspector Spillers. 'You'd have thought that—'

The vicar lifted a finger to his lips and gestured to the two children, each of whom was about to take their first bite of chocolate.

'Now you two, why don't you take your treat into the living room so my daughter doesn't nick any from you?'

The children immediately gave Anna a suspicious glance before re-wrapping their confectionery and scurrying from the room.

'Sorry, darling, I think they've heard enough sad stories to be going on with.'

I can't argue with that, Dad.

'Sorry, I wasn't thinking.'

She breathlessly explained the morning's events. 'And to top it all off, the inspector told us that someone saw Enzo with Ruth Cotton.'

The vicar thought for a few seconds. 'It seems to me you two face something of a conundrum. You either stand down and allow matters to take their course, whether that be your Italian chap ending up in police custody or worse, or you redouble your efforts to find him and risk falling foul of the police.'

Eddie stepped forward and sat himself on the corner of the kitchen table. 'Your father's right. I think you British call it being stuck between a rock and a hard place. I guess the thing we need to ask ourselves is whether we believe Enzo to be innocent, and therefore caught up in a trail of fateful coincidences, or a murderer.'

The vicar nodded while scratching his ear. 'While you two ponder your moral dilemma, not helped, I imagine, by missing lunch, I'll fetch some SPAM that I saved you. You're lucky because it was a struggle to stop the terrible twins from scoffing the lot.'

Tom Bradshaw popped his head round the kitchen door. 'I saw the Jeep parked outside and thought I'd check what you two have done to put my inspector in such a foul mood.' He closed the door behind him and hung his police helmet on a coat hook screwed to the back of the door.

'I think you mean her and not us,' announced Eddie.

'Cheeky,' replied Anna.

Constable Bradshaw shook his head and relieved the vicar of a steaming cup of tea from his outstretched hand. 'You know that he cuts both of you a lot of slack. He's not forgotten you were instrumental in bringing the murderer of two people to justice a couple of months ago. He just wants you to be upfront with him.'

'But we told him everything.'

50

He glanced at Eddie before turning back to Anna, who added, 'Well, almost everything.'

'I thought as much. You need to listen to me, Anna. Be straight with him and he'll give you more rope.'

'What, to hang ourselves with?' laughed Eddie.

Tom waved a finger at both. 'Well, we can use rope for many things, can we not? That said, we police have many forms of restraint at our disposal.' He reached down to the broad leather belt that held several pieces of equipment. 'Take this, for example.' The sergeant held his ebonised truncheon aloft. 'One tap with this on a villain's shoulder brings them to heel, I can tell you.'

The lieutenant pointed to the weapon. 'May I?'

Tom smiled as he handed it over. 'Don't drop it; it'll break the tiles.'

'I bet it would,' replied the American as he studied the benign-looking cylinder of hardwood, which tapered in diameter from one end to the other. 'That could do some damage, all right.'

'Don't you be getting any ideas,' said Anna. 'You look lost in your own little world. Now, give it back to the nice sergeant and eat your SPAM before someone gets hurt with that thing.'

Eddie took a long look at the implement as he cupped its cylindrical shape in the palm of one hand.

'Eddie Elsner, did you hear what I said?'

Anna's sharp tone had its desired effect.

'Er… yes… I… Oh, never mind,' replied Eddie as he handed the truncheon back to Tom.

'Honestly, what's got into you?' said Anna.

'SPAM, I hope,' replied Eddie as he turned his attention back to his meal.

For the next few minutes, Tom's companions tucked into their sandwiches while he finished the slice of cake the vicar had provided.

Eventually, Anna asked something she'd been pondering for several minutes. 'Who was it that said they saw Enzo with Ruth?'

Tom continued to eat his cake before taking a sip of tea and gently placing the bone china cup back onto its saucer. 'You know I can't tell you.'

She snapped at the constable. 'Come on, you can do better than that.'

Tom shook his head, glanced at Anna, then Eddie before taking another sip of his tea. 'Let's say that one person's eyewitness is another person's nosy parker. Anyway, I'd better get back to my beat or my sergeant will have my guts for garters.'

Collecting his helmet, Tom offered his thanks for the snack and closed the kitchen door, leaving the room's three remaining occupants staring at one another.

'You push him too far sometimes, my darling. I may sound harsh, but you need to hear it. Tom is one of His Majesty's police officers first and a friend second. You'll do well not to compromise the man.'

Anna reflected on her father's words.

He can turn me back into a child with one sentence.

'I suppose you're right, Dad. It's… Oh, I don't know.'

The vicar sauntered over to his daughter and gave her a hug. 'I know, darling. Now, how are you two going to spend the rest of your day?'

Her father's embrace gave Anna the time she needed to compose herself. 'Well, I'm waiting for Miss Broadbent. She said she'd be back by four to pick the children up. Also, I promised Mum I'd make tea. After that, I think a second trip to Top Field Farm. Don't you, Eddie?'

The American looked at the vicar with pleading eyes.

'I think the most productive thing Eddie can do is to peel the potatoes for our tea while you keep the little ones entertained.'

* * *

'Got to give it to your mother, she's a wonderful cook. That meal was fantastic.' Eddie licked his lips as he pulled into the now-familiar surroundings of Joe Applemead's farmyard.

Anna chuntered as she climbed from the dust-covered Jeep. 'We did our bit; it took me ages to prep the veg.'

Before Eddie could respond, Joe waddled through the wide front entrance to his Georgian farmhouse and completed the familiar routine, checking the string holding up his trousers as a precaution to keep them in place. 'Twice in one day. You two are gluttons for punishment.'

His visitors stepped over a line of cowpats as they crossed the concrete space and exchanged pleasantries with the happy-go-lucky farmer.

'We wanted to check if you might tell us anything else about Enzo away from the prying eyes of the police. If he's guilty, he deserves everything he gets. But what if—'

Joe strolled to his left before beckoning them. 'You know, those lads are as damaged by war as our boys and girls. Follow me, I want to show you something.'

Turning a corner of the sizeable farmhouse, Joe led the way to a large wooden hut camouflaged by overgrown brambles. 'In my father's day, we used it for chickens. It's stood empty for decades, as you can see from the state of it.' The farmer pointed to the sorry-looking timber structure.

As they neared the hut, Eddie spoke. 'Why has the vegetation been cut back from the door?'

The farmer turned and smiled. 'That's what I want to show you.' He reached forward to twist a recently polished brass doorknob, then slowly opened the tongue and groove door to reveal an astonishing sight. 'What do you think of this?'

His visitors stood in astonished silence as they took in every surface of the richly decorated interior.

'It's the chapel,' whispered Anna.

'Did they do it?' asked Eddie.

Joe Applemead slowly walked towards the altar and crossed himself. 'It's all their own work. Nine months it's taken them, and they haven't asked for a penny. All this stuff, carvings, paintings, everything. They did it.'

What an achievement.

Anna joined the farmer and gave a respectful nod towards the altar. 'I didn't realise you were Catholic?'

The farmer let out a quiet laugh. 'No reason you should, is there? I believe we're all made of the same stuff and experience the same things. I suppose we just react in different ways.'

'Sorry, I'm not sure I understand what you mean,' replied Anna.

Joe stroked his chin stubble between a finger and thumb. 'The way I see it, ordinary folk, civilian or soldier, get pushed around by politicians at the best of times, never mind when we're at war. I mean, just look at that Mussolini fool... there, I've just done it, I called him a fool and dismissed him, when he has the power to send people to war, even have someone, anyone, killed with a snap of his fingers. Well, I think the Italians built their chapel to bring them some peace. A sort of physical statement that all this will pass, and that their faith is stronger than any dictator. If I were one of those men praying on his knees in front of the alter I'd helped build, I'd like to think my loved ones were doing the same thing back home. That would bring me true peace.'

The conversation fizzled out as each withdrew into themselves.

Eventually, Anna gave in to her need to find out more about the Italian. 'Is there anything you can tell us about Enzo?'

Joe hesitated for a moment. 'If I'm honest, I'd say he's a deep thinker who's considerate towards others, at least from what I've seen of him.'

'But what about the girls?' asked Anna.

The farmer shrugged his shoulders. 'I said he seemed a

considerate chap, not a priest. Men are men the world over.'

'What if that led to Ruth's murder? You know, it starts out as fun and for whatever reason gets out of hand, then one thing leads to another?' suggested Eddie.

Joe continued to visit each station of the cross as he discussed Enzo. Meanwhile, Anna sat on a rustic wooden chair while Eddie gazed at the ornate ceiling painting.

'Did you see him with any girls, Joe?'

The farmer turned to Anna. 'Like most of the others, yes, I saw him flirting with the Land Girls. It always seemed a bit of fun to me, so I never felt the need to intervene. I watched on from a distance; you know the sort of thing.'

'There were no girls from outside the farm?'

Joe hesitated again. 'I can't say for certain, but I know Enzo got a ribbing for keeping a picture of a girl. Apparently, he guarded it like the devil and put the image in a locket attached to his crucifix. I've never seen it but assume it's his girl in Italy.'

Before the conversation could go any further, the rumble of heavy trucks filled the air.

Rushing to the flimsy door, Eddie almost swore. 'Da… this isn't good. You better look, both of you.'

A column of four army personnel carriers, headed by a staff officer's car, bounced along the uneven farm trackway before coming to a halt in a toxic mixture of dust and exhaust fumes.

They watched as Major Leonard-White waited for his driver to open the rear passenger door.

Emerging in the warm evening sun, the major puffed out his ample chest before offering a menacing smile to his three targets. 'Tell me what you know of Enzo Conti.'

At first, they attempted to play dumb.

'May I remind you I'm a senior officer of His Majesty's forces and require you to answer my question? Enzo Conti was not present for roll call earlier this evening.'

'And what has that got to do with us?' replied Anna, attempting to sound in control of her emotions and not show weakness to the thug she thought the major to be.

Leonard-White beat his gloved left palm with an officer's stick he was holding in his right hand. 'Don't play with me, Miss Grix. Withholding information from the king's command can have drastic consequences. I'm sure you would not wish me to elaborate what powers are available to me in wartime.'

Eddie attempted to intervene. 'You have no such powers, Major.'

The major snapped back. 'Keep out of this, Lieutenant Elsner. I outrank you by an order of magnitude. You're a visitor to our country. I doubt your superior – General Bob Murphy, I believe? – will be happy with how you're executing your duties. Therefore, you'll remain silent.'

Anna gave her companion an anxious look. Eddie responded by offering the faintest shake of his head.

Before either could react, the major ordered four military police officers to detain them. 'Mr Applemead, don't think your part in this debacle will go unpunished. I shall inform my superiors of your conduct. They will, I'm certain, have something to say concerning who should have a licence to work this farm.' The major turned his attention back to his two detainees. 'Get them into my car. I've had enough of this nonsense.'

'You have no jurisdiction over an American citizen.'

Leonard-White laughed. 'I'm the law around here, Lieutenant.'

In seconds, the military police forced the pair into the staff car.

'You have no right to do this,' protested Anna.

'The army says I do. Now, get in.'

Chapter 5: Cock and Sparrow

Being locked in an untidy storeroom within a British prisoner of war camp was hardly how Anna expected to spend the warm and still sunny Monday evening.

My parents won't believe this.

Floor to ceiling wooden racks, each divided horizontally into four sections, lined the walls except for two narrow sections, one of which allowed space for an ill-fitting door, the other a high-level frosted window permitting a modicum of light to enter the forlorn space. Two lines of low storage cupboards divided the rest of the room into narrow strips, and it was at the far end of one of these that Anna and Eddie found themselves handcuffed, each sitting on a basic chair that hardly seemed fit for purpose.

'You fancy a game of I Spy?' asked Anna as she shifted uncomfortably in the small round seat of her chair.

Eddie gave a wry smile and tried to fold his arms, forgetting that his wrist restraints had other ideas. 'How about something beginning with "S"?'

His companion spent several minutes trying to guess the answer, becoming increasingly frustrated as each of her guesses met with Eddie shaking his head. 'That's it, I give up.'

The American raised both arms from his lap and with what freedom his handcuffs allowed, gestured to the disorganised space surrounding them. 'Stuffed.'

'Stuffed? That's not a *thing*. That's a state of mind in our current predicament. It's also cheating.'

Eddie let out a boyish giggle. 'I suppose if any of my friends back home asked me what you British are really like, the last ten minutes sums it up perfectly.' He glanced wide-eyed at his fellow prisoner.

'What?' responded Anna in a tone that suggested bafflement.

'Well, we find ourselves handcuffed and sitting in a locked room full of blankets, towels and heaven knows what else after being chucked into the back of an army staff car, and what do you suggest? That we play I Spy. Priceless.'

It took Anna several seconds to see the funny side of her companion's comment. 'Well, like the poster says, "Keep Calm and Carry On", and seeing as we don't have any other choice, I thought it might pass the time. I'll apologise for being so predictable, Lieutenant.'

'Don't pull that one, Anna Grix. I may not have grown up around you but if I've learnt anything over the last couple of months, it's to know when you're playing for sympathy.' Eddie smiled and wagged a mildly disapproving finger at his companion.

A comfortable quiet fell across the room as its incarcerated guests listened to a steady flow of Italian voices passing by the high-level window.

'How do you suppose they spend their time?'

This time Eddie's response was more thoughtful. 'If I were an Italian prisoner of war in the British camp, I guess I'd feel a mixture of missing family and loved ones, but also, speaking frankly, relief that I was away from the fighting.'

'What, you wouldn't try to escape and get back to your unit?'

Anna's voice displayed an element of surprise at her companion's apparent defeatist attitude.

Eddie got to his feet and wandered up and down the narrow aisle formed by two lines of cupboards. 'Think about it for a minute. The war might be going all right for the Axis powers, but who's really calling the shots? Your own leader, or Adolf Hitler? Apart from being desperate to get back to your family, what else would make you risk trying to escape?'

She frowned. 'But isn't it every POW's duty to escape?'

'You've been watching too many movies, correction, *films*. Unless you hadn't noticed, a large body of water surrounds the British Isles, so not the most appealing of prospects.'

As Anna was preparing to respond, she heard the sharp snap of the key unlocking the door. A second later, two military policemen entered, one carrying a misshapen aluminium tray on which sat two chipped enamel mugs of water accompanied by four thick-cut slices of bread. Neither military police officer spoke, and they withdrew from the room shortly after without looking at either of their charges.

'Bread and dripping. Still, beggars can't be choosers,' said Anna as she eagerly spied their meagre rations, before picking up a slice of bread and taking a large bite from the crusty refreshment.

'Hungry?'

Anna shot her companion a fierce look while continuing to chew on the ration.

'I'll take that as a yes,' said Eddie as he, too, devoured his share of supper.

The meagre nourishment had a calming effect on both as they sat in relative silence, save for the sound of the tin mugs clattering each time they touched the battered metal trays, and the sound of various Italians chatting amiably to each other in the camp compound.

'What do you miss most about home, Eddie?'

The American hesitated while he finished a mouthful of bread and dripping. 'My folks. If I close my eyes, I can see Grandpa's cattle ranch in the snow-capped mountains. If I concentrate hard enough, I can smell the grass that our animals graze. I can even sense the crystal-clear air we're lucky enough to have there. But what I can't do is touch my family and friends. Sure, I can conjure up their image and see them smiling back at me, but it's not the same as your granny flinging her arms around you and giving you a sloppy kiss on the cheek, or a hug so tight from your grandpa that it almost stops you breathing.'

A reflective mood settled within the dark surroundings as its two occupants mirrored each other's actions, sipping cold water from the misshapen enamelled containers and biting into their bread and dripping.

'Things can't be easy for you, either. You may be in familiar surroundings, but Britain has its back against the wall. How are you coping?'

It wasn't a question Anna had been expecting, though on reflection it seemed obvious Eddie might be curious about her own situation. 'I guess so far we've been lucky compared to what's happening in other parts of the country. At the beginning of the war, it seemed almost unreal. One day we were at peace and the next, our prime minister tells us we are at war. I remember my parents hardly speaking in the days following Mr Chamberlain's radio broadcast. They seemed so sad, which I noticed amongst everyone in their age group. I asked my father why, although his response made me feel quite shallow. He said, "We know what's coming. God help us all".'

Anna turned to Eddie, who had stopped eating and was, instead, staring blankly up at the frosted windowpane.

'For the next twelve months, nothing really happened. The papers called it the phoney war. Looking at what's happened since, that description is both ironic and grotesque. I have at least some understanding now of what my father meant.'

Following a further minute of reflective silence, Eddie threw his chipped mug to the far side of the hut by flicking his handcuffed wrist. The object moved with such force that it bounced off the grubby timber wall before ricocheting off a shelf and coming to a spinning rest on the floor. 'Enough of this depressing stuff. What do you hope to do when it's all over?'

Hearing the tin mug bouncing around the place startled Anna. 'Eddie, you're a fool. You scared the life out of me. The future? Do you think any of us have one?'

The American stood up, walked halfway to the far wall and turned around before giving an impromptu performance of a tap dance. 'One thing I learnt after my pa died is that the sun came up the next morning, the one after that and again the following day. This lot will end like the last time, and there will come a time when you wake up and think about something other than the war. So, come on, what ambitions do you have?'

She rested her head back against the wall of the timber hut and looked at the open roof beams as if searching for something precious. 'All right, Fred Astaire, it's September 1941 now. If a pessimist, I'd say we'll all be speaking German by 1943. On the other hand, if Mr Churchill has his way, we'll send them packing by, what, 1948? I'll almost be in my mid-thirties, and if I'm not married with children, spending my days washing and ironing, my parents will think I'm a lost cause. They're already complaining about the lack of grandchildren, so I guess, depending on how things turn out for our prime minister and Mr Hitler, my future is pretty well mapped out.'

Her companion smiled. 'I don't believe that for one minute, the bit about washing and ironing all day, I mean. You're far too independent to fall for that. I think you'll be at university or have joined the police force. Something tells me you won't go through life quietly without leaving your mark.'

Anna could feel herself blush. 'They say the best form of defence is attack, so what about you?'

'Touché,' replied Eddie as he returned to his seat and swivelled to face Anna. 'A farmer. That's what the men in my family do. I don't think I'll be any different.'

This time it was her turn to laugh. 'I think that's about as likely as the farm cats you must have on your ranch befriending a family of mice. You say I won't go through life quietly, well, cliché alert, I reckon you'll cause an earthquake.'

The friends exchanged smiles as nightfall cast its shadow through the opaque glass of the hut's single window, causing an eerie glow to envelop the room.

'Is that a car?'

'Strange,' replied Eddie.

Seconds later, several muffled voices punctured the air.

'Whoever they are, they're coming nearer. Do you think Leonard-White is going to move us?'

Anna had her answer on hearing the now-familiar sound of a key turning in the door lock, a precursor to Inspector Spillers entering the space.

'It seems you two are a liability when out on your own. Come on, we'd better get going before we have to shoot our way out.' The detective saw Anna's horrified reaction. 'Only joking.'

Joking?

'How did you know we were here?'

'Because I'm a detective, Miss Grix. That's what I do, detect things. Your father rang us with his concerns. Given our brief chat on the edge of Witton Wood earlier today, I spoke to Joe Applemead. He told me what happened.'

'Then I'm correct; the major had no right to detain us?' commented Anna.

'Yes, and no,' replied Spillers. 'However, now isn't the time to discuss the finer points of civil versus military law. I'll give you a lift back to Top Field Farm so you can pick up the Jeep.'

The atmosphere was frosty in the vicarage kitchen as Helen and her daughter finished tidying away breakfast things and cleaning what remained of the flour dust from the previous day's junior bakery school, courtesy of the vicar.

Anna knew that eventually she'd need to account for her absence the previous evening. 'I suppose you're wondering how I came to get myself locked up in a prisoner of war camp?'

Helen at first ignored her daughter's question as she finished dusting the wall clock with a cleaning cloth. After neatly folding the fabric into a square, Helen stepped over to the table and sat opposite Anna. 'You're a grown woman, and what you get up to is your own concern. All I ask is that you consider your father and me. For the second time in almost as many days, we were the ones at home worrying about what had happened to you. Now, enough said about that and it's forgotten. Are you seeing Eddie today?'

Is that a trick question?

'As a matter of fact, Eddie is off doing whatever Eddie does and I'm off to see a couple about the evacuees they have staying. I'm sure I'll see him when I see him.'

Her mother played with the cloth she'd so neatly folded minutes

63

before by repeatedly unfolding it and pressing it flat on the pine table, before re-folding the fabric. 'Aren't you being a little dismissive of the lieutenant?'

Anna bridled. 'It's not as if I'm going out with him or anything, Mother.'

Helen raised an eyebrow. 'And I know that when my daughter sounds so defensive, she—'

'Goodness me, is that the time? I'll be late for the Bancrofts if I don't get a move on. See you later, bye-bye,' said Anna.

She risked a sideways glance at her mother as she opened the back door to the kitchen.

Parents are infuriating sometimes.

Once outside, Anna took a deep breath and rounded the corner of the vicarage, making for the old stables. After retrieving her newly refurbished bike from one of two stalls, she slid her bicycle clips onto the bottom of her baggy trousers and set off down the high street, waving to several locals as she passed by.

The Bancroft family leased a smallholding half a mile outside Lipton St Faith, a distance that Anna covered in less than fifteen minutes. As she pulled into the tiny yard surrounded by a low flint-built wall, a smiling Daisy Bancroft came out of a small washhouse, its chimney smoking from burning dirty coal. 'Nice to see you, Anna. I suppose you're here to check on the two terrors.'

As she spoke, Timmy and Margaret came running into the yard, each waving a long narrow stick. 'We're playing bad guys and good guys. I'm winning,' announced Margaret.

Anna looked at Daisy, whose smile was infectious. 'I see. I hope peace breaks out soon, or else lunch might be late.'

The children gave Daisy a look of horror. 'Say it's not true. You promised us a real sausage each and some bread with butter on,' pleaded Margaret. She turned to her brother. 'That's it, the war's over, and I won, you lost.'

Timmy shrugged his shoulders and took off with his stick, raking it against the flint wall before disappearing into a small barn.

'I rather think they're having quite an adventure, don't you?'

Daisy held Margaret close and toyed with one of her pigtails. 'You know, I don't think either of them had seen a real chicken or pig. After a couple of days, you'd have thought they'd been around them all their lives, poor mites.'

After accepting a cup of tea from Daisy and spending fifteen minutes checking if she needed anything to help the twins settle in and discussing general gossip, Anna took leave of the newly formed family and headed back to the village.

Now for Gertrude. This should be interesting.

With its own small duck pond, the picturesque cottage overlooked the village green and in the front garden, a picket fence in need of maintenance was the only thing that shielded it from the outside world.

As Anna neared the medieval building complete with thatched roof and overhanging first floor, she waved at Gertrude who was busy digging up some potatoes from a small vegetable patch to one side of the pond. 'Good morning. You have a minute?'

'I thought I recognised you on that bike of yours. Come in, I've been expecting you, but you'll have to take me as you find me; I've been digging and cleaning vegetables all morning.'

Anna stepped through the open cross frame of the bicycle and leant it against the picket fence, before picking up one of two open baskets containing heavily soiled potatoes. 'I wanted to talk to you about—'

'Let's go inside, shall we? Big ears and all that,' replied Gertrude as she looked around the quaint village scene with locals going about their business.

'Did you enjoy the scrag end?' she asked, heading down the side of the half-timbered cottage and into a tiny kitchen.

'Mum loved it. I was in her good books for once.'

Gertrude frowned. 'I don't believe that for a minute. You not being in good books with your mother ever, I mean.'

The two women giggled as they rested their baskets on a small round table full of clutter.

Inviting Anna into the low-beamed sitting room, Gertrude pointed to a carver chair, its bright fabric enhancing the little light coming through the small panes of glass in the Georgian bow window.

'This is about Ruth Cotton, isn't it?'

Anna nodded as she gave her host a half-smile. 'You mentioned that you got to know her at the boatyard. Is there anything else, anything at all, you can tell me about her?'

Gertrude brushed dry soil from the knees of her working trousers onto the stone floor. 'What, you mean like family and stuff? For the most part, she kept herself to herself, even if it was a bit odd for such a confident girl.'

'Yes, anything at all to give me a better picture of Ruth. Do you mind talking about her?'

The cottage owner shrugged her shoulders. 'There's nothing any of us can do to make things better for the poor girl, so yes, I'm happy to help if you think I can. She was always a bit vague about her family. Ruth seemed not to want to talk about them and not knowing her too well, I didn't push it. She said she lived at home with her mum and dad. There was a boyfriend, though. Again, she didn't talk about it much, but I knew exactly what sort of bloke he was; still is.'

'Do you know, you're the second person to say something like that. You know him?'

Gertrude got to her feet and played with one of several small brass

66

ornaments on the mantelpiece. 'A bit hot-headed, you might say, so being stuck in a tank blowing things up should be right up his street.'

That's harsh.

'Hot head or not, the man won't even know his girlfriend is dead,' said Anna.

'He does because he's home on leave. He kept it quiet all right. I thought I'd seen a ghost at first, but no, it was him all right. You don't forget Robert Sedwell, or his family. A bad lot, they are.'

I don't know that name...

'I see. Where does he come from?' asked Anna.

Gertrude thought for a moment. 'When he was a lad, he lived about a mile up the road. That's how I came to know him – always making mischief. Not the usual larking about – he liked to break things; the more expensive the better. Then something happened, I don't know what, and they all upped sticks. I hear they're a little west of Norwich now; Easton, I think. But I'll lay a bet he's not with his parents.

'He's a strange one all right. Even as a kid, he liked to camp out in the woods. If you ask me, I bet he's in one of his bolt holes. His favourite was Witton Wood.'

The Cock and Sparrow public house in the lieutenant's home village of Three-Mile-Bottom stood in splendid isolation, set back from the narrow lane that snaked its way through the tiny hamlet. First opened in 1507 by a Mr John Woodman, the pub had been a feature of the Norfolk landscape ever since, nestled as it was by a small stream on the edge of the Norfolk Broads.

It was against this backdrop that Eddie Elsner sat in the near-deserted bar of the ancient hostelry, attempting to understand why Major Leonard-White had asked for a meeting.

As he waited for his guests to arrive, Eddie pondered how things had changed in the Cock and Sparrow since he and Anna had helped shut down a sophisticated betting ring, which operated from the restroom of the pub.

Even the barman is new, and this one smiles.

An officer barking orders at his hapless driver alerted Eddie to the major's arrival. Seconds later, the rotund figure of Leonard-White strode self-importantly into the sparsely furnished establishment.

'There you are, Elsner. Thank you for meeting me. What's your poison?' Eddie watched with suspicion as the British officer thumped on the bar top to alert a member of staff who was already looking straight at him. 'Get me a whisky, no water. Elsner, you want one?'

At this time of day?

'Haven't got any,' said the barman without blinking.

Good, that solves that problem.

Leonard-White exploded at the barman, wagging his officer's stick inches from the uninterested man's face. 'You'd better have another look, because my men say differently, and if you still decide you're out of stock, I'll make sure the Justice of the Peace withdraws your liquor licence. Do we understand one another?'

Without bothering to answer and still staring intently at the major, the barman shrugged his shoulders and slowly disappeared beneath the bar top, only to reappear a second later, holding a half bottle of single malt whisky.

'That's the spirit, old chap,' said the major sarcastically. 'Get it? Spirit, whisky?'

Eddie exchanged exasperated glances with the barman. 'May I get a glass of water, sir?'

Eddie wasn't sure who was more surprised at his form of address, the bemused major or amused barman.

Slouching into his chair opposite the lieutenant with only a small beaten copper-topped, three-legged table between them, the major emptied half of his drink in one gulp.

Likes his drink.

'Why the mystery, Major? A note shoved through my billet's letterbox in the dead of night, instructions not to tell anyone. What gives?'

The barman delivered Eddie's glass of water, and Leonard-White waited for the barman to retreat while looking around to make sure no one else was within hearing range. 'Damn civilians. I don't trust any of the blighters. The police are the same, waltzing around in their little cars and taking turns to blow their whistles. I'd get rid of the lot.'

'What, civilians as well?' Eddie took a sip of his water, having already heard enough from his guest.

The major emptied the rest of his whisky and tapped the empty glass loudly on the small table before extending his left arm towards the barman without looking at the man. 'Another.'

Loser.

Within twenty seconds, the barman refilled his glass. The major retracted his arm without acknowledging the barman's quick service.

'I want to talk to you as one brother officer to another. You know, as do I, that in times of war the military must take command. We lead, others must obey. Get my drift? That's why I didn't want the little lady here. I'm sure she has enough on her shoulders doing what women do, which, by the way, is a complete mystery to me.'

I don't like the way this is going.

'It's a good job Anna isn't with us to hear you say that.' Eddie's attempt to lighten the conversation fell on deaf ears.

'Lieutenant, I don't give a fig what she or any other woman thinks of my views, nor the police. I have little doubt Spillers felt like the cavalry in one of your American Western films. You may wish to know I knew he'd come to your aid and chose not to spoil his little adventure.'

This is sinister.

'Not sure I'm catching your drift, Major?'

Leonard-White drummed the fingers of one hand on the tabletop. 'It's simple, Elsner. I have my orders and I'll carry them out. As one military man to another, I'm sure you understand that?'

He's mad or bad, perhaps both.

'Yes, I do, but perhaps you'd humour me by explaining a little further.'

The drumming of fingers became more intense. 'These Italians are lazy and cowards, everyone knows that. Who'd have thought they ran an empire from Africa to Hadrian's Wall all those years ago. Now look at them, led by a pompous ass in a funny hat playing the hard man, when all the time he dances to the tune of a crazy Austro-Hungarian with a pathetic moustache. England and America must lead, Lieutenant Elsner. You can see that, can't you?'

And a racist.

Eddie worked hard not to rise to the major's incendiary comments which, by now, had attracted the interest of the few regulars who populated the bar.

'What exactly is it you want from me, Major?'

Leonard-White stopped tapping his fingers on the table, lowered his voice and leant towards Eddie. 'You think Enzo Conti is innocent, don't you?'

Surprised at his assertion, Eddie bit back. 'I think no such thing. However, I do believe in due process.'

The officer flared his nostrils as he leant forward. 'Let me tell you a thing or two about the charming Enzo. He has a reputation for seducing young British women, leaving their families to clear up the mess, if you understand my meaning.'

Eddie attempted to interrupt.

70

The major held an open palm toward him. 'Let me finish, Lieutenant. I've had to deal with such families on more than one occasion, and it's not a pleasant thing to do. Enzo Conti is a prisoner of war, always denies knowledge of such girls and has his alibis corroborated by his fellow prisoners.'

Is he playing me?

'You have proof?'

'Better than that, Lieutenant Elsner, I give you my word as an officer and a gentleman.'

I wonder?

Chapter 6: A Sad Loss

Although Harvest Festival had, by common acclaim, been a triumph in the face of wartime adversity, removing the flowers and other decoration to return Lipton St Faith Parish Church to its more usual day to day state of repose was one of Anna's less cherished annual tasks. 'It's such a shame to throw all the decoration away, don't you think, Mum?'

Helen was struggling to untie a stubborn bunch of barley from high on one of the ornate Norman columns that supported a hammer-beamed open ceiling. 'What was that, dear? I have no idea why some people fasten these things so tightly. It's not as if a sheaf of cereal is going to poleax one if it lands on one's head, is it?'

'No, although I suppose one might be a little itchy for the rest of the day.'

'Ah, got you,' said Helen triumphantly as she slipped the barley from its string constraint and popped it into a large brown paper bag to stop the seeds dispersing.

'Be careful on those steps, Mum. We don't want a repeat of last year, do we?'

Helen tutted at her daughter as she gingerly descended an ancient set of wooden stepladders. 'You know perfectly well that was your father's fault for startling me. Why the man is always in such a hurry is a mystery to me. Do you know, I think he was the one who taught the bull how to misbehave in china shops.

'Anyway, that's why I've banished him from the church for the next hour. There shall be no repeat of his knight in shining armour act. Now, I suggest we get a move on since we are a day late in tidying up this year, and it's 3.00 pm already and your father will be itching to make sure all is in order for Evensong.'

Mention of the time spurred both women on to speed up their efforts to clear the church before the last task of dusting the pews and making sure hymn books were at the ready for the early evening service.

Progress continued apace until the new curate, Brian Tidmarsh, entered the sacred building.

'Darling, I thought we agreed the church was ours until four-thirty?' Helen bridled at being ignored by her husband. 'Charles, did you hear me, I said—'

Her daughter's giggles interrupted Helen. Turning around, she noticed the frozen figure of the curate, his face pink with embarrassment. 'Ah, Brian, it's you. Well, one day you, too, will marry and be subject to the strict instructions of your wife. In the meantime, what can we do for you? We are rather busy, as you can see.'

Brian stood silent for several seconds before pointing to a large display of donated foodstuffs that had held pride of place during the Harvest Festival service.

Anna looked at the food, then at her mother. Both women turned to the hapless curate.

'Are you hungry?'

The curate frowned as the women laughed. 'Oh, I see. A joke. Yes, exceptionally funny, I'm sure. No, I wanted to catch you both because I know what a fine job you do in distributing the villagers' offerings.'

'I sense a "but" coming, Brian?' said Anna.

She looked at her mother, who appeared suitably suspicious.

'Brian?' said Helen.

'Well... err... I thought this year we might, how should I put it... pool, yes, that's the word I'm looking for. Why don't we pool our resources with the surrounding parishes so we may have a greater impact on our communities and foster a sense of "We're all in this together" sort of thing?'

Several seconds of silence fell as Anna and her mother processed what Brian seemed to suggest. Helen covered the distance between herself and the curate in slow, deliberate steps while maintaining a warm smile. 'Sit down here with me, Brian. I think we need a few words.'

'Have I offended you, Helen?'

'Not in the least.'

I know that look. Being cruel to be kind, she calls it.

'Brian, you mentioned that your plan would help us all feel we were "in it together". I don't wish to be patronising, but I think that fact is apparent as we listen to the news on the wireless, queue for what rations we're allowed and support friends and acquaintances when they receive one of those dreaded telegrams via the post office.'

'I'm sorry, I don't understand, Helen?'

Anna joined the conversation. 'I think what Mum is saying is that each community deals with things their own way, which helps us to be stronger. Hmm. That didn't come out right. What I mean is—'

'What we both mean is that each village has its own traditions, Brian, especially concerning charitable giving. Honouring those traditions, symbols if you like, is the best way to reinforce a sense of continuity in dreadful times.'

The curate clasped his hands as if in prayer. 'I understand our village has, since 1920, distributed its Harvest Festival yield to war widows, is that correct?'

Helen placed a hand over Brian's clasped fingers and offered a gentle smile. 'Yes, we have, just as Three-Mile-Bottom gives to the Seaman's Mission in Great Yarmouth in memory of a merchant ship sunk during the Great War by enemy action. Several men from the hamlet perished in that tragedy.'

'And the nearby village of Lazenby donates to the local orphanage,' added Anna. 'Not because they lost any men in World War One, but in thanks. Their intention is to help other local communities that did lose men and women. Think of it as their way of saying "We're all in this together".'

Brian unclasped his fingers and gently cupped the hand Helen had placed on his. 'Thank you for making a city boy understand what community means.'

Eddie Elsner interrupted the touching moment, stepping into the church and giving a polite cough to announce his presence.

'Hello, you. I see you timed your entrance to perfection, as in, all the work's done.'

Eddie offered a half-smile. 'Have you got a minute?'

'Go on, you go. Brian and I will finish up here, isn't that right?' Helen looked at the curate, who responded with a broad smile as Anna rose from her pew and wandered up the aisle to the church entrance where the lieutenant was still holding open the door.

'That looked intense.'

'A delicate task that always seems to fall to Mum: inducting the new curate into the ways of rural Norfolk.'

'I see,' replied Eddie.

His companion laughed and led him by the hand until they were in the middle of a waist-high labyrinth of weathered headstones, most of which carried only the faintest eulogy to the departed caused by decades, and most times, centuries, of weathering. 'I'm not sure you do. Now, the fact you turned up when I didn't expect to see you means you've discovered something of interest, yes?'

As they meandered around a hundred graves, some marked only by a tiny raised oblong mound showing the repose of a long-gone villager, Eddie recounted his meeting with Major Leonard-White in the Cock and Sparrow. 'Freaky or what?' concluded the lieutenant.

'You think he has something to do with Ruth's murder?'

Eddie stopped in his tracks and rested his hand on an adjacent headstone. 'I can't say there's a direct link, no. But I think he's unhinged and if he gets his hands on Enzo, well, heaven knows what he'll do to the man.'

Anna wandered around a grave as she pondered Eddie's revelation before sharing her encounter with Gertrude and news of Ruth's boyfriend. 'Two people, independent of each other, have told me Robert Sedwell is a bully. Ruth even said he likes to disappear into his hideaways. What if he found out Ruth was seeing Enzo and killed her in a jealous rage and ran for it?'

'But it sounds so far-fetched,' replied Eddie. 'We have one person who's convinced herself he's a bad lot and thinks she saw him and deduces he must be Ruth's killer?'

'Don't patronise me. Gertrude made no such link and for your information, she grew up with the man. She knows the family and is convinced she saw him. All I ask is that you keep an open mind instead of disappearing down your own rabbit hole and assuming everyone else is wrong.' Anna felt the blood rushing through her cheeks as her anger grew.

Eddie wasn't for backing down. 'Well, there's one way we can sort this. I'll check whether he's still with his unit. It's as simple as that.'

'Is it really? You think because you do whatever it is you do, that you can pick up the phone to the British army and demand to know where one of their soldiers is?'

'I don't need to demand anything, Anna.'

His bitter reply stunned Anna.

I don't know him at all.

Separating to inspect headstones whose writing they could not decipher allowed tempers to cool.

'Of course, there's one person neither of us has spoken to yet,' said Eddie in a low, conciliatory tone.

Here we go again. Clever clogs rides to the——

'Geoffrey Lenox,' exclaimed Anna, the recent bad blood between them now forgotten.

'Only one problem. We don't know what he looks like, so we must spin a tale or two to get at him.'

'Well, Lieutenant Elsner, that shouldn't be a problem for you.'

The sign read:

'Dingle Boatyard: Makers and Repairers of River Craft'.

Less clear was how Anna and Eddie might gain entrance to a site contracted to the government for war work.

'Any ideas?' said Anna as her companion brought the Jeep to a halt fifty yards from the heavily guarded entrance to the sprawling boatyard.

Seems strange seeing soldiers with rifles on such a lovely day on the Norfolk Broads.

The gravel-covered patch of ground on which the Jeep stood allowed for partial concealment from the armed troops as the pair pondered their next move.

'Nothing for it but to go in hard.'

77

'Are you mad? You mean to ram the entrance? They'll shoot us,' replied Anna, her voice tinged with incredulity.

'I may be an American, but John Wayne I'm not. But we're in an army Jeep and I'm in uniform. If nothing else, they'll be curious. We'll use that to our favour.'

Anna hung on for dear life as he rammed the gearstick forward, took his foot off the clutch and pressed the accelerator. The Jeep's tyres spun wildly, throwing a stream of small stones behind the vehicle as it picked up speed.

'I knew it, you've gone mad. I'll say you kidnapped me and flutter my eyelashes at them. You can fend for yourself.'

The noise of the engine roaring away meant that Eddie failed to hear Anna's dire warning. Seconds later, the Jeep stood idle a few feet away from an army private and lance corporal pointing their rifles at the vehicle's occupants.

'In a rush, are we?' said the lance corporal as he joined his subordinate in smirking at their visitors.

'Salute, soldiers,' snapped the lieutenant. Eddie's stern tone and unsmiling face snapped the guards into action. In a second, both had shouldered their weapons and raised their right arms in salute. Eddie acknowledged the protocol by returning the salute. 'Stand easy, soldiers. Open the gates now. I cannot reveal my orders to you, except to say I have a WVS welfare officer with me, whom one of those workers will need when I do my sad duty today. Do you understand, soldiers?' Eddie emphasised his last sentence by almost barking the words at the confused guards.

'Good heavens, it worked,' whispered Anna as the private and lance corporal scrambled to open the iron-framed gates in double quick time, offering a second salute as the Jeep passed them by.

'That was the easy bit. Now for whoever manages this place,' replied

Eddie as he eased the Jeep forward at a sedate pace into the complex, bringing the vehicle to a halt directly in front of a huge, dilapidated timber building, its cavernous interior concealing several crafts in various stages of construction.

A man wearing smart working clothes walked towards them. 'It's not every day you see an American serviceman around here. May I help?'

I can't believe our luck.

Eddie stepped forward. 'Nice to meet you, sir. I have orders to talk to a man who works here. His name is Geoffrey Lenox. My colleague here is with the WVS on vital war work. Do you know where we might find the gentleman?'

The lieutenant's confident manner did the trick. 'I see,' replied the man. 'I'm his foreman. He's having his tea break over there. On his own, as usual. Do you want me to take you to him?'

'No. no, that won't be necessary,' replied Eddie. 'The matter is delicate and one that I'm not mandated to share. You understand?'

The foreman touched the rim of his flat cap with two fingers. 'Of course. Well, I'll leave him to you, shall I?'

'So kind,' replied Eddie.

I've got to admire your front, Eddie Elsner.

As the pair neared Lenox, he took notice of them before finishing a plastic cup of tea and throwing the remnants into the Broad.

'Can I help?' he said politely.

After introducing themselves, Anna revealed the reason for wanting to speak to him. '...So, we wanted to know if you might tell us about Ruth since you worked with her. Is that all right?'

Lenox gave his visitors a suspicious look. 'You know what Mr Churchill says about careless talk costing lives.'

'Friends of the family. The uniform need not alarm you. I'm just passing through.'

'She never mentioned any Americans…'

Anna was in like a shot. 'You know her?'

The man shrugged his shoulders. 'What kind of question is that? Of course I do. I work with her every day… or at least, well, she hasn't been in for a few days. Is she OK?'

'She's dead, Geoffrey, or to be more precise, murdered.'

Anna watched for Lenox's reaction.

Hasn't batted an eyelid…

'You know, Mr Lenox, all kinds of rumours fly around. Some are baseless tittle-tattle that can do more harm than good.' Anna warmed to her theme. 'You're a case in point.'

Lenox frowned. 'What's that supposed to mean? Has someone been saying something about me? Well, it's not true. I didn't touch her. She's not… I mean wasn't my type.'

'That's as may be, Mr Lenox, but Ruth told one of her friends you were always trying it on, and she didn't like it. Is that what you did, Geoffrey?'

The man turned from his interrogator and peered out over a silken-smooth stretch of Broad. 'I'm not interested in having a girlfriend; they're all the same.' Lenox turned. His eyes burned into Anna.

'You know, Mr Lenox, there's one thing that's puzzling me. Why haven't you enlisted? You must be what, twenty-five?' said Anna.

'Twenty-six, if you must know. And before you say what all the others say, I tried to, but the army turned me down. I have haemophilia and I look after my mother who's bad with her nerves; there's only the two of us at home. Father died in the Great War. I can't remember him, and no one talks about him. He's not even named on the war memorial in our village.'

Crikey, where did all that come from?

Anna and Eddie exchanged surprised glances as the lieutenant

80

picked up the conversation. 'I'm sorry to hear that.' I guess that's more reason for you to live life to the fullest. You know, flirting with young women even if they don't want to know. After all, speaking man to man, we know it's only a bit of fun, don't we, and it sure beats shooting a rifle at the Germans, eh?'

Instead of responding to Eddie, Lenox turned on Anna. 'I told you, women are all the same. My dad was a hero, and it wasn't his fault.'

What's going on?

'Are you all right, Mr Lenox? You're sweating.'

'Some say my mother was messing about while dad was away fighting. Whatever happened, I only know he didn't come back.'

Eddie held his palms out. 'Steady on, fella. It sounds like you've had it tough and we're privileged that you've shared that with us, but we're only here to get as much information about Ruth as we can. After all, we don't want those rumours getting so out of hand that the police take an interest in you, do we?'

'I told you I—'

'And I'm telling you, you have quite a temper, Geoffrey. Did Ruth make you angry when she turned you down?'

Before Lenox replied, the foreman called out. 'Back to the line, Mr Lenox, if you don't mind.'

Lenox responded immediately by raising his hand to acknowledge he was on his way back. As he passed his unwanted visitors, Lenox glared at Anna while completely ignoring the lieutenant.

'Did you notice he aimed all his anger at you?'

'Or perhaps women in general. Anyway, you're convinced Enzo murdered Ruth, aren't you?'

'I may lean that way, but there's no harm in seeing where this rabbit runs, is there?'

Anna smiled as they walked back to the Jeep. 'I tell you what, why don't we see if Ruth's parents will talk to us? You never know, they may have heard her talk about a strange character called Lenox.'

'Do you know where they live?'

'Yes, Tom Bradshaw told me. It's about five miles from here.

Tuttingdon took them over twenty minutes to reach, remote even by the standards of East Norfolk. The long, twisting, narrow roads with deep drainage channels and high hedges on either side made for treacherous going as the Jeep neared its destination.

'I reckon that's it.' Anna pointed to a gap in the hedges a hundred yards ahead. Squeezing the army vehicle as far to the right as possible, Eddie just got it off the road, so enabling any other traffic to pass by without obstruction.

The Cottons' house was modern by any standard, built as a farm worker's cottage before the outbreak of war. Instead of a thatched roof, it boasted concrete tiles. Rather than tiny Georgian squares of glass, the window frames allowed for a generous amount of plate glass.

After unhooking the latch on the garden gate, Eddie stood aside to allow Anna through. A ten-yard walk saw them standing at the dark green-painted front door with an oval piece of opaque glass occupying the upper section of the construction.

Two gentle taps of the wrought iron knocker saw the door open, whereupon a dishevelled woman stuck her head around the doorframe.

She looks ill, poor woman.

'Mrs Cotton?' Anna whispered.

The woman gave the briefest of nods. 'Can I help?'

Anna explained who she and Eddie were and the circumstances through which they came to discover Ruth's body.

'The police said a couple had found our Ruthy while out walking in the woods. We are ever so grateful you both took such good care of my daughter. Please, come in.'

She's thanking us.

Inside the spacious lounge, Mrs Cotton stood nervously, seemingly not sure what to say or do.

Anna picked up on the woman's predicament. 'Is Mr Cotton at home?'

The bereft mother looked towards the back window. She pointed. 'He's tending his vegetables. It seems to help him cope. You know how it is.'

I can't imagine.

'Please, sit. Would you like tea?'

The visitors sat next to one another on a cottage suite-style sofa, its beech arms and legs polished to within an inch of their life. Other than two matching chairs and an old mahogany sideboard, there was little else in the room apart from a few family photos and a business card, which Anna realised was from an undertaker.

'We had tea a little while since, but thank you for asking, Mrs Cotton.'

Eddie broached the difficult subject of why they had called in. 'Mrs Cotton, there is no way that we can understand the pain your family is going through right now. Please know this, there are so many people thinking of you in your time of loss. And we want to help find out what happened to Ruth. Will you allow us to do that?'

Mrs Cotton nodded without hesitation. 'Like it or not, you're involved in this terrible thing. If you can bring my husband and me some peace, we should be so thankful.'

What a dignified woman.

After what seemed like an age of silence, Anna spoke. 'I wonder if you might tell us a little about Ruth?'

83

Mrs Cotton gave the merest of smiles at the mention of her daughter's name. 'Loving, that's the first thing that comes to mind. She never gave us a minute's trouble and was always helping around the house. And she was a hard worker at the boatyard. Everyone says so. She loved going to the pictures, especially to see Hedy Lamarr and James Stewart. Oh, what were they last together in?'

'*Come Live with Me*,' said Eddie.

'Yes, that's it, she loved that film. Do you know she's watched it at least four times…? I mean, did. Who would do that to my girl?' Mrs Cotton broke down, the tears rolling down her cheeks.

'That's what we're helping the police to find out, and we shall, you have my word on it,' said Anna.

Mr Cotton's sad frame appeared from the kitchen doorway, holding a small bunch of carrots.

'They want to help find who hurt our Ruthy.'

Mention of his daughter's name caused the burly man to tear up.

Mrs Cotton sprang to her feet to put her arms around her husband. 'Now, Jim, that's enough of that; blubbing won't bring her back. We have to be strong for Ruthy.'

Jim Cotton gave Anna and Eddie a determined look. 'If I get my hands on him, I'll…'

'I know, Mr Cotton. But best to leave it to the police and anything we can do to help them,' replied Eddie in a compassionate tone.

Well, it's now or never.

Anna steeled herself for the question she knew needed asking. 'Did Ruth have a boyfriend?'

Ruth's father exploded in a fit of anger. 'If you mean that worthless Sedwell, I'm a Dutchman. Trouble was, Ruthy wouldn't be told. We reckon he was her first real fella, if you know what I mean.'

Anna got up from her seat and placed a hand on Mr Cotton's arm.

'I know it's hard for any father when his daughter dates for the first time, but why do you dislike him so much?'

Ruth's father glanced at his wife, who shook her head. 'No, Jen, we must say it. Because we think he was two-timing her.'

'Why do you think that?' replied Anna.

'Because he's a Sedwell. Like father, like son. They're all the same. Brothers, uncles, the lot of them. Ruthy wouldn't listen. We told her, didn't we, Jen?'

Mrs Cotton looked at the tiled floor rather than answer her husband.

'When was the last time you saw him with your daughter?' asked Eddie.

'I dunno, don't much care anymore.'

Mrs Cotton rallied. 'Come on, Jim, these people are trying to help.' Turning to Eddie, she continued, 'If you think he had anything to do with… with what happened to Ruthy, I'm afraid you'd be wrong. He got sent to Italy months ago and Ruth had this letter from him only last week. I never read Ruthy's letters, I mean, it's not proper, is it? But I thought it might help us understand and…' Her voice tailed off as she scrutinised the envelope.

'What's the matter, Mrs Cotton, are you feeling unwell?'

She's seen something.

'Why didn't I notice that before?' said Mrs Cotton, pointing to the stamp.

'May I look?' asked Eddie. After scrutinising the post office date and time on the cancellation mark, he held up the envelope for all to see. 'It was posted in Southampton a week ago. That means he's in England, not Italy.'

Chapter 7: The Neglected Evacuee

'Do you think we'll ever eat when normal people have their meals? That lamb stew your mother conjured up from the – what did you call it, scrag end? – looked fantastic.'

Anna looked at her wristwatch.

6.30 pm and driving into the middle of nowhere.

'Well, it can't be helped. My WVS supervisor sounded concerned. We rarely get reports of an evacuee being mistreated, but when we do, we jump on it straight away.'

Her mind raced at what they might find as she glanced up at a sky dotted with fluffy white clouds that bathed the patchwork of fields into soft shade as they danced in front of the evening sun.

'Do they get paid for giving the young ones food and board? Why would anyone bother if they disliked kids enough to neglect them?'

I can't bear to think about it.

'It gets a bit complicated and depends on which group the evacuee falls into. For the lad we're on our way to see, the family will get ten shillings and sixpence a week. As for neglecting their charges, the placement officers don't consider whether the host family wants to take them in, or even if they're comfortable looking after young children.

If they have room and the amenities required by the government, they must accept them.'

Eddie temporarily removed his hands from the Jeep's steering wheel before banging it with clenched fists. 'That's asking for trouble. Do you mean to tell me that's how you're trained?'

Oh dear.

'Look, if I get a bad feeling about a family, I won't put children in their care, no matter what the training manual, or my supervisor, say. Luckily for me, she's a good, caring woman. Unfortunately, it's kids from the poorest backgrounds that seem to get the dirtiest end of the stick. Families with money and influence will often have friends or family they can send their children to when the evacuation order comes.'

'So what's new?' replied Eddie, shrugging his shoulders. 'Looks like we're here.'

A weather-beaten board warned visitors of danger, courtesy of a rough hand-painted message in large white capital letters:

'KEEP OUT, DOGS OFF LEAD. YOU HAVE BEEN WARNED.'

The sign set the tone for the general state of dilapidation of the smallholding.

'I'll get the gate open. You keep your eyes peeled for the hounds of hell.'

Many a true word said in jest.

The lieutenant jumped from the stationary vehicle and wrestled with a wide five bar gate, which refused to budge. 'Do you think this thing has ever been opened?'

'It's as good a way as any of keeping folk out,' replied Anna. 'Try undoing the rope on the bottom left corner. That should help.'

Her companion muttered under his breath as he realised what held the gate in place. Solving the last of several knot puzzles, Eddie finally pulled the rope clear, only for the gate to topple towards him.

As he jumped smartly out of the way, the gate crashed to the ground, covering the American's uniform in a thin film of fertile Norfolk soil. 'Don't you dare laugh.'

'Me? How can you think such a thing?' answered Anna with a broad smile.

'Hmm, let me think about that. In the meantime, this thing is far too heavy for me to lug around, so there's only one thing for it.' Eddie completed a final brush of his uniform before clambering back into the driver's seat.

'You're not going to… I see you are.'

As Eddie plunged his right foot onto the accelerator, the vehicle roared forward, making short shrift of the fallen gate as the Jeep bounced over its crumbling construction.

A hundred yards down the meandering track, which had a line of grass running down its centreline, denoting a lack of regular use, the pair observed the worn-out roof thatch and stained net curtains of a farmhouse in urgent need of repair.

Within seconds, a scruffily dressed elderly man, wearing wellington boots and a pair of patched trousers held up with an ancient set of braces, poured himself out of what passed for the building's front door.

'What do you be wanting on my land?' The man gave special attention to Eddie.

Anna held up her WVS identity card and attempted to make their introductions.

'You're one of them nosy parkers, are you?'

'I'm doing my job if that's what you mean. I'm here to see Vincent O'Conner,' Anna responded in a calm, assertive tone.

The man shrugged his shoulders. 'Him not 'ere; 'im gone with the missus. Dunno when them's comin' back. You knows what women is like with shoppin' and the like.'

'Then you won't mind us looking around?' Eddie unfolded himself from the driver's seat of the Jeep.

'I doesn't care if you is an American; no one is pokin' their nose around 'ere. Now get off my land or I'll—'

'Or you'll what? It's Mr Larson, isn't it? Take me to the boy now or I'll call the police. We've had reports of him being ill-treated and I want to see him.'

'I knows no Larson fella. You got the wrong place, girl.'

Anna stepped from the vehicle before taking several more steps towards the increasingly angry farmer. 'I've had enough of this nonsense. You're Larson.' She pointed to an open-fronted outbuilding, its roof almost collapsed, in which stood a wooden cart with faded lettering spelling the Larson name on one side. 'Don't take us for fools. I want to see the boy, now.'

Larson shrugged his shoulders again. 'Who's been sayin' things?'

At last.

'That's no concern of yours. Now, you have a choice. Show me the lad or you can explain matters to the police. Which is it going to be?'

The farmer scowled at Anna, then turned his attention to Eddie. ''Im is simply accident-prone. And all for ten bob a week. You two wait there, get my drift, boy? I'll see if 'er's back.' Larson sniffed the air as he turned towards the farmhouse before disappearing back through the door.

'What do you make of him?'

'I wouldn't trust him as far as I could throw him,' replied Anna.

'I'm with you. He'll need watching when he brings the boy back. There's something not right here, but I can't put my finger on it.'

'Vincent O'Conner. That's what.'

'No, it's not that. I don't swallow what we see here. Unless he's got land elsewhere, he isn't growing anything. How does that work when every villager has dug up their garden to grow vegetables?'

89

Their deliberations came to an abrupt halt as a thin, pasty-looking boy emerged alone from the farmhouse, his clothes hanging off his tiny frame. Dirty knees and grubby hands completed the sorry sight.

'Soft lad said you wanted a chinwag. Who are yous, anyway?'

Wow, I've heard about cocky Liverpudlians, but I didn't expect this.

Eddie offered Anna a confused look. 'What did he say? Is he English?'

The boy took umbrage at the American's comment. 'Listen 'ere, la', I'm from the 'pool. Yous two are the foreigners, not me.'

Anna laughed. 'My friend may come from America, but I'm as British as you.'

The young boy shook his head. 'That's what you say, but yous talk funny. I suppose you must be one of them woolly backs, or a carrot-cruncher.'

Eddie leant into Anna. 'What's he on about?'

She smiled as she whispered back, 'It's Scouse for people who live in rural areas. It's a sort of put-down.'

'Scouse?'

'That's how people from Liverpool refer to themselves. Don't ask me why.'

'Anyway, I've got things to do, so you'd better tell me what you want or I'll be off,' said the boy.

The Scouser's proclamation provided the opportunity for Anna and Eddie to introduce themselves.

'Me ma says you lot are always late. Don't know what she means, but if she says it, it must be true. Anyway, what you doing here? America's that way,' said the boy as he pointed to his left.

Eddie pointed to the right. 'As a matter of fact, it's that way.'

'Posh as well. Only posh people say, "As a matter of fact". If I said that around our way, I'd get me 'ed stoved in.'

Anna closed in on the boy and gently took hold of his hands.

'What's your game, missus? Get off me or I'll punch you one, girl or not. I don't care.'

'I'm not going to hurt you. It's Vincent, isn't it? I—'

'Too right you ain't, missus. I'll give you a Scouser's kiss if you try any funny stuff. Same goes for you, la'.' The boy squared up to Eddie.

'What on earth is a Scouser's kiss?' asked Anna.

'Are you stupid or what? It's a headbutt. Ma says it's like a Glaswegian kiss, only with a smile.'

Eddie grinned and raised his arms in mock surrender. 'Sounds like you come from a tough place, young Vincent. Tell me about it.'

The young boy gave Eddie a suspicious look. 'If you must know, I live on the Scottie Road with me ma. Pa used to work at the docks until a German bomb blew 'im up.'

'Heck, I'm sorry about that. That's a real tough deal.'

Vincent shook his head. 'Don't matter. Ma says 'e was a waste of space, always spending her housekeeping getting bladdered in O'Flanigan's on the Dock Road.'

Poor little one.

'You've had it tough, Vincent.'

'Are you stupid or what? The O'Conners stick together. All the family live a few streets away from each other, or they did until one road got flattened by them Germans. Ma says the Nazis are a waste of space as well.'

Anna and Eddie exchanged astonished glances.

I think that's what's called being streetwise.

'Then you didn't mind being sent away?'

'Don't care. Ma said it's too risky to stay, so they sent me to somewhere in Wales first. Couldn't be doing with the lingo, so I sagged off. Some nomark in a posh suit and bowler hat said if I did a runner from this place me ma will be in trouble, so I'm stuck with soft lad and his Judy.'

Eddie looked totally confused. Anna said, 'I assume you mean the farmer and his wife?'

The boy looked at Anna. 'Yous don't half speak posh for a carrot-cruncher, missus. I bet you eat beans on toast with real cutlery and that.'

Anna smiled at the impish boy. 'Something like that, Vincent.'

'Don't call me that. Only me ma and nan do that when they're mad at me. Me pals call me Vinny.'

'We're your pals now, are we?'

A frown spread across the Scouser's forehead. 'You will be if 'e gives me some chocolate. Every American soldier packs chocolate. That's what me mate Alf reckons. 'E says his older sister is always getting chocolates and stockings and stuff from them. I think they all must like her.'

Bless.

Eddie beamed at the boy and rummaged in his jacket pocket. 'I must get some more supplies – that's twice in as many days,' he whispered to Anna.

Vinny's eyes widened as he caught sight of the Hershey's. In a flash, the boy grabbed it before Eddie knew what was happening.

A now-familiar ritual unfolded as the boy carefully unwrapped the confectionery, looked on in wonder for several seconds and sniffed the intoxicating blend before carefully taking a tiny bite, savouring every morsel.

It's horrible what war does to kids.

Anna took care to glance at Vinny's upper arms as he concentrated on his chocolate.

Those bruises are not accidental.

Noticing the lad appeared more relaxed with them now, Anna pointed to one of his arms. 'How did that happen, Vinny?'

The Scouser stopped looking at his treat for the shortest time, before shrugging his shoulders.

'And that bruise? Plus the one on your other arm… It looks like someone has grabbed you?'

Vinny carefully wrapped his chocolate bar, holding the precious gift as if it were a bar of gold. 'Soft lad thinks 'e can tell me what to do. When 'e comes near me now, I kick him in the shins. It's what I used to do to Pa when 'e came home drunk and started throwing his weight around.'

It's a different life, poor lad.

'I see you've had practice,' commented Anna, trying to lighten the mood. 'What about food, Vinny? Do they give you enough?'

Vinny took another look at the Hershey's bar. 'The one thing I miss about me pa is that when 'e was in a good mood, he'd bring stuff home he'd nicked from his job on the docks. Even with the bombing and that, there was more food at home than there is here. Soft lad keeps saying stuff about shortages, but have you seen the size of his belly? His Judy is the same. I tell you this for nothing. I'm sick of jam butties 'cos it's not as if he's short on ration books.'

The farmer showed himself. 'It's time for young Vincent's bath. I need him in.'

Vinny almost bent himself double, such was the intensity of his laughter.

'What's so funny?' asked Anna.

'They don't own a tin bath, at least, I've never seen one. Those two stink; I usually have a swill in that pond.' Vincent pointed to a small pond with two ducks minding their own business in its murky waters.

'You thinking what I'm thinking?'

'Yes, but where do I put him?' replied Anna.

Eddie smiled and raised an eyebrow. 'Your dad's great with kids. I'm sure he'll help you while you get the young lad sorted with a new billet.'

Eddie turned to the boy. 'Fancy a ride in an army Jeep?'

Vinny's eyes lit up as he ran towards the military vehicle without requiring a second invitation.

'Oi, what you doin'?' protested the farmer.

'Taking your ten shilling and sixpence a week away. Now I suggest you go back inside before I really call the police.' Anna held her ground as the farmer closed the distance between them.

One more step and I'll wallop you.

'Is that real meat?' The boy gave an enormous smile as he rushed through the vicarage kitchen door and caught the smell of a lamb stew.

Astonished to hear a strange voice and at the sight of a bedraggled young boy invading the spacious room, the vicar put down his paper.

'Sorry, Mum, Dad. This is Vincent from Liverpool and I need your help.'

Eddie brought up the rear and deftly closed the kitchen door.

Helen extended both hands to encourage Vincent to move closer. 'Hello, Vincent from Liverpool. You like lamb stew, eh?'

The boy concentrated on a large, glazed earthenware container that held pride of place on the AGA. 'If you let me scoff some of that, you can call me Vinny, missus.'

Anna smiled at her mother. 'That privilege means you're his friend.'

'Now that you've met my mum, Helen, let me introduce you to my dad. His name is Charles. Why don't you say hello?'

'Yous one of them bible punchers?' was the boy's greeting.

'If you mean do I teach the word of God, yes. If you imply that I force the Almighty's words down people's throats, I most do certainly not.'

Vinny looked at Anna, his face a picture of confusion. ''Es posh as well. What does "imply" mean, missus?'

After explaining the meaning of the word, Anna laid down a challenge. 'Right, young man. You either call us all aunt and uncle or use our first names. Enough of this "missus" and "soft lad" stuff, yes?'

Vinny remained silent for a few seconds before giving a firm nod to show a contract now existed and turned his attention back to the vicar. 'Fair enough, Charlie, our local one gives us apples from his orchard, or 'e did until them Nazis got busy.'

The vicar said, 'It's Charles, Vinny, not Charlie, and I'm so sorry to hear he died.'

'Er, no. I meant his apple trees. Them Germans bombed his apples. He got off with a singed beard and burned cassock or whatever it is you call it. He looked a right div.'

The room erupted into laughter.

'Right, that's enough about religion for today, Vinny. Get yourself sat down at the table while I dish up.'

Vinny squinted as he looked at the upside-down headline from the paper Anna's father held.

'Raider Sinks US Steamer off Iceland.' The boy turned around to look at Eddie. 'That's them Germans at it again. What are you lot going to do about it?'

'You take an interest in what's in the papers?' responded a surprised Eddie.

Vinny scowled. 'I'm not thick, you know. I can read and write and stuff. You think 'cos I'm a kid I don't understand? Watch them bombs fall in Liverpool for a couple of nights and you will too.'

A silence fell over the room as the adults took in the young boy's profound comment.

'I guess I asked for that, Vinny, and I'm sorry.'

Vinny looked at the American. 'That's all right, you're only a grownup.'

Out of the mouths of babes, thought Anna.

Meal over, the young boy yawned.

'Now, young Vinny, there are a couple of things I need to talk to my parents about. How about Eddie and you go through to the other room? I'm sure he'll find you a comic book or something to read.'

Seemingly too tired to put up a fight, Vinny got to his feet. 'Thanks, missus… er, I mean, Helen, that stew was boss.'

Helen looked bemused as the boy left.

'I assume he means the food was excellent, which it was, my dear!'

Now alone with her parents, Anna explained what happened in the run-up to her arriving with Vinny. '…As you see, I'm stuck. Would you mind awfully if he stayed here until I can arrange a new billet for him?'

Her parents exchanged a knowing look.

'Something tells me the next few days will be quite educational for us all,' said Charles. 'I think the best thing to do with the boy is to keep him busy. Heaven knows what my parishioners will think of him.'

'The change will do them good,' replied Helen with a twinkle in her eye.

'I'm all for change. Let's hope they survive the whirlwind that's our streetwise young Liverpudlian.'

Parents and daughter shared a nervous laugh.

'Right, now the fun starts. It's bath time for that lad. Can you take charge, Anna, while I nip down to the thrift shop to see if I can find him some fresh clothes?'

After ten minutes of heated negotiation, resolved with the promise of a further bar of chocolate when supplies allowed, Vinny agreed to bathe, and once in the tub, took great delight in scrubbing himself clean.

Keeping watch outside the bathroom, Anna and Eddie discussed the day's events as they stood on the landing. 'I've been thinking about what Vinny said about those ration books. Seems a bit odd, don't you think?' said Anna.

Her companion thought for a moment. 'Now you mention it, yes, I suppose it is.' Eddie sighed. 'Something tells me it's another thing you want to get your teeth into. Don't you think we've enough on our plate with Ruth Cotton?'

Anna shook her head. 'I've a hunch I want to follow. We'll need Tom Bradshaw's unofficial help to put a bit of gentle heat under the Larsons' backsides. It's his off-duty day tomorrow, so we should head over to his first thing.' Anna suddenly stopped talking. 'It's gone quiet in there, you'd better look to see that Vinny hasn't drowned, or sagged off as he might put it.'

The journey to Tom Bradshaw's place took less than fifteen minutes as Anna updated Eddie on her young lodger. 'He slept like a log. Mum had to wake him up for breakfast. You should have seen his face when she gave him his new clothes. To top it off, the lad had his first real egg in I don't know how long. His face was a picture.'

He's not listening.

'Yes, yes. Tell me again what you expect to gain by getting Tom to speak with Larson?'

I give up.

'Oh, it's a feeling I have.'

Before the conversation could progress, she caught sight of Tom tending his father's vegetable patch in the front garden of their semi-detached home.

'My dad's cabbages are bigger than your dad's.'

Tom lifted his head on hearing the familiar voice and laughed. 'Have you two got nothing better to do than tease a busy police officer on his day off?'

Several minutes passed as the threesome exchanged good-natured banter.

'OK, so what brings you to my father's door? I assume it's not the need for fresh produce?'

It took Anna less than two minutes to explain about Vinny, her concerns about his welfare and the remark he'd made about the ration books.

Tom appeared hesitant. 'The problem is that his place isn't on my beat. If my sergeant finds out, he'll want an explanation of what I'm up to.' He thought for a moment. Anna realised he'd found a solution as a smile stretched across his face. 'I know, I'll say we had a spate of reports about farm outbuildings and sheds being broken into and I'm visiting all the local farmers to offer advice.'

Anna beamed. 'What a clever police officer you are. I asked Vinny this morning which building he's seen the ration books in. It's one around the right side of the farmhouse. It has a number six painted on the door; I've no idea why, but at least it will be easy to spot.'

Tom cautioned Anna. 'If he won't let me look, I don't have the powers to make him without showing my hand, which I assume you don't want me to do at this stage?'

'You're a treasure, Tom. What would I do without you?'

Oops, don't want to give him the wrong idea.

Quickly changing the subject, she asked Tom about where the police investigation into Ruth's death had progressed.

The switch in tone and direction took Tom by surprise. 'Err... well, not far. We spoke to her parents about boyfriends, but you know all about that, don't you?'

Better not to dwell, I think.

'We were in the area and—'

98

'And nothing, Anna. Remember what I've said about helping my inspector, not working against him. You and I know he can spike your guns any time he wants.'

Hmm.

'What about the POW camp commander?' asked Eddie.

'What about him, apart from the man being an upper-class twit? The truth is, we don't know where he's coming from. One minute he cooperates, the next he's a right pain.'

Anna sensed Tom's unwillingness to share anything further and concluded they should take their leave of the police officer. Moving forward to plant a kiss on his cheek, she thanked him for agreeing to help.

Her action made him blush, which he attempted to disguise by asking a question. 'And where are you two off to next?'

'I fancy a game of "Catch the squaddie",' offered Eddie.

'What?' replied Anna.

'I think he's referring to Ruth's boyfriend,' laughed Tom. 'What makes you think he's back in the country?'

'Because a postmark on an envelope proves he was in Southampton a week ago,' replied Eddie.

Chapter 8: The Strange Squaddie

The fields around Witton Wood were a hive of activity as Land Girls and POWs busied themselves gathering in the last of the harvest. A cold but dry winter and wet spring had provided the perfect ingredients for Mother Nature to do her work.

Apart from tractors pulling unwieldy stacks of hay along some of Norfolk's most challenging rural roads, little traffic troubled Anna and Eddie on their way to their destination.

'I thought you'd decided that Enzo Conti is responsible for Ruth's death. What changed your mind?'

'I haven't, but it'd be crazy to ignore the possibility that her cracked egg of a boyfriend is AWOL or wangled a furlough.'

'Cracked egg? That's a new one on me.'

'Perhaps you should learn to speak American.' Eddie gave Anna a sardonic glance. 'It means… well, many things, but in this context, that Sergeant Sedwell is flaky, you know—'

'Yes, I get you. Honestly, why you can't say what you mean is beyond me.' The irony of Anna's response hit home as both laughed.

Ten minutes later, they stood in the middle of a dense clump of trees in Witton Wood. The familiar sound of wildlife and creaking

100

trees filled the afternoon air as the dense canopy shimmied in the light breeze.

'I don't mean to be picky, but this is a big place, and one tree looks much like the next. What is it you expect to find?'

Eddie continued to lead the charge deeper into the rich green undergrowth. 'It's your fault. You gave me the idea. Remember, you told me your friend, what's her name… Gertrude? Well, she said Sedwell liked to do his own thing and camp out. What better way to stay out of the way, especially if you're absent without leave from your fighting unit?'

'Isn't that a bit of a leap, you know, from a letter to prime suspect in one fell – ouch.'

He turned to see Anna nursing a slight cut on her forehead. 'What happened to you?'

She gave the American a disapproving look. 'You're what happened. There you are charging through this jungle stuff and letting branches go once you've passed by. Does it not occur to you I'm close behind?' Anna dabbed the cut with a handkerchief as her displeasure with Eddie continued to intensify.

'Perhaps you should keep your eyes open. Remember, you can see me. I was in front and haven't got eyes in the back of my head.'

'Don't you shout at me. Not content with running me over a couple of months ago, now you attempt to put my eye out. The trouble with you, Eddie Elsner, is—'

'Shush, did you hear that?'

That old trick.

'Don't you shush me… Oh, yes, I hear it too.'

Bother.

'Someone or something is on the move. It'll be quicker if I go. Will you be OK here?'

101

Anna gave her forehead one last dab with her handkerchief. 'I'm not a child, you know.'

Patronising American.

As the minutes passed, she began to think about Vinny and the other evacuees in her charge.

What must go through their little heads when they have a brown paper tag tied to their collar, and they're put on a train? I suppose children adapt quicker than adults, or am I fooling myself?

I wonder if it's worth trying to arrange a get-together so they can all meet up and have some fun.

'Over here, Anna.'

Eddie's familiar voice snapped Anna back into the present.

Where's "Over here"?

He shouted again. 'Follow my voice; I'm about fifty yards from you.'

The man must think I'm a magician.

Following several failed attempts to locate her erstwhile friend, Anna caught sight of the American. 'You've no idea what I've stepped through and brushed out of my hair to find you. This had better be good.'

Eddie didn't answer. Instead, he pointed to a spot six feet in front of them.

Seconds passed as Anna looked in vain to see what he could see.

We're playing party games, are we?

'What?' she eventually replied. 'Either I'm blind or you're hallucinating.'

Eddie continued to point without making further comment. Tiring of the game, she stepped forward, hoping to discover what transfixed her companion.

'Stop,' barked Eddie. 'It's two feet in front of you.'

The abruptness of his call shook Anna. 'If you do that again, I'll punch you. Do you understand?' Returning her gaze to the tree loam underfoot, she glimpsed something glinting.

'It's a double-edged Fairbairn-Sykes Commando knife.'

'It's a what?' replied a dumfounded Anna.

Eddie stepped forward and took a handkerchief from his trouser pocket. Crouching down, he carefully retrieved the fearsome-looking weapon. 'It's not your run-of-the-mill weapon. The name gives it away. This is special forces stuff. The question is, what's it doing in the middle of a Norfolk wood?'

Anna watched as Eddie examined every surface of the glistening object. 'Are you saying there are commandos operating around here?'

'Who's to say?' replied Eddie, shrugging his shoulders. 'One thing's for sure, this knife hasn't been here long. It's as clean as a whistle, which means whoever it belongs to wiped it clean after they dropped it, or it's unused and fell from their belt. Either way, it didn't hide itself. I bet whoever owns it will be back looking for it as soon as they realise it's missing.'

The thought sent a shiver down Anna's spine. 'Let's get out of here. Have you ever had a feeling you're being watched?'

Eddie smiled as he wrapped the knife in his handkerchief. 'There's something else I want to show you.'

I've had enough of this.

Anna retraced her steps.

'I'm being serious; this is important. Look, through those trees, it's brilliant.'

She turned back and followed her companion. 'Wow. Who do you think built it?'

Both now stood next to a low-level hide ingeniously constructed out of broken branches, over which a camouflage net had been spread.

103

'I'm less than six feet from it and can hardly see it. Are there any signs of life?'

Eddie carefully lifted the net and looked inside the secret construction. 'Only this. It's the lid from a British army emergency ration pack.'

Anna looked on in fascination. 'If we take the knife and this together—'

'We may have our killer,' replied Eddie.

After the shock of their recent discoveries, Anna concluded a pub lunch beckoned. 'Don't get your hopes up. It'll be a cheese sandwich and a pickled egg from a jar on Betty Simpson's bar.'

Eddie licked his lips as he pulled the Jeep onto a small patch of grass next to the King's Head public house in Lipton St Faith. 'I'm getting to like your British food.'

'Are you mad?' replied Anna as she led the way into the medieval building. 'Don't forget, watch your… Oh dear, are you OK?'

Her warning about the low door entrance came too late for Eddie as he walloped his forehead on the door lintel, which had a small sign attached to it that read in capital letters:

'DUCK'.

'It doesn't refer to the wildlife, you know. I thought you'd have learnt your lesson from last time.'

Eddie wasn't in the mood for a lesson on the difference between winged fowl and stooping as he followed a giggling Anna into the small bar.

'I heard the thud. I hope you haven't damaged my pub, Lieutenant Elsner. Anglo-American relations are one thing; wrecking my livelihood is quite another matter.'

A couple of regulars momentarily stopped puffing on their pipes as they watched Eddie wander towards Betty in an almost straight line while rubbing his brow.

'That'll be enough from you two. Are you going to order another pint, or nurse those all afternoon? I'm not running a charity, you know, or a daycare centre for old men their wives want from under their feet.'

The regulars averted their gaze from Betty and began puffing furiously on their pipes.

The interlude gave Eddie enough time to recover his wits. 'Afternoon, ma'am, I apologise for any damage I've caused and—'

'Give over, you daft lump. If you think an American skull can dent a 400-year-old slab of English oak, you're concussed. A pint for you and a glass of my special lemonade for Anna?'

Anna laughed as she looked at Eddie's swollen forehead. 'Does it hurt?' she said, touching the afflicted area.

Eddie cried out in pain and jumped back from his companion.

'Oh, sorry, I assume it does. Never mind, beer will make it better, or at least dull your senses, so I'm told.' She winked at Betty as the widowed pub owner poured a brown-coloured liquid from a glazed pitcher into a pewter tankard.

'Have you eaten?' asked Betty.

Anna eyed up an enormous bottle of pickled eggs sitting to one side of the bar. 'Have you any cheese to go with a couple of those?'

Betty smiled. 'You're lucky, I got some fresh in this morning with a nice bit of bread to go with it. You two sit down and I'll bring it over.'

It took a couple of minutes for Eddie to recover while Anna took in the pub's atmosphere.

If only these walls could talk.

Next to a large sign ordering customers not to spit that sat over an inglenook fireplace, hung a handsome watercolour of a Norfolk wherry plying its business on Hickling Broad. The unmistakable image of its single, high-peaked sail was set against the lush surroundings of the flat farmland. On the horizon, a traditional windpump went about its important business of draining the fields and helping to keep the waterways at a healthy level.

'There you go, me dears. You can pay me later. Something tells me young Eddie here will need more than one pint to clear that head of his.'

Lunch soon revitalised Anna's companion and as the predicted second pint did its work, Eddie returned to his jovial self. 'Gran pickles anything she can lay her hands on back home. She says it helps during the winter months, though I think it's a hangover from when times were tough in the twenties.'

It hadn't occurred to Anna that America enjoyed anything but an abundance of all things. 'Is there much rationing in the States?'

Eddie wiped the beer froth from his lips. 'Not half as bad as you have it over here, but yes, there's some. Still…'

His attention fell on two strangers entering the bar. 'Do you know them? Betty's giving them a cool look.'

Anna turned to take in the scene. 'Nope, not seen them before, but it looks like they've got a few bob, judging by the way they're dressed.'

The pair of heavyset, clean-shaven men approached the bar with a determined step. Anna struggled to hear what they were saying to Betty.

'Perhaps they're commercial travellers. If they are, Betty will give them short shrift. She has her regular suppliers and from what I've heard, doesn't take kindly to people trying to muscle their way in.'

Within seconds, their peaceful surroundings erupted as a loud bang of one hard surface hitting another reverberated around the small space.

'Get you out of my pub. I'll pay protection to no one. This is my place. Tell your boss he can take a running jump.'

Anna turned towards the bar while Eddie shot to his feet. The loud noise had been Betty bringing a gnarled cricket bat crashing down on the mahogany countertop.

'You all right, Betty?' asked Eddie as he moved forward.

The landlady held the cricket bat up and gestured for the American to stay where he was. 'I can deal with these two.' Betty pointed the willow bat at the well-dressed strangers. 'Why are you still here? Do I have to throw you out? Because mark my words, I've dealt with far worse than the likes of you over the years. Out, both of you.' She gestured toward the door with the cricket bat.

Both men half-turned, smirked at Eddie and made their way to the pub exit. One man stepped back into the bar.

'Think of our offer as insurance, Mrs Simpson. A woman on her own with dodgy punters around… We wouldn't like anything to happen to you or your pub. We want to keep you safe. See you soon, lady.'

The two regulars continued to puff on their pipes as if nothing untoward had taken place. Anna stepped over to Betty, who looked pale and was shaking.

'It ain't fear, my love. If they come back, I'll swear they won't walk away.'

Eddie walked around to the rear of the bar, ducked under the counter and retrieved a half-bottle of whisky. He poured a double measure into the nearest glass he could lay his hands on. 'Here, get this down you.'

Betty neither chastised Eddie for invading her space nor refused the drink. After taking it down in three gulps, Betty placed her glass on the bar with such force that it shattered. 'Insurance. I'll give them insurance.'

Anna tidied the shards of broken glass away as Eddie leant on the bar next to Betty. 'You know where I come from, we'd call what those two were trying on a protection racket. I didn't realise you Brits had imported the idea.'

Betty offered a half-smile as she bumped shoulders with the American. 'Call it what you like, but they're not getting any of my money. I doubt they're from Norfolk. Probably London thugs from their accents. With a bit of luck, they were trying their luck and won't be back.'

'I hope you're right, Betty, but they knew your name.'

Betty smiled. 'It's written above the entrance. The law says the licensee must do so.'

Letting the matter drop, Eddie helped Anna clean the rest of the mess away before taking their leave of a now more relaxed Betty. As they wandered back to the Jeep, Eddie caught sight of a limousine making off. He could barely make out the silhouette of two heads as the car disappeared up the narrow lane.

'What do you reckon?'

Eddie turned to Anna. 'I think Betty's in trouble. They'll be back. If she doesn't cooperate, they'll either rough her up as a warning, or give her up as a lost cause and burn the King's Head to the ground.'

Disturbed at what she'd witnessed, Anna persuaded Eddie to drop in at Lipton St Faith police station. 'We have to tell the inspector. If we do nothing and Betty gets hurt, or worse, I'll never forgive myself.'

Having left the Jeep outside the pub to at least give the illusion Betty had friends, the two companions walked the few hundred yards to see the inspector.

'Have you thought Betty might be mightily annoyed if she knew what we were doing?'

'I'm certain she would be, but I'll risk that temper of hers if we can help. Now all we have to do is persuade Detective Spillers to see us. Do you think he's still angry?'

Eddie laughed. 'What do you think?'

In the event, the matter resolved itself as Spillers stepped from the police station entrance as they neared the sandstone steps to the Victorian building.

'Don't tell me you've found another body?' Spillers sighed as he lifted his hat as a courtesy to Anna.

'Not yet, but I'm worried we shall soon if we don't do something.'

The detective's smirk vanished. 'Miss Grix, if you're about to send me on another of your wild goose chases, I shan't be pleased. What on earth are you talking about?'

Without the slightest consciousness that the three of them stood in full view of anyone that might pass by, Anna explained what had taken place. As she continued to relate the unpleasant incident, Spillers gave her more attention.

'So, it's started?'

'What has?' replied a surprised Anna.

The inspector pointed towards the police station entrance so they might have a measure of privacy. 'Three months ago, Norwich headquarters sent a confidential briefing out to senior ranks, citing intelligence that a London mob intended to move onto our patch.'

'A protection racket?' asked Eddie.

Spillers nodded. 'They're well known and feared in the East End of London. For some, wars mean hardship. I'm afraid others see it as an opportunity to get rich. The Mr Bigs don't care who gets hurt because they never get their hands dirty. Well, from what you've told me, they've started their operations. I bet they're based in Great Yarmouth; they can get a quick getaway by boat if the need arises.'

Anna looked stunned. 'Why our tiny village? Betty can't make that much money from her regulars?'

Spillers shook his head. 'You misunderstand. For now, it won't be about the money. Their game will be to terrorise small local pubs. That way they stay out of the police's way, knowing pub owners talk to one another. By the time these thugs put the screws on the city pubs, word will have got around. In their eyes there's nothing better than a few owners ending up in hospital with broken ribs, or a few pubs mysteriously catching fire, to make their actual targets pay up.'

For once, Anna was stuck for words.

Eddie took off his cap and inspected his regiment's insignia. 'Dumb question, I know, Inspector, but do you think these hooligans have anything to do with Ruth Cotton's murder?'

Inspector Spillers put his hands in his pockets and looked up and down the high street. 'Directly, no. They have nothing to gain in random killings; it would bring too much attention their way. However, who knows what her boyfriend is up to or, come to think of it, why the Italian did a runner?'

Chapter 9: A Burglary

'I thought Inspector Spillers was going to put you in one of his cells,' said Anna as she led her companion out of the police station and back towards the King's Head to pick up the Jeep.

'I'm not sure he had the power to arrest an American army officer, but I didn't want to push him too far and find out.'

Anna laughed as she linked arms with the lieutenant in a sign of solidarity. 'At least it's made him get serious and order a full search of Witton Wood. Don't you think he should have done that in the first place? Eddie, I'm talking to you.' The American was too busy looking first one way, then the other. 'What's got into you? Do you think we're being followed or something?'

'Oh, sorry. I'm looking for a telephone box.'

'A telephone box?'

'Yes, you know, one of those big red things with little windows and a door that's impossible to open.'

She slipped her arm from his and stood rooted to the spot. 'Do you want a slap because you're going the right way for one? Adopting British humour is one thing. Being sarky is quite another, and it doesn't suit you.'

You might well look shocked.

'And you a vicar's daughter. What might your father say to his daughter threatening violence?'

You're getting too good at this.

'He'd say the end sometimes justifies the means, providing one is repentant.'

They exchanged smiles, which allowed the pair to move on from a tense moment.

'That's religion for you. Do your worst, say sorry and start again with a clean plate.'

Anna gave him a scornful look. 'You want this to go the full distance, do you? Because I'll win; my father's celestial contacts give me a head start.'

Eddie held his hands high. 'I surrender, one round in the ring with you is quite enough for me… At last, a phone box.'

Before Anna could enjoy the moment, the lieutenant dashed across the deserted lane that led back into the village centre and grappled with the phone box door. 'Damn these things. Are they designed specially to keep people out?'

'I hadn't thought about it before, but perhaps it's an anti-kid device to stop them rifling the cashbox,' replied Anna while savouring her companion's tussle with the cast-iron door.

Serves you right for trying your hand at British satire.

Minutes passed as Anna watched the lieutenant first struggle to select the right button and then insert coins into the slot.

What's so complicated? It's button "A".

Eventually, Eddie opened the door and crossed to Anna when she called out to him, 'Have you checked for leftover coins?'

'What?' asked the lieutenant as he gave Anna a confused look.

'It goes to show you Americans have got too much money for

112

your own good. Go back into the telephone box and press the other button. The one with a big letter "B" next to it. If the post office owes you money for time you've paid for but not used, you'll get it back.'

Still wearing a look of bemusement, Eddie retraced his steps, once more fought with the telephone box door and did as instructed. 'Will you look at that,' he cried out as he crossed the lane, holding two one-penny coins aloft.

'Of course, you realise you've deprived one of the village young-sters of those coins, not that they'd have anything to spend them on.'

Eddie looked at the pennies, then at Anna. 'What do you mean?'

She laughed. 'Let me tell you a secret, but only on the proviso you say nothing to my parents?'

'Er… OK,' he replied, frowning.

'Coming home from school as a child, it was the done thing to check all the public phone boxes to see if the last caller had forgotten to check for leftover coins. One press of button "B" could yield as much as a thruppence, and thruppence bought a lot of sweets before the war.'

'You're a criminal! Anna Grix, I'm shocked and disappointed in you… Er, how often did you get lucky?'

'To be honest, not too often. You see, Billy Spragg had it all sewn up. He'd push a small piece of cloth up the money-return slot on his way to school and make sure he was first to collect on the way home. He was much bigger than us and a bit of a bruiser. Come to think of it, he still is.'

'Cloth?'

'For an American, you've led a sheltered life, Eddie Elsner. Don't you get it? By blocking the chute, anyone pressing the button after their call might simply assume the leftover change mechanism broken; these phones are always breaking down. Anyway, when Billy Spragg came to pick up his loot, he'd simply pull the bit of cloth out and, hey presto, a pile of coins usually toppled out. Safe to say Big-Belt, as we called him out of earshot, never shared. I suppose that's why he's the size he is now.'

'He's in the forces?' replied Eddie.

'Oh yes,' replied Anna. 'He couldn't join the catering corps soon enough. Billy Big-Belt is no fool.'

By the time the pair had stopped laughing, they were next to the King's Head pub.

'Perhaps we should check on Betty?'

'Good idea,' replied Eddie. 'I'll give the door a knock.'

A familiar sight rounded the side of the pub, carrying a hammer and some of the longest nails Anna had ever seen. 'What in heaven's name are you going to do with those?'

Betty held the hammer aloft as if impersonating Thor, the god of thunder. 'Those goons ain't going to get back into my pub. These are for the windows. If I can keep the Nazis from breaking my glass with tape, I can keep those two out with six-inch nails.'

'But what if they get in? After all, you live here on your own,' asked Eddie.

Betty chortled. 'If you think these nails look fierce, wait till you see what I've done inside. If they mess with me, all I can say is they won't be having kids anytime soon, if you get my meaning.' She winked at the lieutenant.

With that, Betty strode past the pair and disappeared around the far side of the pub. 'Don't you worry about me and don't be a stranger. I need the business.'

'I think we can safely leave Betty to it for the time being, don't you think? Let's hope Detective Spillers has his bobbies monitor the place,' said Anna. Climbing back into the Jeep, she turned to Eddie. 'You didn't say who you telephoned.'

Driving the vehicle off the patch of grass and back onto the firm surface of Long Lane, Eddie left his response for a few seconds. 'Oh, no one important.'

Eddie Elsner, I wish you'd stop keeping secrets.

The sound of water splashing onto the floor of the vicarage bathroom prompted Helen Grix to shout from the bottom of the stairs. 'Anna, what are you doing up there? I thought you said you were washing your hair, not swilling out the bathroom?'

Several seconds of silence followed before her daughter appeared on the landing, her head swathed in a large towel. 'Sorry, Mum, but it needs cutting. It's too long and a nightmare to wash in the bowl.'

'Well, you're a big girl now, so I'm sure you can arrange a visit to the hairdressers. Make sure you clean the mess up before you come down.' Helen didn't wait for an answer before wandering back into the lounge.

Ten minutes passed before Anna joined her parents and Vinny.

'You look a right divvy, girl. Good job your American boyfriend can't see you or he'd run a mile.' The young Liverpudlian turned his attention back to an old copy of *The Hotspur* comic without making further comment.

'Cheeky,' replied Anna while smiling at the youngster. 'And anyway, he's not my boyfriend.'

She watched as her parents exchanged knowing glances.

'What?'

'Nothing, my dear,' responded the vicar. 'Nothing at all… except you're being a tad defensive. Have you anything to tell us?'

'Father, really,' replied Anna as she stomped out of the room with the laughter of her mum and dad ringing in her ears. No sooner had she moved into the vestibule when the brass front door knocker announced a caller.

For goodness' sake.

Forgetting she still wore the towel like a ridged pyramid of whipped cream, Anna opened the door. 'Yes?' she said sharply.

Her barbed question met with silence. In fact, Tom Bradshaw didn't know what to make of the sight before him. 'I hope it gets better soon.'

'Don't you start. One comedian in the house is quite enough, thank you.'

Tom laughed as he closed the front door behind him. 'Vinny's still with you?'

She saw the funny side of things. 'Do you know, it's impossible to take offence at anything that little boy says or does. He fizzes like a glass of Epsom Salts from the second he wakes until his head hits the pillow after his mug of hot milk.'

She led her police friend into the kitchen. 'Tea? it's freshly brewed.'

'Just the job after the time I've had with your mysterious farmer.'

Anna's eyes lit up at the possibility of gaining information. Passing Tom his cup of tea, she sat opposite him and sipped her own drink. 'Good news or...?'

Tom took a healthy swig of his tea before placing the cup back onto its colourful saucer. 'He was far more interested in telling me he wanted the American who smashed his gate with a Jeep prosecuted than anything I had to say about securing his property.'

Anna almost choked on her drink at the mention of the gate. 'Are you serious?'

'No, I'm not, but he is. Our Mr Larson is far from a pleasant fellow and clearly someone that holds a grudge. I spun him a line about me not having the powers to investigate an American soldier. I'm not sure he believed me, but he let it pass.'

Cleaning the last dribble of tea from her chin with the back of her hand, Anna leant into the kitchen table. 'Did you get a look at the outbuildings?'

'Not a chance,' replied Tom as he lounged back on his chair. 'Larson said he could quite look after his own property, and if anyone dared trespass, he'd see them off with his shotgun. I warned him about the use of undue force, but he shrugged his shoulders at me.'

Anna mirrored Tom's posture. 'Can't you get a warrant or something to look around?'

The police officer shook his head before Anna finished her sentence. 'Not enough proof. Without at least something to put before a magistrate, I've no chance of a search warrant.'

Getting to her feet to bring the teapot from the AGA, Anna wore a thoughtful look. 'Eddie and I shall have to break in. That's all there is to it. We'll go as soon as it's dark.'

Tom looked aghast. 'You can't do that, or at least you can't tell a police officer you're going to break into someone's property. For goodness' sake, Anna, don't say another word.'

His companion laughed. 'Had you going there, Tom Bradshaw. I always could make you fall for a joke. I wouldn't think of breaking into Mr Larson's farmhouse.'

Tom gave his friend a sceptical glance as he made for the kitchen door. 'One of these days, Anna Grix…'

Once Tom was clear of the house, Anna rushed into the vestibule and picked up the telephone handset.

Come on, answer.

'Anna, why are you ringing? I've told you before, my superiors paid to install this line strictly for military business. What do you want?'

Pompous American.

117

Anna explained. 'So that's it… we have to do it ourselves. Pick me up at sunset. We can be there by 11.30 pm.

The Larson smallholding looked a picture of rural serenity as a cloudless sky allowed the full moon to bathe everything it touched in a soft-edged glow. Having parked the Jeep well out of sight on the lane next to the farm entrance, Anna and Eddie walked with hunched shoulders, keeping close to a tall, overhanging unkempt hazel hedge.

'I can't believe you talked me into this, and why is your hair damp?' Anna ran her fingers through the long locks.

Men have no idea how long a girl's hair takes to dry after a good shampoo.

'Shh,' said Anna, keen to move the conversation on. 'Someone will hear you.'

As they progressed up the long, winding track that led to the farmhouse, Eddie pointed. 'Look, it's in darkness. We might be lucky and they're in bed.'

Anna continued to inch carefully forward, then came to a sudden stop and looked skyward.

'What's up?' whispered Eddie.

She shook her head. 'Nothing, at least not yet, but that clear sky is an open invitation to enemy bombers.'

After a brief silence during which Eddie, too, looked to the heavens, he replied. 'And our lads may well be on their way in the opposite direction.'

How did it come to this?

'Do you think there will be a raid tonight?' Anna involuntarily moved towards Eddie.

'Who's to say, but it's late, speaking of which, we should get a move on.'

Eddie's prompt refocussed Anna. 'You're right, come on, Vinny said the shed was to the right of the main house.'

After stealthily walking a further fifty yards, the sudden cackle of ducks pierced the still night air. Anna squealed in surprise. Both hunkered down into the hedge and looked with trepidation at the farmhouse to see if the sudden noise had roused its occupants.

'Our luck's in tonight all right,' said Eddie as the house remained in total darkness.

Anna wasn't listening; she was too busy keeping an eye on a bat that flitted about yards from where she was hiding.

'It won't bite you, come on,' said Eddie as he urged her to get back to her feet. 'Then again, this is Norfolk. Perhaps Count Dracula has a place around here; there are enough old graveyards to pick from.'

'Not funny,' replied Anna. 'Come on, let's get going.'

Skirting around the far side of the duck pond, whose occupants had settled back into their slumber, gave the pair an unobstructed view of the darkened farmhouse and the outbuilding beyond.

'It shouldn't be difficult to spot with a number six painted on the door.'

Sure enough, as they passed by one run-down timber building after another, their target came into view. It was a shed measuring eight feet square with a felt-covered pitched roof, sporting one small tightly fitting window. The numeral painted onto the door stood out from its unkempt surroundings.

'Do we smash it off, or can you pick it?' Anna pointed to a large padlock that passed through a heavy metal hoop, which was, itself, bolted to the shed frame.

'And wake half the neighbourhood? I don't think so. Give me two minutes and I'll have it open.'

Anna stood back, all the time keeping an eye peeled for signs of life in the farmhouse.

Who's a cocky one?

After several tense minutes and a great deal of Eddie muttering under his breath, a sudden 'click' interrupted the stillness as the padlock snapped open. 'Quick, let's get out of sight.'

Anna required no second invitation as she pulled the door to behind them. Although it was a bright night, the single small window did not allow the moonlight to penetrate all corners of the shabby building.

'I never thought to bring a torch.' Anna's confession came with due humility.

'It's a good job I did.'

Smug so-and-so.

Eddie's narrow torch beam illuminated a tumble of shelves and cluttered work surfaces with all manner of tins, boxes and hand tools mingling together.

'This will take us all night.'

'I reckon we have about ten minutes, so start looking,' replied Eddie.

In her hurry to check the contents of the various containers, Anna knocked a rusty paint tin from a chest-high shelf onto the floor. Landing with a thud, the lid sprang off, making a sound like an orchestra symbol being hit – hard.

Eddie rapidly silenced the reverberating metal and urgently looked out of the shed window towards the farmhouse. 'Damn it, there's a light on. Don't move.' Eddie switched off his torch and continued to watch for signs of life. 'Thank God for that, all quiet now.'

Anna let out a sigh of relief. 'Thank goodness that sign for dogs being off their leads was fake, too, or the *Hounds of the Baskervilles* would've been all over us.'

'Come on, Anna, we'd better get a move on and be out of here.'

Dropping to her knees, she rummaged in a box stashed in the far corner of the shed at floor level. 'Give us the torch, will you?'

'Have you found something?'

After flicking the torch on, it took several seconds for Anna to interpret what she held and extract herself from her uncomfortable position. 'Only if you enjoy reading the newspaper – there are dozens down there.'

Eddie's disappointment was palpable. 'I suppose they've been there ages. Perhaps he's a hoarder of such things.'

Meanwhile, Anna studied the paper in more detail, carefully skipping across the front page with Eddie's torch. 'I don't know about that; this one's only two days old, look, September 22nd.'

'This may be Larson's escape from his wife, perhaps, to read the paper, then he stores them under there?'

Setting the paper aside, Anna continued to search the dishevelled interior of the shed, checking first one shelf, then another, muttering to herself each time something that looked interesting turned out to be the detritus of a man who appeared to never throw anything away.

Five minutes passed as the pair continued their fruitless endeavours.

If we don't turn something up soon, we'll have to leave it. We're bound to be discovered if we hang around much longer.

She looked back into the corner where she came across the papers. 'Wait a minute, what happened to yesterday's and today's papers?'

Spurred on by her sudden flash of inspiration, Anna crossed to the far corner of the shed again, crouched and scrambled to pull a large cardboard box forward. Disappointed that the missing newsprints were nowhere to be found, she brushed the pile to one side in frustration, which revealed the top of a decorated tin box. 'Look at this,' she said, retrieving the tin from its secluded position. It's a Huntley & Palmer biscuit box.' Anna showed Eddie the container decorated with a snowy village streetscape and the wording 'Enjoy a Christmas Biscuit' across its lid.

'Is there anything in it? I'm starving.'

Anna frowned at her companion as she prised the lid clear. 'Well, will you take a look at what we have here.'

'How many do you reckon are in there?' asked Eddie.

Anna picked out a handful of ration books. 'I'd say there're at least a hundred.'

'I think this proves Larson is a hoarder, but not in the conventional sense,' said Eddie. 'I suggest we take a couple as proof and carefully put the rest back. We don't want him spooked until we know what his game is.'

Anna nodded, picked up the biscuit tin lid and was about to replace it when something caught her attention.

'You look as though you've seen a ghost.'

Anna slowly turned to look at her companion. 'Sort of, but this one is the ghost of Christmas past.'

The lieutenant frowned. 'What on earth are you on about? Come on, we have to…' His words tailed off as he saw what Anna was pointing to on the inside of the lid.

'*With Best Wishes and Season's Greeting from the Officers of Top Field Camp.*'

'Why would Larson have a tin of biscuits issued by Major Leonard-White?' said Anna.

'Perhaps the more apt question is whether Larson is in league with someone at the camp, perhaps even—'

His words were cut short by a man shouting. 'Show yourself. I've a gun and will use it.'

Eddie sprang into action. 'Follow me, now. Make for the field.'

Anna didn't hesitate. As they rushed from the timber building and cleared a low fence, a shot rang out.

Silence.

Chapter 10: Tea and Trouble

Eddie scanned the moonlit landscape. Gone were the soft shadows; now they were replaced with sinister shapes competing for space as he bore down on a crumpled figure amongst the unkempt vegetation. Kneeling beside his fallen companion, Eddie continued to watch Larson, shotgun in hand, who hadn't left the confines of the farm-yard. 'Are you hurt?'

He moved nearer to Anna's still body to brush an untidy layer of grass and wildflowers from her face. His touch caused Anna to open her eyes. Both jumped in surprise at the other's actions.

'Where do you hurt?' asked Eddie as he scanned his companion for signs of blood.

'My side hurts, but if you move your lump of a knee, perhaps my right lung will re-inflate.'

Shocked at her response, Eddie shifted his weight and focussed on her right side to detect the bullet's entry point.

'What are you doing? I tripped over some rubbish and winded myself, that's all. It's your knee that was causing the pain.'

Eddie's posture deflated with relief like a collapsing souffle. 'I thought Larson had shot you.'

123

'I thought you were going to suffocate me,' whispered Anna as she attempted to get her breath back. 'Is he still after us? We need to get out of here.'

His attention shifted to the farmhouse. 'No, I can't see anything moving and the houselights are off. I guess he assumes he's seen the intruders off. Can you move?'

'Yes, I think so, but let's take it easy, shall we?'

Eddie helped his companion to her feet, and they made for the treeline. 'Now we're safe. Out of sight, out of mind, I hope.'

'What now?' asked Anna as she bent forward slightly and put a hand on each knee to catch her breath.

'I've got to go back to tidy up after us and shut the shed door.'

'What? Are you mad? The man likes to shoot things.'

Eddie shook his head. 'I've no choice. If Larson finds out someone's been in that shed, he'll assume the game's up and get rid of the evidence. Anyway, it's your fault.'

'My fault?'

'Yes. You were the one who insisted we come on this little caper.'

I suppose he has a point.

'Will you be OK here? Remember to stay well out of sight. If Larson catches me, you'll have to make your own way back home. Whatever you do, don't show yourself. Understood?'

Anna nodded as Eddie set off for the outbuilding.

Maybe I need to stop mucking about like this. Looking after my evacuees should be more important to me than chasing down ne'er-do-wells.

Time felt as though it were standing still as Anna waited for Eddie to return. Overhead, she heard the rumble of a single aeroplane heading for the coast.

It's a heavy bomber heading back to France or wherever he took off from. I wonder where he's been raiding tonight. Perhaps he didn't drop

his bombs and turned back instead. I suppose he could always say he had
engine problems or suchlike. I'd like to think that, anyway.

The sight of Eddie running across the field, all the time crouching
to minimise his profile, interrupted Anna's thoughts.

'Thank heavens you're safe.'

'When I clicked the lock shut, I convinced myself the noise might
bring Larson out again. I guess I got lucky.' Breathing hard from his
exertions, Eddie took a last look at the farmhouse. 'Right, let's get
out of here. You've still got the ration books, yes?'

Where did I put them?

She checked each pocket of her jacket and trousers with growing
alarm until at last she felt the valuable cargo deep within an inside
pocket. 'Yep, got them.' Anna tried to sound as nonchalant as possible
to hide her momentary panic.

Wading through the undergrowth in semi-darkness made the short
trek back to Eddie's Jeep more taxing than Anna expected.

My ribs still hurt from his knee.

Each time one of them stepped on a dry stick, which resulted in
a loud cracking sound as the timber shattered, the other would offer
a rebuke.

'That's the third time, Anna. Be careful.'

I'll 'be careful' you.

'Thank God for that,' remarked the lieutenant as the Jeep came
into sight. 'Quick, get in so we can beat it.'

If you hadn't almost crushed me, I might move quicker.

As the engine roared into life, Anna took her revenge. 'Shush,
you'll wake the dead if you carry on like that.'

'It's like that, is it?' replied Eddie as he eased the vehicle forward
and slowly gathered speed.

Suddenly, Anna's attention moved to a figure standing beyond the trees, one made almost translucent by the effect of moonlight lazily bouncing from one surface to the next. 'What's that?'

Her urgent tone startled Eddie. 'What?'

'Look, over there.'

By the time the American understood his companion's message, the Jeep was almost past the spot that she'd seen the man. 'I can't see anything. Do you want me to stop?'

She shook her head urgently. 'No, it was a soldier, I'm sure of it. But what's he doing at this time of night?'

Eddie momentarily slowed the Jeep before accelerating away. 'If you saw what you think you saw, there could be many reasons. The most likely explanation is that he's with his sweetheart. Who knows what the military gets up to in these remote areas? Remember, we've already found one knife, who knows, there may be a military operation going on that the civilian authorities know nothing about.'

You seem well informed.

'As you say, Eddie, who knows?'

The downstairs rooms of the vicarage were remarkably calm compared to the excitement of the previous few days. In the kitchen, the vicar sat reading the daily paper, Helen tidied the last of the breakfast things away while Anna busied herself poring over one of the ration books taken from the Larsons' smallholding.

'What's that you're looking at?' asked the vicar as he neatly folded the paper and placed it on the table in front of him.

Anna hesitated for a few seconds.

How much do I tell them?

'I could say I found it and assumed someone had lost it…'

'But that wouldn't be true, would it, my darling?' Her father's voice had a gentleness to it that Anna couldn't resist.

'It would, Dad, besides which it hasn't got a name stamped on it.'

Helen wandered over to the table and picked up a second ration book Anna had laid on the pine surface. 'And neither has this one. Do you want to tell us what's going on, darling?'

She looked at each of her parents. 'I don't know. Vinny mentioned Larson had a great number of these and—'

'And he brought them here?'

'No… no. Eddie and I, well, we…'

The vicar reached over the tabletop to gather in the ration books. 'Are you telling me you broke into someone's property to get your hands on these?'

Anna could see her father stiffen. 'Dad—'

'This won't do. What if news of this gets out…? I shan't ask why you did this stupid thing because I assume you have your reasons, but if people find out, how do you think it will affect your… all of our standing in the village? What has got into you? I'm starting to think Lieutenant Elsner is proving to be a bad influence.'

The vicar stood and shared a concerned glance with his wife.

'No, no, you've got it wrong. The first part, at least. Yes, Eddie and I found evidence that might uncover a disgusting fraud. We couldn't tell the police in case they blundered in and gave Larson a chance to destroy the ration books before we confirmed Major Leonard-White's involvement, and—'

'Anna, my dear, you're making no sense. Fraud, the camp commander, your evacuee? Are you ill?'

Why won't you listen?

Anna's frustration caused her to break down. Her tears had an immediate effect on the vicar. Meanwhile, Helen stood back as if objectively observing unfolding events.

'Please, Dad, let me speak.'

Charles nodded and quietly resumed his chair.

'It's easier if I don't go into the ration book thing now, but you have my word. I'll tell the police as soon as I'm certain they'll take Eddie and me seriously. I promise, Dad.'

Helen moved forward a few feet until she stood directly behind her daughter. Extending a hand, she gently stroked her offspring's flowing locks.

I love your touch, Mum.

The vicar reached over the table to cup Anna's hands. 'My dear, if I sounded sharp it's only because I… we, love you with all our hearts and would not wish to see you hurt. However, I, of course, accept your word. All we ask is that you tell us if you're in danger. The fact you're a grown woman does not mean your parents stop worrying about you. In fact, it's the reverse, since when you were a child, we could keep you safe. Now you're out in a madcap world on your own, which makes us feel helpless.'

I get it, Dad.

A smile spread across Anna's face as the friction within the room melted away.

'One thing, my darling, could you ask your American not to ring so early? I assumed a parishioner had died, and the matter required my attention. Most natural deaths take place overnight and around breakfast, you know.'

Her father's unknowingly witty explanation made Anna smile all the more. 'It wasn't Eddie, Dad. My WVS supervisor rang in a bit of a panic. The billet she had in mind for Vinny wouldn't take him. I know she could have made them, but what's the point of doing that, and it wouldn't be fair on Vinny. By the way, I thought it was quiet. Where is the little imp?'

Her parents laughed as Helen pointed to the rear of the vicarage. 'He was up with the larks digging his own veg patch in the back garden.'

Anna's smile vanished. 'The poor mite is making himself at home, isn't he? He'll hate me when I take him away. I love what I do, but I can't treat it like any old job. They're so vulnerable, all of them, no matter how cocky they come across.'

Helen walked around the table to sit next to her. 'Be careful, Anna, or you'll hurt yourself. There's only so much you can do. One day, soon if we're lucky, all these children will go back home, whatever home will look like or mean to them. Your job is to make this bit easier for them, not to be a surrogate parent.'

Tears began to well up once more in Anna's eyes. 'But—'

'Before you say anything else, your mother and I have been talking. Yes, Vinny drives us to distraction and his cockiness takes our breath away, but do you know, in the couple of days we've looked after the little devil, we've grown rather fond of him.'

Anna's eyes opened wide. She looked at her mother, who was too busy giving her husband the sort of look Anna knew only people with a deep love and respect for one another could pull off.

'Are… are you sure? He'll be a lot of work and I won't be able to—'

'We know you have your work and, er… investigative duties to perform, but yes, we spoke last night. I take it as a sign of the influence I have with my heavenly boss that your supervisor woke us up this morning.'

Vinny ran into the kitchen, holding several dahlias by their tuberous roots. 'These weeds were in the middle of the veg patch I'm digging. Should I chuck 'em in the bin or what?'

The three adults looked at each other and burst out laughing.

'Are yous lot laughin' at me?'

The vicar quickly reassured the boy. 'Laughing with, not at, you,

129

Vinny. I'll explain later. Meanwhile, there's something we want to talk to you about.'

By the end of their explanation to Vinny, all four had tears in their eyes.

Anna broke the moment by making an announcement. 'Well, I can't stay here all day. I'm off to the hairdressers to see if she'll fit me in at short notice.'

Vinny paid close attention to Anna's hair. 'Me ma says long hair encourages nits. She has a special steel comb to get 'em out. It doesn't half hurt, though. She makes me kneel on the floor with me 'ed over a newspaper on her lap. When she combs one out, she squeezes it between two fingers. Ma has really long nails and they squirt all over the place when she squeezes 'em.'

The room fell into an enthralled silence, listening to the young Scouser's memories of home.

'Just as well I'm having it cut, Vinny. We don't want any steel combs in this house, do we?'

Anna left the kitchen, watching Vinny shaking his head with vigour.

Once on the high street, Anna didn't get far before being stopped by Tom Bradshaw as he walked his beat.

'Morning, Tom. Everything OK?' She could see something was wrong.

'Larson rang the station early this morning. He says someone tried to break into his place last night.'

Anna froze.

'You were lucky. He can't find anything disturbed, but swears someone was on his land. I assume it was you two?'

Anna smiled, hoping to disarm the bobby. 'Are you going to arrest me?'

He smiled. 'I'm not that brave, but on the QT, did you find anything?'

'You bet – and more, but we can't talk here. Listen, I'm meeting Eddie later this afternoon. Why don't you join us at the Smuggler's Rest Inn at 2.00 pm?'

'Will they have much on the menu?'

'If you mean can you expect a meal with a salad course, rib-eye steak and pumpkin pie to follow, no. If you'll settle for boiled pota-toes, suet pudding and semolina with a dab of strawberry jam for afters, you'll be pleased.'

Eddie didn't respond as the Jeep cleared the brow of a small hump-back bridge that spanned the River Thurne. Immediately after the bridge lay the turn-in to the hostelry. A weather-worn red-brick exterior with one gable, white-washed to provide a reflective surface for fruit growing on the south side of the building, blended together under an impressive thatched roof.

'Do they have a problem with foxes here? Are you sure it's safe to eat in?'

'Foxes? What on earth are you… Oh, hilarious I don't think.' Anna realised Eddie was pointing to the hazel twig figure of a fox on the ridge line chasing a goose, also sculpted in hazel. 'It's Tommy Green's work. Every thatcher has his own trademark. You know, a rabbit, hare or stork, that kind of thing.'

As they pulled to a stop next to an old car that had seen better days, Tom Bradshaw's cheery smile greeted them. 'Good to see you're on time, you two.'

'They shut at three, so I knew it would by tight, but you already knew that since you make regular checks on our pubs to make sure they're obeying the licensing laws,' replied Anna.

'Ouch, I felt that,' said Tom as he slammed the driver's door of his father's pride and joy.

131

'Day off?' asked Eddie as the trio sauntered toward the front door of the Smuggler's Rest.

'A long story. Let's hope inspector Spillers doesn't cop me.'

Inside the seventeenth century structure, its exposed beams, blackened from centuries of fire and pipe smoke, leant atmosphere to the building, which Anna mused must hold many secrets of past customers.

Settled in the snug, they discussed Larson and the ration books while waiting for their boiled potatoes and suet puddings to arrive.

'What I don't understand is why you think there may be a link between Larson and Major Leonard-White,' said Tom.

'What, other than a tin of biscuits gifted to him as a Christmas present from the POW camp?'

'Are you sure?' replied Tom.

Anna sighed. 'Yes,' she said, leaving no doubt about her conviction.

They each sat back in their chairs as an unshaven man in a stained chef's uniform, complete with a misshapen toque hat, pushed a squeaking trolly laden with three main courses to the snug entrance. 'I'll leave this here so you can serve yourselves. The cutlery is on the shelf yonder. Think on not to use too much ketchup and the like. There's a war on, you know.' With that, the man turned unsteadily on his heels and left the room.

After a few minutes of organising, all three tucked into their lunch with varying degrees of enthusiasm.

'What did you say the pudding's made of? I don't mean the inside, I've given up on that, I mean this grey stuff that sticks to the top of your mouth?'

'You're a philistine, Lieutenant Elsner. It's suet. Lovely stuff. Try a swig of beer. It'll stop the suet attaching itself to your pallet,' said Anna.

The tall, slim figure dressed in a calf-length coat and blocking the entrance to the snug interrupted the moment of levity. 'Enjoying ourselves, are we?' said Detective Inspector Spillers.

'Inspector Spillers, what a surprise,' said Eddie.

Anna gave Tom a confused look, not knowing why he'd turned pale. 'Are you OK, Tom?'

'Yes, Tom, are you OK?' said the inspector.

Anna and Eddie exchanged confused looks.

'Is there anything wrong, Detective?' asked Anna.

Spillers rounded on his subordinate. 'Perhaps my constable might enlighten us?'

Tom placed his cutlery back onto his plate to show he had finished with his meal. 'I'm sorry, Inspector, I—'

'Sorry for what, Tom?' asked Anna.

Spillers moved towards the table and looked down on the three diners as if they were schoolchildren awaiting their fate outside his office. 'Constable Bradshaw pleaded with me to give him a couple of hours off so he could attend to an urgent personal matter. Now, the only reason I'm here is that I saw the lieutenant's Jeep as I drove past and thought I might call in to say hello. But what do I find? A scene worthy of Macbeth's three witches—'

'Hang on a minute, Inspector.'

'I'm sorry, Lieutenant, this is official police business. I don't expect to be misled by a member of my staff, let alone in a time of war, so they may have a pleasant pub lunch while discussing a murder that his superiors are responsible for solving.'

Anna threw her napkin on the table and stood up. 'Stop, Inspector. This is my fault. I asked Constable Bradshaw to meet us here. He had no idea why. It was I who told him it was a personal matter and that I needed a trusted friend's help.'

Tom's eyes remained focussed on his half-eaten lunch, while Spillers seemed for a second to relent.

'Help you how?'

Got to think quick.

'Child cruelty. One of my host parents has been mistreating their evacuee. I needed PC Bradshaw's help, but in a private capacity.'

Spillers' gaze burned into Anna before shifting to Tom Bradshaw. 'Is this true? Or has it anything to do with your brief visit to Mr Larson the other day? I've checked, there's nothing in your report book to say you were there. However, unfortunately for you, PC Bradshaw, Mr Larson phoned back for a second time this morning, wanting to know why we couldn't catch a burglar after lecturing him on keeping his buildings secure as part of some "project" or other. The description of the officer attending fits you to a tee.'

Anna resumed her seat. Neither of the other two spoke.

'I see you have nothing to say for yourself and I had intended to speak to you tomorrow, but events force me to suspend you on full pay as of now. You'll hand in your warrant card and other particulars to the desk sergeant this afternoon without making comment or conversation with him. Do I make myself clear?'

Chapter 11: Anna's Mistake

'That was awful. Poor Tom. We've got him in a load of trouble.'

'Not "we", Anna, you. I said it was a madcap scheme and now look what's happened. He could lose his career over yesterday's antics. Will you never learn?'

Go on, rub it in, why don't you?

The rest of the few seconds it took to walk from the pub back to the Jeep took place in silence. Anna grabbed a handle on the vehicle frame and slumped into the passenger seat.

To cap it all, I need a favour from him.

'Look, I'm sorry. I should have thought about the trouble I might cause for Tom. I'm not proud of myself but thought I was doing the right thing.'

Eddie loosened his grip on the steering wheel, sighed and turned to look at his companion. 'I apologise for being rude to you. I know you mean well. It's…' After a few seconds of silence, Eddie slowly extended his left hand, bringing the back of his fingers to a gentle rest on Anna's cheek. 'We'll call on Tom later, shall we, to see how he's doing?'

Making no attempt to move Eddie's hand, Anna gave a faint smile and nodded.

'Right, let's get you back home.'

The Jeep roared into life, causing a plume of grey smoke to envelop the rear of the vehicle.

'I have a favour to ask.'

'You're pushing your luck, aren't you?'

She gave him a coy smile. 'I know, but I promised Dad I'd pick up some papers from his vicar friend in Holkham. It's not that far, I promise.'

Her companion shook his head as he observed for anything coming over the humpback bridge before turning onto the main road. 'Have I guessed correctly?'

'You have – keep going along this road. I'll tell you when to turn off.'

The rest of the journey to Holkham was a subdued affair. Anna knew she had hurt Tom and thought she might have damaged her relationship with Eddie.

She looked at her watch.

'Are we late?'

'No, I told Dad we would call sometime this afternoon. He said the vicar should be around all day.'

Eddie huffed. 'Something else you forgot to tell me.' Anna bit. 'I'm joking, Anna Grix. What did you say the name of the church was?'

Anna gave him a sideways glance. 'I didn't, but it's St. Withburga. You can see the Norman tower in the distance. You can't miss it. The church sits on top of a small hill which, as I'm sure you've noticed by now, is novel for Norfolk.'

Within a few minutes, Eddie had parked the Jeep by the side of the church.

'What's up?' said Anna, noticing Eddie looking at the church noticeboard, positioned next to a thatch-roofed lychgate.

'How do you get what you called this place from a spelling like that?

Anna laughed. 'Don't forget that the Vikings were big around here. Forget the "GA" bit on the end of the name and you'll be fine.'

Shaking his head, Eddie clambered out of the Jeep and followed Anna through the thatched construction. 'We have these back in the States but call them The Resurrection Gates. Oh, and we don't bother with the straw stuff. We use cedar shingles; they're much stronger and smell nice, too.'

'Well, Lieutenant Elsner, I don't suppose the men or women in their coffin who rest here before being carried into the church much mind, do you?'

'Suppose you're right, Miss Grix. One thing we don't have, though, is that.' Eddie pointed to the magnificent place of worship. 'We sure don't have any of those. How come a lot of these churches in the middle of nowhere are so big?'

Anna joined her companion, looking up at the tall square bell tower with its castellated top and the flag of St George fluttering in a gentle breeze. 'We call them wool churches. Norfolk got rich literally off the backs of sheep in the middle ages. I guess the landowners wanted to bribe their way into Heaven by paying for one of these.'

Before they could spend more time admiring the ancient place of worship, a spectacled man, dressed in black and sporting a white clerical collar to signify his office, wandered down a steep slope. 'You must be Charles's daughter. Anna, isn't it?'

She smiled and extended a hand. 'Nice to meet you. My father said you have some documents I should collect?'

The vicar shook Anna's hand, then pointed toward the church. 'I do. Your father always was one for history, although what he expects to discover in our parish records I don't know. Anyway, I'll take you in through the vestry. I've a young couple who requested some private

137

time in the church, so I've shut the front door, which is rare for me. Who knows, the young man may have to fight for his country in a few weeks.'

After trekking up the steep slope on a narrow path that cut through a multitude of old headstones leaning at perilous angles, the vicar lifted a huge iron key from his waist and opened a heavy, nail-studded oak door.

Inside the small stone-walled room, he reached for a smaller key that hung on the side of a door frame and gestured for them to follow. 'Please be mindful of the young couple I told you about and respect their wish for privacy.'

Doing her best to comply, Anna concentrated on the iron-bound wooden box that rested along one wall of the vestry. The charcoal surface that covered one edge of the medieval container fascinated her.

'Ah, I see that, like Charles, you too are a lover of history,' whispered the vicar. 'Well, we have Oliver Cromwell to blame for the damage. During the English civil war, the parishioners moved the chest for safekeeping into the vicarage cellar. For reasons that continue to mystify me, the Roundheads burned the house to the ground while leaving the church untouched. Luckily, the box is so well made that its contents remained undamaged as the upper floor of the house collapsed into the cellar.'

After fiddling with a small lock for such an important chest, the vicar gained entry. He lifted two great leather-bound volumes from its cavernous interior, then rested them on the red and white tiled floor. 'You'll be careful with them, won't you? They're so precious to our community. They contain the records of births, marriages and deaths stretching back many hundreds of years, and some family names still exist in the area.'

Anna marvelled at the ancient records before being interrupted by a gentle nudge from Eddie.

'Look over there,' he whispered.

Much against Anna's better judgement, she took a sly look at the two people the vicar had said wished for privacy.

This doesn't feel right.

Her attention fell on the man. 'It can't be?' she whispered back as the vicar busied himself securing the magnificent chest.

'Can't do anything now. We'll wait for them to come out.'

Having completed the pleasantries of thanks and saying goodbye to the vicar as quickly as possible so they could take up position, Anna tasked Eddie with carrying the two heavy tombs.

'You've no time for tea?' asked the vicar with a tinge of disappointment shown by his sentence dropping a tone as he completed the last word.

'I'm so sorry, Vicar, but my father is expecting me back for Evensong.'

The vicar appeared to cheer up. 'Oh, yes, of course. I almost forgot myself, so much have I enjoyed your company. Please forgive me for being so selfish; of course, you must go. Have a safe journey. Remember me to your mother and father, won't you?'

Walking carefully down the steep slope that led from the church, Eddie tried twice to say something.

'Go on, get it out. Yes, I know. I told a lie. I can see the headline in the Sunday papers now: *"Shock Horror, Vicar's Daughter Tells Untruth".*'

'I was about to say no such thing.'

Anna laughed. 'Really? Well now I see a second headline: *"Second Scandal, American Officer Tells Porkies".*'

The following fifteen minutes were tame by comparison as the pair observed the church from a discreet distance, waiting for the young lovers to appear.

'There they are. Coming out now.' Anna pointed to the heavy

front door and gasped. 'It isn't just Enzo. Remember that girl we came across on Sunday, arguing with the older man? Either I'm going bonkers or that's her.'

'Where do you think they're going?'

'Only one way to find out – let's get after them but be careful, if they get wind of us, they'll be off like a shot,' replied Eddie.

Within a minute, Enzo and the woman left the narrow lane that passed for the main road into Holkham and made for a narrow dirt track that meandered its way through a wooded landscape.

'They've chosen well. No one will find them in here. Do you reckon Enzo's holed up here?'

'It makes sense,' replied the lieutenant. 'He solves two problems in one move. Somewhere to hide and a place near his girlfriend. They must have planned it together.'

As the pair whispered, the woman stopped and began to turn around. 'Quick, in here, Anna.'

Before she had time to react, she found herself being pulled into a bed of brambles off the track. 'Will you get off me? And if my face gets scratched by these rotten things, you'll live to regret it, my American friend.'

After a few seconds, they carefully untangled themselves from their thorny refuge.

Anna noticed the back of Eddie's left hand was bleeding. 'Serves you right.'

Her companion dismissed the minor injury and instead poked his head out of the bushes to check they were in the clear. 'Come on, they're rounding the corner.'

I must be mad.

They followed around the corner with particular care to ensure their quarries were not about to spring a surprise.

140

Eddie gave the all-clear as they rounded the bend. 'Looks like they've come to a stop. They're looking at something, but I can't see what it is.'

Anna walked a few feet so she stood next to the lieutenant. 'I'm sure I recognise that woman as the one from Wells-next-the-sea.'

'Never mind the woman. One thing we now know for sure is that the man is Enzo, and we have to get to him before either the major or Inspector Spillers, or he'll be for it.'

The pair continued to creep along the hedge line to see how close they could get without alerting Enzo and his companion.

'Why don't I casually walk up to them?' said Anna.

'Because there's a chance he'll recognise you. If he does, he'll run.'

'What do you suggest we do?'

Come on, you're supposed to be the clever clogs.

'We wait. Let's see where they go.'

Seconds later, the pair vanished from sight.

'Come on, but quietly.'

If you say that to me one more time, I'll make sure you're the one who stays quiet.

The pair drifted forward until a break in the hedge came into view.

'Perhaps they've both bolted into the field?'

Eddie shrugged his shoulders. 'Only one way to find out. Follow me.'

Yes, Oh Master.

No sooner had Eddie walked forward than he came to an abrupt stop. So abrupt that Anna crashed into his back.

'What are you doing, silly American? You could have broken my nose,' she whispered.

Again, ignoring her protestations, Eddie crouched down and risked a look around the hawthorn hedge before quickly retreating. 'There's an old cottage. It looks as though it's about to fall down.'

141

Anna strained to see the place. 'Do you think that's their hideout?'

'Dunno, but what other reason do they have for being all the way out here?'

'Let's go for it.'

Eddie let out a gasp as he tried to stop his impetuous friend.

Enzo spotted the sudden movement and bolted, leaving the young woman stranded, before she too turned and ran.

The pair stood motionless, shocked at the speed of events.

'Shouldn't we—'

'We do nothing, Anna. Are you happy now? I told you to be careful but no, as usual, you know best. You always have to push things. Wasn't Tom enough for you? Now you've lost us the best two leads we have in finding Ruth Cotton's murderer. When will you learn? When, Anna?'

His booming voice and contorted face alarmed Anna.

I've never seen this side of him. Do I know this man at all?

'And you? What about you?' she shouted, arms flailing with rage. 'All you wanted to do was wait… but wait for what? The pair of them to walk over to us and wish us a pleasant afternoon?'

Eddie snatched the cap from his head and began pulling at it with both hands. 'To pick our moment. That's what we should've done. Pick your battles, Anna; don't simply rush in. Today it lost us the prime suspect and his girlfriend. Tomorrow your recklessness may cost someone, perhaps one of us, our lives. I've told you before. This isn't a game. You might see yourself as Miss Marple, or whatever her name is, but this is real life, not a book.'

'I know full well it's not a game, Mr. You say pick your fights, well, sometimes you can't. You of all people should know that. After all, your father didn't choose to go on that reconnaissance flight over France in 1918. He obeyed an order. He didn't choose, and it cost him his life.'

142

'Don't you dare bring my father into this. Who are you to lecture me on picking fights? What does a vicar's daughter know of the real world? You have no idea what it feels like to face an enemy whose sole intent is to kill you.

'You have no idea of the fear that floods through your body at the thought of never seeing the people you love again. No, instead you attend Evensong, help sort old clothes in a thrift store and play mother with evacuees. Don't dare to consider yourself qualified in losing a father, and I pray it will be a long time until that day comes.'

Exhausted, the couple glared at each other, neither prepared to be the first to break angry eye contact.

Eddie broke the stalemate. He thrust his hands into his pockets and pushed the gravel at his feet around with the sole of his shoe. 'I've nothing more to say, Anna,' he said in a low, hoarse voice. 'I think it best if you make your own way back home. We both need time to think.'

Anna didn't reply. Instead, she watched the lieutenant walk at pace back along the track until, a minute later, she stood alone, even the birds seemingly too afraid to resume their song.

Not knowing quite what to do except make sure Eddie was long gone before she walked back into Holkham for a bus home, Anna busied herself by observing every inch of the old cottage for no other reason than to pass ten minutes.

She almost failed to notice a small, slim figure gingerly making her way out of the cottage.

It's Enzo's companion, the girl from last Sunday. She must have entered the cottage through the back.

'It's you.'

The young woman, seemingly under the impression the coast was

143

now clear, jumped in fright. 'I don't know you. What do you want?'

'Don't be afraid. My name's Anna. Remember, last Sunday? You argued with your father.'

The woman scrutinised her inquisitor. 'I... yes... yes, I remember you. That man, the one you were arguing with. I recognised the uniform when I looked out of the cottage. He was with you on Sunday, wasn't he?'

Anna felt her eyes starting to moisten.

No, don't cry now. Come on, fight it.

'Yes. You heard us argue? I'm sorry, that couldn't have been pleasant,' said Anna.

'It wasn't difficult to hear. It sounded terrible. My name is April. April Rider.'

The women walked back into Holkham, exchanging general conversation as they strolled along the deserted track.

Got to do this.

'I have a confession to make, April.'

Her companion stopped walking. 'What do you mean?'

'I know Enzo,' said Anna.

'Who?'

'I thought you might say that, and who can blame you? You see, I, and my friend, well, we're looking into the death of a young woman. This man, Enzo, we think he might be connected to the tragedy in some way. Of course, we couldn't be sure the cottage was connected to him, but it was too good an opportunity to miss.'

'You came to spy on him? Who is this Enzo anyway? He sounds foreign?'

'No, we didn't. We came to see the vicar, but when we recognised Enzo in the church, we were nonplussed.'

April walked off. 'Why should I care about some Italian prisoner of war?'

Anna caught the woman up and stopped her. 'I didn't say he is an Italian, or a POW, April. You're correct on both counts, but how did you know?'

'I heard him out of the window like I heard you and the American, that's all.'

'Look, April, unless you have a doppelganger, we know you were in the church with Enzo, so please, let's stop this silly game. Believe it or not, I'm trying to help both of you.'

'I don't know what you're talking about. I've never heard of any Enzo person. Now leave me alone or I'll call the police.'

'Are you sure?' responded Anna. 'And by all means call the police because I think you'll find they're looking for you anyway. You accompanied him from the church to this cottage, and you know him to be a POW. So what's going on?'

April began to cry, tears streaming down her cheeks.

'Come here, let me give you a hug. Please believe me when I say I'm here to help.' The girl collapsed into Anna's open arms. 'That's it, don't hold it back. It'll be fine,' said Anna as she held April tightly to her.

As the minutes passed, April began to calm down until all that Anna could detect was the occasional heaving of the woman's chest as she let out a sob. Eventually, the two women simply held each other. It felt to Anna like April might never let go.

'Enzo clearly means a lot to you. How did you meet?'

After a few seconds of silence, April responded. 'Some POWs came to work at one of my father's factories. They weren't there long, but Enzo and I got to know one another. He was easy to talk to and we hit it off. When the POWs left, we agreed to carry on seeing one another.'

Anna gave her charge a final hug before gently prising herself away then holding Apil's hands in her own. 'Well, when it happens, it happens, doesn't it? War makes no distinction when it comes to bumping into "that special person", does it? Now, let's get you cleaned up.'

Heavens, you look a picture, thought Anna as she caught sight of April's blotchy checks and reddened eyes.

'Here we go, that's it, let me wipe those tears away,' said Anna as she gently dabbed with a handkerchief.

Chapter 12: Friends in Need

What was I thinking?

Anna wandered aimlessly towards the open fields on the edge of Lipton St Faith, wanting to shut out the endless replay of her argument with Eddie the previous day. The scene stole her night's sleep and continued to haunt her.

What have I done?

Ashamed she'd used the death of the lieutenant's father to score a point, Anna tortured herself with the likely ramifications of her outburst.

What if I never see him again? Heaven forbid this war kills him without us making up. How many sweethearts live with that awful outcome already?

Anna stopped walking and checked herself.

We're not sweethearts. Why did I think that?

'Good morning, Anna. A lovely day,' said Flo Bassett as she passed the sad figure, on her way to start her day volunteering at the thrift shop.

Anna heard, but couldn't bring herself to speak. As she began walking slowly towards an opening in a tall hedge that provided access to open fields, Beatrice Flowers, the village gossip, attempted to harangue her.

'…And do you think it's fitting that the vicar's daughter should walk the streets in that state? Knees should be covered at all times, except when exercising, where shorts should be worn so that men can't… well, never mind that. What will your father say?'

Oh, do shut up, thought Anna, unable to summon up the energy to defend herself.

At last, the isolation she craved materialised as she stepped aimlessly through the field opening and into unfettered countryside.

Thank you, God.

Anna knew that invoking the Almighty wasn't something she did regularly, despite her upbringing. She often inwardly chastised herself for not being closer to the faith her parents built their world around. She knew the outbreak of war changed her. She spoke to other people of her age and knew some of them felt the same.

What gets me is that the older ones have been through it before and were promised by those who should know better that a world war could never happen again. Why should any of us care what happens? We're not the ones in control.

'Hello, you.'

The familiar, cheery voice snapped Anna out of her self-imposed isolation. Looking a few feet to her right, she saw Vinny laying on his tummy. 'What are you doing?'

Vinny held up an ear of wheat by placing an elbow onto the golden carpet of straw left over from the recent harvest. 'It's clever, you know. An old bloke chucks some seeds around, waits for it to rain and comes back months later and gets this.' Vinny surveyed the single stalk cereal as if it were a bar of precious metal.

I adore this little boy.

'I'm not sure it's quite that simple, but I get your point. Why do you suppose it was an old man that scattered the seed?'

Vinny scrambled to change position and now sat cross-legged on the straw. A field mouse, disturbed by the sudden movement, scurried past the soles of the Scouser's well-worn shoes without Vinny bothering to react. 'Well, all them about twenty have gone to fight. That means there're only the old ones left.'

For the first time in twenty-four hours, Anna smiled. 'So you think anyone over, say, twenty-five is old?'

'Ma says she's twenty-one, an' she looks dead old, so I reckon anyone who coughs like Ma does, or keeps saying the same thing over and over, must be ready for the knacker's yard. That's what I tell Ma.'

Why do we have to grow up?

'And what does your mother think to that?'

'She clouts around me ears. Doesn't half sting but I always get jam butties after. Anyway, what's wrong with you?'

His question took Anna by surprise. 'What do you mean?'

Vinny pointed a finger. 'You've got a face on like a wet weekend. Ma has that look sometimes, usually when the tally man's been round an' she can't pay 'im. She says he gets bad-tempered, so she throws a piece of coal to get rid. I have to go out and pick it up before 'er next door nicks it. She ain't half quick for an old gal with one leg.'

Anna so wanted to laugh, but the events of the previous day overwhelmed her. Her eyes began to moisten.

'I said you was sad. 'Ere, take this.' Vinny held out several sheets of loo paper. 'And don't waste 'em. I've got a stash in me bedroom to take to Ma. The newspaper squares we use in the outside lav don't 'arf scratch. That's when there's any to use. People nick it, you know.'

Anna's combination of laughter and tears continued as she joined Vinny on the rich bed of flaxen vegetation.

'I'm sure that's most inconvenient, Vinny.'

'What does that mean?'

Anna's explanation led to Vinny shaking his head. 'That's one word for it. We call people who nick your lav paper—'

'Let's not go into that, shall we, young man?'

'Are you going to clip me round the ear now like Ma does?'

Anna leant over and gave the boy a hug. 'No jam butties this time, young man.'

Following a few minutes' silence during which Vinny did not escape Anna's embrace, she explained why she felt sad to the little boy.

What am I doing? He's still a baby.

'Ma says it's best to make up as soon as you can, unless it's with your old man. She says you should make 'im sleep on the couch until he sobers up.'

'I'll remember that,' replied Anna, the tears now rolling down her cheeks.

'Don't cry, Anna. If you does what me ma says it'll all be all right. She reckons making up is the best part. Me ma always liked it 'cos it meant she got a bar of Fry's Chocolate Cream off 'im. Mind you, I bet it was nicked from the docks. Once she'd scoffed it, they always went out into the backyard for ten minutes. Don't ask what they did, but when they came back, they'd be smiling like Cheshire cats.'

Moving on.

'Yes, well, I'm sure that's all remarkably interesting, but you see, I did something bad. I hurt someone I think a lot of. Do you understand?'

Vinny didn't hesitate. 'Sure I do, but does that mean I don't get more Hershey's chocolate?'

Anna riffled the young man's hair with her fingers. 'Oi, you little scamp. How did you know I was talking about the lieutenant?'

'That's easy. I see the way you look at each other. Jed and Mary do that back home. They're always taking off and coming back smiling. Don't know what they do, but do you do it?'

Help.

'I don't know what you're talking about, young man, I'm sure.'

'Well, how are you going to put it right with Eddie? I need more chocolate.'

Oh, Vinny, what a lovely world you inhabit.

She shuffled a few feet away from the Scouser and pivoted herself so she sat directly opposite him. 'What should I do?'

Vinny picked up a handful of wheat stalks before releasing them into the pleasant September breeze. 'That's easy. When I fall out with me best mate, Freddy, I leave it a little bit, then take him a present. It's usually some of me marbles. Not me best ones; usually a couple of me second best. If I've been a real blert, I might give three. That way you don't need to say nothing. You know, he takes the marbles, and you have a good laugh and start playing again. Easy.'

'You might have something there, young 'un, but I think it'll take more than a few glass marbles.'

The walk into Three-Mile-Bottom helped calm Anna's head as she took in the fresh air and sounds of birdsong. She'd rehearsed what she intended to say and do. As Anna neared Eddie's billet, doubts set in.

What if he slams the door on me?

The hamlet presented its usual sleepy self. Apart from one or two vehicles and a line of tarred telegraph poles bringing electricity and a few phone lines into the hamlet, the scene hadn't changed in hundreds of years, Anna supposed.

Approaching Hilda and Albert Crossman's cottage, she felt the fluttering in her stomach turning into a leaden weight.

Anna stood inches from the front door, raising her right hand and lowering it three times, not wanting to find out what reception awaited her.

Eventually, she summoned up the courage to knock and took a step back.

151

The snap of a lock being unbolted alerted Anna to fear the worst. Instead, the smiling face of Hilda Crossman appeared around the edge of the door.

She knows.

'Thank goodness you're here. He's had a face on like a man who's found a sixpence and lost a shilling.' Hilda opened the door wide and turned into the small living room. 'Albert Crossman, get yer baccy and change out of them slippers. We're off out.'

A minute later, a confused looking Albert followed his smiling wife out of the front door.

'Get Eddie sorted, will you? He's in a right spin,' Hilda said and winked at her visitor before ushering her husband to get a move on.

What do I do now?

She waited. The silence continued.

Nothing for it.

Anna slowly crossed the threshold and shut the door behind her. She discovered a deserted living room, save for the rhythmic ticking of a mantle clock. She passed through into a tiny kitchen, which too, remained empty.

Where's Eddie? He must be here, or Hilda would've said.

Anna resorted to looking in the only place left, the long, narrow back garden of the cottage.

There he is.

Beyond a small patch of lawn and much longer spread of vegetables growing in raised boarders, was the lieutenant.

He looks so lonely.

Anna wasn't sure if Eddie realised she'd arrived but guessed he came into the garden once he heard Hilda greet her. Now it was too late for either of them to shy away from each other.

'Eddie,' said Anna. She stood less than six feet from the American, who continued to look at the ground. 'Eddie, I've…' Anna looked down at the brown paper bag she had with her. Uncrumpling the rolled-over top, she reached in for something. 'Eddie, a wise person told me that when you do something wrong, you should make it up to the person you upset by bringing a gift. Something that means a lot to the person who was wrong.'

Please, Eddie, look at me.

At first, the lieutenant continued to ignore his visitor, but slowly, almost imperceptibly at first, he shuffled his feet on the cinder path.

Come on, Eddie.

'I've brought this.' Anna held out a pristine bar of Hershey's chocolate. 'When we first met, you gave me this. I can't tell you how much I wanted to eat it. It's been so long since I've eaten chocolate.' She watched as Eddie reacted. 'Instead, I saved it for a really important day. The day the war is over, whichever way it goes. After the wise person explained things to me, I realised that it was no use keeping precious things if I had no one to share them with. What's the point of waiting for the war to be over if you're on your own?' Slowly, Eddie began to lift his arm and reach for the confectionery, his eyes rigidly fixed on Anna's gaze. 'I'm sorry, Eddie, I had no right to—'

'Don't say it, Anna. We both got angry and I shouldn't have left you. That was unforgivable.'

He took the chocolate bar from Anna's hand. 'Equal shares?'

I'm an incredibly lucky girl.

'I think you deserve the lion's share, don't you?' Anna offered a coy smile, not wishing to push things too fast.

'Equal shares, Miss Grix. It's that way or no way.'

Anna couldn't help herself. She rushed forward and gave the lieutenant a hug. She sensed he wasn't responding with his own arms.

153

That's OK, I'll settle for this.

Over the next twenty minutes, they gently explored each other's feelings, being careful not to say anything that might upset the other.

'We need to move on.'

For a split second, Anna froze.

Oh, no, he's had enough of me. I guess I deserve it.

'I think we should get back to finding out who murdered Ruth Cotton. I've only got another week before I have to report back to London, and I'll be away for a couple of months.'

Anna's emotions overwhelmed her. She could feel herself shaking as she continued to hug Eddie.

'What's the matter, do you not want to carry on with our investigation?'

'You try to stop me.' Tears of relief trickled down Anna's cheeks. 'And have I got some news for you.'

Continuing to be careful with each other, Anna and the lieutenant settled for genial conversation as they made their way from the Crossmans' to Holkham to track down where April lived.

It's like meeting him all over again.

Once in the village, they headed for the nearest newsagent.

'If they don't know where the Riders live, I don't know who will.'

As they entered the tiny shop, a woman dressed in a green cardigan, pleated plumb-coloured calf-length dress and stout brown shoes offered a neighbourly smile. 'Good afternoon.' The middle-aged woman looked up at a wall clock. 'Yes, it's passed the noon hour. What can I get you? It's not every day we see an American officer in our tiny village.'

Eddie looked at the small, cluttered counter covered in the day's newspapers sorted by title, a muddle of sewing accessories for sale, and a half-full mug of tea perching precariously on the edge nearest the shopkeeper.

'I'll take the *Express*, please,' said Eddie as he fumbled in his pocket for a penny.

Retrieving a copy of the *Express* and rearranging the remaining papers so they regained their tight formation, the shopkeeper sighed. 'Poor Russians. They're fighting so hard to stave off the Nazis.' She pointed to the headline:

'*Leningrad Fights 2-Day Stuka Blitz*'.

Eddie took hold of the paper and handed over the coin. 'Ma'am, the Russians will see them off just as your brave country won the Battle of Britain.'

Anna felt her heart swell as she looked on at the beaming shopkeeper.

Now, Eddie. Ask Her Now.

It was as if Anna's thoughts beamed themselves into Eddie's head. 'Tell, me, ma'am. As you can tell, we are strangers in the area. We're looking for some folks and wondered if you might help us?'

'Oh, I'm sure I can. As you'd expect, everyone uses my shop. Who is it you want?'

Eddie gave the woman one of his beguiling smiles. 'That's so gracious of you, ma'am. Them folks go by the name of Rider. Do you know them?'

The shopkeeper's demeanour stiffened as she folded her arms.

She knows the husband, that's for sure.

'I hope you mean Mrs Rider and her wonderful daughter?'

Anna stepped in. 'Oh, yes, of course.'

The woman nodded. 'I should think so too. Far be it from me to gossip, but the husband is a cad and I shall say no more. You can't miss the house; it's up on the left. The largest one in the village.'

Thanking the shopkeeper for her kindness, Anna and Eddie left the woman busying herself once more, rearranging the lines of paper on the countertop.

Leaving the Jeep parked up outside the newsagent, the pair set off for the Rider house.

'She was correct – you can't miss it, can you?' said Eddie.

Anna stood back to admire the fine building. 'Do you know, it looks like a house designed by Edwin Lutyens.'

'Edwin Who?'

'Philistine. He's a famous architect. Oh, never mind, let's get on with it.'

Leaving a confused Eddie at the entrance to the substantial residence, Anna headed for the front door.

April Rider's face came into view as she opened the door. 'Anna, what are you… how did you find me?' She caught sight of Eddie walking up the drive. 'That's the man who—'

'We've settled our differences, April, but we need to speak to you. Are your parents in? Is it OK to speak?'

April shrugged her shoulders. 'Uh, my father's visiting his fancy woman; he won't be back for hours.' She looked over her shoulder at the attractive oak staircase. 'And Mum's in bed. She's taken some more sedatives.'

'I'm so sorry, April. We—'

'Don't be. We're used to my father's ways, but it still takes its toll on Mum. Come in, but you know I won't tell you anything.'

April showed her guests into an exquisitely furnished lounge decorated in the country manner style.

'April, I know this is hard, but we have to talk about it. I'm not sure you're aware of how dangerous things are for Enzo.'

April shook her head. 'They won't find him. Nobody will. I'll keep him safe whatever happens.'

Anna looked at Eddie, who said, 'Miss Rider, if the police or the army catch him first they will put him on trial. Based on the facts as they know them, they will convict and… April, this isn't the time for me to use vague language. If he's convicted, he'll hang.'

Anna could see Eddie's words had cut through April like a knife.

'But he didn't do it. He explained everything to me.'

'That's as maybe,' said Anna as she stood and walked over to her host. 'Listen to me. We have no time to lose. If you tell us where to find Enzo, we can get his side of the story and, if he's telling the truth, try to find the evidence to prove his innocence. We can't do any of that unless you help us. Do you understand, April?'

The lounge door burst open. In the doorframe stood a massive man, his face purple with rage. 'You two again. What are you doing here? Get out or I'll call the police, or perhaps you'd like me to deal with you myself?'

April ran over to her father. 'What are you doing back?'

'It's none of your concern, but as well I'm here. What do they want with us?'

He doesn't know about Enzo.

'They're my friends, Dad, that's all.'

'Rubbish. You only met them a few days ago and that was because they wouldn't mind their own business.' He turned to them. 'Have you any idea who you're messing about with? No? I suggest you leave while you can and find out. Get out of my home, now.' He pointed to the lounge door.

'It's all right, Dad, I'll see them out.' April encouraged Anna and Eddie to move toward the door and led them back to the front of the house.

'Will you be OK with him?'

April nodded. 'He's overprotective, that's all. He won't touch me. Anyway, he'll be drunk and asleep within the hour.'

'April?' Her father's voice boomed from within.

'Tomorrow morning. I'll meet you back at that old cottage at eleven.'

157

Chapter 13: Who Speaks the Truth?

Saturday morning arrived and with it a drizzle that clandestinely soaked everything it touched, making the drive back to Holkham a miserable affair.

'The farmers will be pleased they got the harvest in on time. Dad says the weather forecast looks bad for the next week.'

'Let's hope the roof on that old cottage is intact or we'll get soaked.'

The journey continued in a comfortable silence until Anna brought up the subject of Tom Bradshaw. 'We said we'd see how he's doing. I feel as guilty as I did in the Smuggler's Rest. We ought not to have left things like that.'

Eddie slowed to a snail's pace as they came up behind a military convoy of army troop carriers. As soon as the soldiers in the rear lorry saw the Jeep, complete with an American officer and civilian woman, a roar of cheers erupted. They both did their best to ignore the unwanted intrusion.

'Good on yer, mate.'

'Who's a lucky boy?'

'Got any spare silk stockings, Yank?'

The lieutenant determined the best course of action was to drop back and leave enough distance between them to make their comments impossible to hear.

'About Tom. You saw the inspector. He'd have arrested us if we'd tried to intervene. I also feel guilty, but Tom's a grown man. He'll deal with it. The last thing he needs is us going to see him and Spillers finding out. Let's leave things be for a few days, then decide what to do.'

The convoy, plus the intensifying drizzle, did little to improve their mood. However, eventually, they arrived at the derelict cottage.

Anna checked her watch. 'We did well to arrive spot on eleven, considering the weather and what was in front of us.'

Her companion didn't answer. Instead, he was already out of the Jeep and standing in front of the decrepit building, feet slightly apart with a hand on each hip. 'Come on, let's get on with it.'

'Who's the one that says fools rush in?'

Eddie looked back and smiled. 'You're not suggesting you're an angel, I hope?'

Anna offered a friendly sigh as they crossed the broken threshold of the front entrance. Inside the old cottage, a scene of devastation met them. Heaps of lime plaster littered the floor, leaving the wooden laths, which anchored it to the wall, exposed. Most of the glass had gone from several rotted windows and as Anna looked up, she could see small shafts of light allowed access by a rotten first floor and decaying thatched roof covering.

'April, are you here?' Anna's call went unanswered as the pair continued to explore the wrecked building. 'April, it's Anna. I have Eddie with me. It's OK, no one knows we're here.'

After a few seconds, Anna thought she heard whispering coming from one of the broken-down bedrooms.

'They're here,' said Eddie.

Soon, two pairs of footsteps broke the silence as April and Enzo showed themselves on the rickety staircase.

'It's OK,' said Anna in a reassuring voice. 'We want to help. That's it, come down.'

April and Enzo cleared the staircase and stood opposite Anna and Eddie like two opposing armies sizing each other up before battle.

'I know how difficult this is, Enzo. And you, April. Thank you for trusting us.'

'Why you bring police and soldiers into woods if you here to help?' Enzo turned to Eddie. 'All British and American soldiers the same.'

April laced the palm of one hand on Enzo's cheek. 'Listen to what they have to say, my love, please.'

Her appeal worked.

'Enzo, you know how much trouble you're in. Let us help you.'

'But first things first, Enzo,' said Eddie. 'Look me in the eye and tell me you did not murder Ruth Cotton.' Eddie's firm stance and cold eyes caught everyone's attention.

The Italian hesitated, and his look varied from April to the floor and back. 'I not kill girl.'

Anna touched Enzo's arm. 'Tell us everything you know. You were seen with Ruth on the day she died. Give us something we can check so we can prove your innocence.'

Enzo shuffled from foot to foot.

April nudged his arm. 'Go on. Tell them.'

'I see her again that day. She—'

'Again?' exclaimed Anna.

Enzo looked surprised to be asked the question. 'Yes… I come to woods most days when I work on farm. I like the place. That lady comes sometimes, too. She say she like place also. We talk about things. Not war, but nice things. She tell me she knows Italy. Her

160

family visit before war and I gave her coin to remember my country. We like same things, so we talk.' Enzo looked at his girlfriend. 'April know all this. No secrets for us.'

Eddie took off his cap, only to feel a drip of water splash his forehead courtesy of the leaking thatch. No one reacted to the comic scene. 'Tell us what happened.'

'That day she worried. She say a man at work not leave her alone and if boyfriend thinks she cheating, he hurt them both.'

Let's see what he knows about Sedwell.

'But her boyfriend is away fighting,' said Anna.

Enzo shrugged his shoulders. 'How can he be if she say she meet him that night? Lady say they like to camp out but other boy somehow knew this and she frightened he will come. Lady not want to go but boyfriend make her. She frightened. I tell her not to come. Am worried, too many secrets. More people get hurt.' He turned to April.

The poor girl's in tears.

'Do you think Enzo believed us when we said we wouldn't tell anyone about meeting him?'

'I don't know,' commented Eddie as he pulled out onto the main road through Holkham and made for the boatyard beyond Wroxham. 'The lovely Geoffrey has some explaining to do. Do you think the yard will be open?'

'It's certain to be. I imagine they're working seven days a week, twelve hours a day on war work. Whether he'll be on shift is another matter.'

By twelve-thirty, the Jeep stood stationary in the place Eddie parked it during their first visit. 'Thank God it's different guards on the gate by the look of things. Let's hope they're more helpful than the last lot,' said Eddie.

'Lenox, you say. Hang on and I'll ring the production office,' responded the guard.

While one soldier stepped into the tiny guardhouse, the other engaged the pair in amiable conversation. 'It's rare we see an American serviceman around here. Are there more of you to come, or are you staying out of it this time? I wouldn't blame you if you did.'

Eddie smiled. 'Not up to me, soldier. Anyway, I'm here so it'll all be fine.'

Both men laughed as Anna kept her eye on the guardhouse.

'Nope, he's not on shift today, sorry. Was it important?'

'Well,' started the lieutenant.

He's got a plan.

'To be truthful, it's both urgent and important. I can't say too much, you understand, but I have to see Mr Lenox today before—'

'A bit hush-hush is it?' The soldier tapped a finger against the side of his nose to reinforce his point.

Eddie sighed. 'Soldier, you've seen through me and my commander won't be happy, but us fighting boys know how it's done, don't we?'

You sneaky so-and-so.

'You wait there. I'll see if the office will give you his address.'

Five minutes later and the Jeep was on its way back toward Holkham.

'I swear the thing can drive itself back to Holkham given how often we've done this journey lately.'

'You'd better make sure you tell it to stop when we see the sign for Foxley,' replied Anna.

'You mean if the locals haven't turned the road signs around again.'

Fortunately for Eddie, the road signs for Foxley remained in place, allowing him to bring the vehicle to a stop off the main road. On the corner, set back from the road, stood the red-brick cottage of Geoffrey Lenox.

'How shall we play this?' said Anna.

'We haven't time to muck around, so I suggest we push hard. With luck, he'll tell us what we need to know.'

The American's firm knock on the paint-chipped door resulted in Lenox opening it in seconds.

Judging by his horrified look, he's got things to hide from us.

His eyes bulged on seeing callers, before he looked over his shoulder into the cottage's run-down interior. 'What do you want? How do you know where I live?' Lenox pushed his way through the half-open door and closed it almost silently behind him before stepping several feet into the small front garden. 'Mother is ill and needs me. What do you want from me? I told you everything I knew last time.' He turned his attention to Anna. 'Get away from my house or I'll—'

'You'll do nothing, Geoffrey,' said Eddie as he and Anna joined Lenox in the garden.

He fears my American.

Lenox visibly shrivelled into his frame. 'I… well.'

'That's better, Geoffrey. I cautioned you the other day about that temper of yours.'

The front door creaked open to reveal an elderly lady, her head covered with a long black shawl, her unsteady gait supported by a walking stick in each hand. 'Who are these people? I need you inside with me, now.'

Lenox turned to Anna after briefly glancing at his mother. 'You must go, or I'll call the police.'

'Mr Lenox, you'll talk to us now or *we'll* call the police. Your choice,' said Anna.

'Get inside, Mother. I'll be with you in a minute.'

There speaks a loving son, I don't think.

Lenox crossed his arms as he swivelled back to his unwanted visitors. 'Tell me what you want or leave. I've had enough of this.'

'As I'm sure Ruth Cotton's had enough of being dead. Do you think the lieutenant and I have nothing better to do? Do you know, you may be correct? After all, now we have proof you were bothering Ruth, perhaps we should tell the police and be done with it.'

Lenox erupted with rage. 'I told you, I look after Mother. That's all I have time for. Are all women as stupid as you?'

'Enough, fella or I'll put you on the floor. You get my drift?' Lenox's glare remained on Anna. 'Look at me, Lenox. Do it now.' Both Anna and Lenox jumped at Eddie's terrifying command. 'Don't let me hear you talk to a lady like that again. Understand? *Do you understand?* The American's repeated question filled the air with menace.

Forced to look at Eddie, Lenox spoke in an urgent tone. 'Who says they saw me? 'Cos it's all lies. Prove it.'

If he calls our bluff, we're done.

'Geoffrey, a woman is dead, and we have proof, an eyewitness, who saw everything.'

Lenox glared at Anna.

Eddie acted immediately. 'Keep looking at me. Do it now.'

This time the repeated order was met with a quiet steeliness. Giving a surly look, Lenox complied with the lieutenant's order. 'She was always leading me on. That hair, the lipstick. Who comes to work like that unless she's—'

'Unless what?' spat Anna.

'You know exactly what I mean. And then I see her with that Italian last Saturday. That's consorting with the enemy, that is.'

The look of hate and menacing tone took Anna and Eddie by surprise.

This is going to get nasty.

Eddie rapidly stepped between Lenox and his friend. 'Stay still. I've warned you; I'll put you on the ground.'

164

The sound of a police patrol emergency bell cut through the icy atmosphere. The car moved at speed toward Lipton St Faith. Anna had a fleeting look at the occupant in the rear seat before the car disappeared into the distance.

'They have Enzo.'

Eddie gave Anna an urgent glance while trying to keep tabs on Lenox. 'We must've been followed.'

Chapter 14: On Watch

Afternoon tea at the Heron's Perch café, overlooking Hickling Broad, would, in normal circumstances, thought Anna, be the ideal spot for relaxing and enjoying the rural idyll.

What the heck are we going to do now?

'We've got some thinking to do,' said Eddie as the waitress motioned them from the far side of the spacious tearoom to select which table they liked.

Anna waved at the young woman dressed in a blue gingham dress and white apron. 'Nice to see you again, Shelia. Mum and dad OK?'

'Mum's rushing around doing all sorts as usual, while dad mucks about in his shed.'

They exchanged friendly smiles as Eddie placed his cap on a table next to a large window.

'Looks like we'll sit here, Sheila. May we have two of your delicious afternoon teas, please? Have you any sausage rolls left? We're starving.'

Shelia winked. 'I'll see what I can do. You're lucky, it's been slow, so I thought of shutting at half past three, but I held on for half an hour to catch any latecomers, and here you are.'

'You're a treasure, Shelia.'

As the waitress passed through into the kitchen, it left Anna and Eddie as the room's only occupants.

Eddie was first to speak. 'How are you getting on with Vinny?'

She raised her eyebrows. 'Still getting used to the pace he lives his life at. Anyway, he starts school on Monday, so that should use up some of that energy.'

'School? They won't know what's hit them, poor kids.'

'You mean poor teachers. I couldn't cope with a class-full like him for ten minutes.'

The levity ended and the conversation dwindled to a stop as they both gazed out of the large window and stretch of still water beyond.

'What do you make of Geoffrey Lenox, you know, as a bloke?'

Eddie studied Anna's expression. 'We need to put each other in a pigeonhole,' he said. 'Call it survival of the fittest if you like. No man will admit it, but each of us compares ourselves to those we interact with. Am I stronger than him? Is he cleverer than me? I suppose a sort of pecking order. As for Lenox, he strikes me as a typical bully. He'll look for people he can dominate, but the second they bite back, he crumples.'

'You're saying he's a coward? You know, bark worse than his bite and all that, so unlikely to be our killer?'

Eddie shook his head. 'No, I'm not. I've come across his type before. He won't confront the person who, in his eyes, belittled him. Instead, he'll bide his time until he can hit back with minimum risk to himself. That temper of his. He thinks he can control it, but he can't.'

Anna turned her head from her companion as she spotted Shelia pushing a wood-framed trolly from the kitchen. 'Thanks, that looks scrummy. Wow, you found us a sausage roll each.'

The waitress beamed at delighting her customers. 'Enjoy your treat,' she said before withdrawing.

'I'll be mother this time,' said Eddie as he took charge of the teapot and began dispensing two cups of the refreshing drink.

'I'm going to save my sausage roll until last,' said Anna as she picked up two delicate cucumber sandwiches and placed them on a china-patterned side plate.

'What, you mean until after you've had cake? Ugh.'

Anna smiled as she bit into the crustless bread. 'You've never lived.'

Quiet fell for a few minutes as they tucked into their afternoon tea.

'So are you saying Lenox could, or could not, have killed Ruth?'

'We're all capable, Anna. In Lenox's case, I think he's more than capable of murder. Think about it. He concludes Ruth has played him after leading him on, which, by the way, I don't believe for one second. Then he finds out she's meeting her boyfriend in Witton Wood; don't ask me how –perhaps he'd been following her around for some time. Let's assume for the sake of discussion that he killed her. What better place for a bully to get his revenge? No one to challenge him and the possibility of setting Ruth's boyfriend up for murder. Oh, yes, I'm certain he's capable of doing that.'

Anna shook her head as she finished her sandwich. 'But you're convinced Enzo Conti killed Ruth, aren't you?'

'As I said, I'm not sure, yet. However, you asked me about Geoffrey Lenox, not the Italian.'

She shrugged her shoulders. 'I have this terrible image of men queueing up to kill that poor woman. This is all getting too confusing. All I know is that I saw the way Enzo looked at April. He's either one heck of an actor, or he's telling us the truth. We need to see him.'

Eddie looked at his sausage roll, gave it a poke with his fork and instead selected another cheese sandwich. 'To quote your famous Sherlock Holmes, "When you have eliminated all which is impossible, whatever remains, however improbable, must be the truth".'

'You're making that up.'

'On the contrary, dear Anna, he made the comment in *The Adventure of the Blanched Soldier*, published in 1926.'

Anna sighed, before taking Eddie's sausage roll.

'They won't let us near Enzo today,' he said, 'so I think we should stake out the Lenox place for a couple of hours tonight and again early tomorrow to see if he runs. Oh, and I hope that sausage roll makes you sick, greedy guts.'

'Can you feel your bottom?'

'I beg your pardon?' exclaimed Eddie as he rubbed his face to keep himself alert.

'You heard what I said. I know Jeeps aren't as comfortable as a Rolls-Royce, but I ask you, do they have to be so hard? I'm numb.'

Eddie wasn't sure where to look. 'Too much information, Miss Grix. Anyway, I guess we should be on our way from here. Three hours last night and another two this morning. If I never see Geoffrey Lenox's place again it'll be too soon. But at least we know he's still in there. He's one cool character – or innocent.'

Anna wriggled on the seat to restart the blood flow. 'I thought you said the likes of him were devious.'

'You're right. I've changed my mind and reserve judgement on that odd dude.'

'Heck, we'd better get moving or I'll be late for Dad's Sunday Service. He'll know if I'm not there. Dad reckons he can see everything from his pulpit.'

Eddie laughed. 'We'd better get you to the church on time.'

Is that supposed to be funny?

Eleven-thirty saw Sunday worship finished and the congregational ritual of commenting on the weather, the state of the war and how measly the ration allowance was, met with a sympathetic nod and handshake from the vicar. It also meant that Anna was free to leave the church grounds.

'Remember, darling, lunch will be ready in thirty minutes, so don't be late... *again* or your mother will have your guts for garters.'

Anna gave a dutiful nod before grabbing Eddie by the arm and pulling him down the narrow path through the small graveyard. 'Come on, let's get to the police station.'

Their visit turned out to be all too brief. Within two minutes of entering the police station, they found themselves on the high street again with a flea in their ears from the inspector, who told them to return later.

As Anna crossed the high street, a car exiting the police station's old stables caught her eye. 'Look at that.' She pointed to an old car driven by Tom Bradshaw. 'How curious.'

Still smarting from Spillers' brush-off and pondering what Tom was doing at the station, Anna led Eddie into the vicarage kitchen to the sight of her father and Vinny chomping at the bit to start Sunday lunch.

'Well done, my darling. You're in time.'

'Sit yourselves down,' said Helen. 'Here's your lunch. Sorry, there's no beef again, you must make do with SPAM.'

A contented air filled the kitchen as its five occupants tucked into their meals.

'It's school for you on Monday, Vinny?' said Eddie.

'You trying to put me off me dinner, or what?'

Vinny's melancholy response caused a ripple of gentle laughter to cascade around the dining table.

'I'd have thought you couldn't wait,' said Anna.

The boy laid his knife and fork back on the table in their assigned positions and pulled himself up as if about to deliver a speech of great importance. 'What's there to love about sitting at a desk being shouted at all day? And when you try hard, they still shout and throw chalk at you, or belt you with a book or whatever.' Vinny picked up his cutlery and took a mouthful of mashed carrots and turnips without making further comment.

Poor nipper.

'Don't worry, Vinny, we don't do it like that in this village,' said Anna.

Vinny looked confused. 'Why not?'

There's no answer to that.

The rest of lunch passed without further issue while Anna sensed her father wanted to know what she'd been up to. 'Vinny, why don't you go through to the lounge?' she said. 'You may find my old wind-up train set waiting for you.'

The young man bolted from his chair without asking permission to leave the table, a novel rule he'd not yet got used to.

'It's nice to see the boy smiling,' said the vicar. 'We adults forget the trauma our young ones are going through. It seems we've learnt nothing from the Great War.'

'What do you mean?' said Anna.

'I was talking to a chap about it yesterday. Shellshock, I mean. For those who survived the war, so many are still affected, yet their plight was, and still is, all but ignored. Think what Vinny must have heard and seen during the bombings. Like old soldiers, children say little when they hurt inside. If the chap I spoke to is anything to go by, in years to come, some of these children will jump at their own shadows or at the slightest noise and have flashbacks. It's too horrible to contemplate.'

I hope Dad's wrong.

'Enough of this gloomy talk,' said Anna's mother. 'How's your investigation going?'

Her daughter sighed. 'Don't ask.'

Having spent a couple of hours passing the time by walking the fields, Anna and Eddie inspected the wreck of a Spitfire, which Air Force personnel were busy recovering onto a flat-bed lorry.

'Did the pilot survive?'

One of the boiler suited men nodded. 'He got lucky when he bailed. The fella landed a couple of miles up the road. Not a scratch on him apparently, unlike this sorry thing.' The man pointed to a twisted pile of aluminium on the back of his lorry. The only thing that identified it as an aircraft was its huge Merlin engine and enormous twisted propeller.

By the time the servicemen left with their tangled booty, Anna considered enough time had elapsed since their earlier visit to the police station. 'Come on, let's get it over with. I doubt even the inspector will chuck us out twice in one day.'

Although their reception was cool, on this occasion, the inspector agreed to see them.

'Two minutes, that's all the time I can give you, so please tell me what you want, as if I didn't know.'

'That's the issue, Inspector Spillers,' said Eddie. 'You know quite a lot. In fact, you followed us yesterday, didn't you?'

Oh, heck, we're going to get thrown out again.

Spillers turned on the lieutenant. 'Yes, we followed you. The two of you think so highly of yourselves as Agatha Christie characters that you lose sight of the real world and how the police work.'

'The cottage?' said Anna.

'Yes, Miss Grix, and if I didn't know before where Mr Conti hid, I do now.'

I feel stupid.

172

'Conti gave himself up as soon as he heard my voice outside that ramshackle place. I imagine he was glad. It can't have been much fun being held up there on his own.'

Anna flashed her eyes at Eddie without alerting the inspector.

He doesn't know about April.

'Er, no, I don't suppose it was.'

'Anyway, we have our killer and justice will now take its dread course. The man will hang.'

'Hang? What do you mean, Inspector?'

Spillers sat heavily into his chair and placed his arms on the desk. 'Enzo Conti confessed to murdering Ruth Cotton, half an hour ago.'

What has Enzo done?

After several seconds of stunned silence and anguished glances between Anna and the lieutenant, Spillers spoke. 'What? Come on out with it. I've been around you two long enough to know when you're holding something back.'

'It's just… well. Oh, you'll find out sooner or later, I expect,' began Anna. 'We spoke to Geoffrey Lenox earlier. He said he'd seen Enzo talking to Ruth on the day she died, but—'

'But nothing, Miss Grix. It's beginning to look pretty bleak for your Italian friend, isn't it?'

'I don't believe that man for one minute.'

'But a jury may, Miss Grix. Now, if there's nothing else?'

'May we see Enzo? He has no one to speak up for him… please, Inspector.'

Spillers toyed with a paperclip while he considered her request. 'Five minutes and that's your lot.'

Unlocking the heavy cell door, the desk sergeant repeated the inspector's order. 'And I'll be around the corner, so no funny stuff or you two will end up in a cell of your own.'

Inside the stark Victorian enclosure, which measured eight feet by four, sat Enzo, slumped on the thin straw-filled mattress, head in his hands.

'Let me do it,' whispered Anna.

Eddie stood as far back as it was possible to do in the cramped space.

'Enzo.' She spoke softly while keeping a little distance between them to save alarming the prisoner. 'Enzo, you know who we are. The inspector told us what's happened.' She waited for the Italian to respond. Instead, the crumpled figure continued to sit, statue-like. 'Let us help you. If nothing changes you know what will happen.'

'You were telling us lies all along. You killed that woman.'

What are you doing?

The American's tactic worked. Enzo shot to his feet, his angry look burning into Eddie.

'No choice. Too many hurt people.'

Chapter 15: Confusion

What must April be going through, I wonder? She sounded desperate on the phone last night with good reason. Let's hope whatever it is she wants to show me today will help prove why her boyfriend was in the woods. I so want to believe he isn't a killer.

The bicycle ride to Witton Wood was no small feat, especially on an empty stomach since Anna left the vicarage so early to make her rendezvous on time.

At least it isn't raining.

The roads were empty, and Anna made good use of the shortcuts she knew. Nevertheless, the journey still took almost an hour.

Thank heavens that's done. Now, where's April?

She glanced at her wristwatch.

9.00 am on the dot.

Leaving her bike leaning up against a substantial elm tree inside the entrance to the wood, Anna looked for any signs of life. Apart from the morning chorus of birds and occasional squirrel scuttling between undergrowth and tree canopy, all remained silent.

I hope she turns up.

A few minutes later, the sound of a car's breaks squeaking to announce its arrival put Anna's mind at rest.

At last.

'Thank you for meeting me, Anna, and sorry for ringing you so late last night. I lost the bit of paper you gave me with your number on. And a second apology for being late today. My father gave me the third degree, wanting to know why I needed the car because he's short on petrol coupons. I think he wanted to know who I'm meeting.'

'He sounds like my parents. I guess sometimes being treated as children is the price we pay for still living with them.'

'I suppose so,' April replied, laughing nervously.

'Is everything OK between your dad and you?'

April sighed. 'We're never going to win happy family of the month or anything like that, but somehow we rub along. It's Mum I feel sorry for, but she's a strong woman.'

'Has he always been, you know... that way?'

April gazed around her tranquil surroundings. 'Funnily enough, no. At least, I don't think so. Something happened when I was little. They don't talk about it but dad had some sort of accident at one of the family businesses. I remember he was in hospital for ages. Somehow things changed when he came home.'

'Sorry,' said Anna, 'I didn't mean to pry into family stuff.'

April shrugged her shoulders. 'It's OK, what goes on behind closed curtains and all that.'

The two women walked into the wood, Anna allowing April to take the lead. Minutes passed in genial conversation.

She's doing anything but talk about Enzo.

'Your call, April, why did you ring me? Rather than the police, I mean. And why didn't you want me to bring Eddie?'

In the distance, the deep roar of rutting red deer stags reminded Anna that other worlds existed and that they too had their battles to fight.

'I... I didn't know what to do... you know, who to trust. I watched

176

the police arrest Enzo. It was horrible. They were so rough with him, even though he gave himself up without a struggle. You should have heard what one or two of them were calling him.'

'They've got their man, April. Enzo's confessed.'

'He's what?' For a moment she began to lose her composure, before adopting a defiant stance and giving Anna a determined look. 'I don't believe you, but even if he did, they must have beaten a confession out of him. They've arrested a prisoner of war they think no one cares about and can accuse of anything they want, even murder. After all, he's the enemy, isn't he?'

I can't believe Inspector Spillers would do that.

A few yards further on, April came to a stop. 'It's here.'

Anna scanned her surroundings.

I recognise this place; it's the hide Eddie found.

'What is? What is it you wanted me to see?' replied Anna, keeping the fact she'd seen the clandestine construction before to herself.

Let's see how she explains this away.

'You don't see it? That's because it's so clever.'

She watched as April took two strides forward and picked up a handful of leaves. 'Good camouflage, isn't it?' said April as she continued to lift the leaves, which Anna now saw were attached to a net.

'Well, I'm blowed. I'd never have found that in a month of Sundays. Did Enzo build it?

Come on, April, give me something to help him.

April shook her head. 'No, I mean yes… well.'

'You're not making sense, April.'

Anna's companion flipped the camouflage net over the top of the hide to expose its small interior.

'Yes, this is where we used to meet before Enzo ran away from the camp, but Enzo didn't build it. How could he? He didn't have access

177

to any of this stuff.' She pointed to the waterproof sheeting and other materials used to construct and fit out the secret hide. 'He told me he found it one day when he came here from the farm and thought it might be a safe place for us to meet.'

Anna ducked to enter the small space and then sat on a small tree stump, around which the hide stood. 'It's quite comfy in here, isn't it? I wonder who built it, and why. It makes little sense.'

April joined Anna and sat on a bed of dry lichen and other materials that looked to be specifically chosen so they would make no noise when trampled on. 'Enzo says the guards from his camp are always doing exercises in here. And he says there's another soldier, a lot older than the others, who talks to himself about German paratroopers and seems to appear then vanish like a ghost. He reckons he sees him either on a Thursday or Saturday night.'

Saturday night?

As Anna processed the additional information, something caught her eye when April shifted her position. Leaning forward, she recovered a small disc-shaped metal object.

A coincidence? Surely not.

'What's that?' asked April.

Anna held up a silver disc. 'It's a coin. It's an Italian coin, April.'

I'm not enjoying this one bit.

'April, Eddie found a coin like this a few feet from Ruth Cotton's body.' She could see the seriousness of the situation hadn't sunk in. 'I want you to listen carefully to the question I'm about to ask. I don't expect a response now, but it's something you must answer honestly to yourself. Can you be sure Enzo is innocent?'

April's reaction was at first to stare at her companion with glazed eyes, as if looking without seeing. 'I'm as certain as I can be that Enzo is innocent.'

178

That's not as convincing an answer as before.

'Listen, April, the purpose of my question wasn't to catch you out. I just need you to be sure of how you feel, because things will get a great deal more difficult before this is over. Why don't you go home and have a think about things? I know you can't talk to your father, but you have your mum. Please talk to her about Enzo, what he's charged with and that he's confessed. If nothing else, talking out your feelings might help you decide what you want to do next. I have a feeling that only you will get Enzo to talk. Am I making any sense to you?'

I need you thinking straight if you're to help Enzo.

'April, do you understand what I'm saying?' Anna placed a hand on her companion's shoulder, hoping it might stir April from her thoughts.

'Yes… I… I understand. Perhaps I should go?'

Anna offered a friendly smile and reassuring pat of her hand on April's shoulder. 'Good, it's the right thing to do and I'll catch up with you soon. Off you go. I'll be in touch shortly, I promise.'

Anna remained in the hideout once April left, to digest their conversation and fathom her own thoughts about Enzo.

It's a terrible cliché, but they say love is blind. What if Enzo is the killer and I somehow convince the police he's innocent because of what April wants to believe? What if she frames another man and I fall for it? Oh, this is crazy. I need food; perhaps that's why I'm thinking such stupid things.

Brought back to her senses by an unusual sound outside, Anna nervously checked her watch for want of something to do while she processed what the noise might be.

One-thirty already and April left at least fifteen minutes ago, so it must be an animal out there. I better get going so I'm home in time to pick Vinny up from school.

Concentrating on a concrete task helped Anna regain her composure.

Anyway, I suppose it's those rutting stags?

179

Lifting the camouflage net, she froze as two booted feet came into view. Instinctively, she fell back.

What have I got myself into? Why didn't I wait for Eddie?

Seconds later, the net lifted to reveal the lower half of a uniformed man.

'What are you doing here?'

'Anna? No, she went out early this morning after a phone call late last night. She didn't even have any breakfast. We assume it's something to do with evacuees; you know how passionate she is about her job.'

Funny, she said nothing to me...

Eddie stepped away from the front door of the vicarage to allow Anna's parents to step out, the vicar checking the lock as he did so.

'When you catch up with my wayward daughter, can you remind her to pick Vinny up from school since we'll be in Norwich having lunch with the Dean?'

'Sure will, Sir... I mean, Charles.'

In seconds, the pair disappeared from sight as they made their way to a bus stop on the edge of the village.

What is Anna up to, I wonder?

The lieutenant remained rooted to the spot at the gate to the vicarage as he pondered what to do next.

Guess I'll fill my time fooling around with Major Leonard-White to see what I can shake out of him.

Eddie knew it was uncertain the major would see him. However, his intuition told him differently.

He'll be curious as to why I've turned up after our exchange at the Cock and Sparrow.

Sure enough, thirty minutes later, a curious Leonard-White sat behind his almost clear desktop to face Eddie.

'Nice of you to call in, Lieutenant. However, after our brief chat, you're the last person I'd have expected to see crossing my threshold, so to speak.'

The American smiled as he settled into a utilitarian chair. 'I've been thinking——'

'Always a dangerous thing for a military man to do, don't you think? Orders are what's important, don't you agree?'

Here we go.

'In my mind, Major, that rather depends on their legitimacy.'

The men exchanged perfunctory smiles.

'There you go again with your idealistic view of the world, Lieutenant. Come, tell me why you're here. I'm sure it's not to debate the morals of the military.'

There's a lot not to like in you, fella, but let's play your game and see where it takes us.

'You're correct, Major. You see, far from seeing the world through rose-tinted glasses, I see things for what they are. War is a cruel thing. You know, the survival of the fittest and all that?'

Leonard-White sat forward and leant into the table. 'Not only survival, my American friend, but to thrive and profit, if you get my drift.'

Where's this going?

'The other day you talked about the military taking control in times of crisis so that the population knew who to look to.'

The major roared with laughter, checking his belt to ensure his sizeable stomach hadn't escaped his shirt. 'I suppose that's one way of looking at things. Personally, I like to think in terms of beneficial crises.'

'I'm not sure I understand, Major?'

Leonard-White got to his feet, strode purposefully to the door and turned the Bakelite doorknob. 'Two teas, now,' he barked, before resuming his seat. 'No, you don't, do you? Let me explain.' The officer slouched into his chair back and pointed to one of three windows that punctured the timber wall of his office. 'Out there, anarchy rules, or should I say under carefully controlled circumstances it can. From crisis come certain opportunities. I like to call such circumstances beneficial crises. Now do you understand?'

Before Eddie could answer, an orderly came rushing in with two mugs of tea, spilling the major's as he set it down before his superior.

'Idiot. Confined to barracks this weekend, Perkins. You'll learn.'

The young private snapped to attention before leaving the scene of his disgrace. 'Sir.'

'Get out.'

Without further exchange, the private retreated at pace.

What an operator you are.

'Treat 'em hard, Lieutenant. That way they know where they stand in the pecking order. Now, what was I saying?' The major took a gulp of his tea, not bothering to clear the spilt liquid from the desktop. 'Oh, yes, benefits. You see, I'm a man in a hurry. This war won't last for ever and there's money to be made. By controlling what the local population do and think, there's ample opportunity to return to civilian life a rich man. Would you like to be a rich man, Lieutenant?'

Bribery? Extortion?

'Are you making me a proposition, Major?'

Leonard-White let out a second throaty laugh, this time not bothering to check his uniform. 'After all, wealth needn't be rationed, need it?'

Let's play his game.

Eddie hesitated for effect. 'You know, back in the twenties, my country had a president who banned alcohol. Some men grew rich off the back of bootleg liquor. I suppose that's what you might call a beneficial crisis, yeah?'

'It is, Lieutenant, and you touch on another opportunity to profit. However, history also teaches us stark lessons. If I take, for example, the reality of life during prohibition in your country, for each of those who got rich, at least one other ended up on the wrong end of a Tommy gun. I have many such weapons at my disposal, Lieutenant. Do we understand one another?'

Chapter 16 : Missing

'It doesn't matter who I am; what are you doing here?'

He means business.

Anna watched nervously as the tall man, around her own age, she thought, toyed with the popper on the end of a short leather strap that held a huge knife in its sheath.

The handle of that knife looks the same as the one Eddie found.

She picked up a familiar smell.

Smoke. He's been living rough for a few days and his uniform is grubby. He must be on the run. It's got to be Ruth's boyfriend, Robert Sedwell.

'Come out of there before I pull you out.'

Scrambling to her feet, Anna ducked under the low canvas top and blinked as she emerged into the relative brightness of the early afternoon.

'Who are you?'

'I might ask the same of you. Why aren't you with your unit?'

Anna, behave yourself, he's the one with the knife.

'Look, I'm sorry. I was out walking when I tripped into this.' She pointed back to the hide. 'I didn't see it. Did you build it? It's really clever and must take a lot of practice.'

184

Anna sensed the soldier relaxing a little as she praised his efforts.

Come on, we all like a bit of praise.

The soldier looked over the hide. 'It's not bad, is it? Not one of my best, mind, but I didn't have much time.'

That's better.

Anna joined the man in admiring his creation. 'If I hadn't have tripped, I'd have missed it altogether. Is that what they teach you in the army?'

He laughed. 'No chance. I've been building these all my life. Means you can get away from everyone. Wildlife never lets you down.'

It's got to be him. What if he did murder Ruth? I'm in real trouble. Time to stay calm, girl, and look for a way out.

'I heard some stags before; they were making a heck of a din.' Anna's mention of wild animals caught his interest.

'They're fighting for territory… and stuff, if you know what I mean… you know, err…'

Anna tried a smile. 'Yes, I know what you mean. Sorry, what's your name?'

She watched the man tense. 'What's it to you?'

'Nothing. Nothing at all, it's, well, here we are talking. How rude of me, my name is Anna.'

The soldier tilted his head to one side.

'That's a nice name. My nan's name was Anna.'

'Was?'

'She died when I was about ten.' He shrugged his shoulders. 'Don't matter now; I'll be dead by the time this lot's over. It's always the squaddies what get it, never the senior officers sat behind their desks.'

Do I keep him talking or try to make a run for it?

'You must have been dreading being called up?'

He shook his head. 'Me? You must be joking. I signed up in

185

September '38. Anything to get away from home. Trouble is, they don't tell you what it's really like. You know, killing and stuff.'

Let's see how much I can get out of him.

'But I thought you said you liked your nan. Is your family not close?'

The man played about with the camouflage net and ignored Anna's eye contact. 'I said she had a nice name. I suppose you could call my family thick as thieves, because that's what most of them are.'

Wow, I didn't expect that.

'Look, I can't keep talking to you without calling you something. What's it to be, Private, or should I make a name up? I know, Bob. Will that do?'

He shrugged his shoulders again. 'Bob's as good a name as any, I suppose. Do what you want; I don't much care anymore.'

Anna moved a few feet from the hideout to gauge the soldier's reaction.

That's a good sign; he didn't flinch.

'Tell me about your family. Surely they can't be that bad?'

For the first time, he engaged Anna's eye contact. 'Do you know what it's like to be treated like a criminal all your life? Just because your father and brothers steal, and your mum can stick up for herself, everyone in the family gets tarred with the same brush.'

A red admiral butterfly began to flit around the two strangers. The man slowly lifted his right hand and turned his palm upwards. The butterfly flirted with his fingers before settling in the middle of his palm. Anna watched on in amazement.

'They like the moisture, and I was cooking this morning, so there'll be stuff it likes on my hands.'

That's astounding.

'You have a gift, Bob. Comes from spending so much time outdoors, I guess.'

186

'I didn't say I spent a lot of time in the wild,' he responded without taking his eyes of the red admiral.

'I'm sorry, it's a feeling I get from how comfortable you are with animals and stuff.'

Raising his palm and gently lowering it again, he encouraged the butterfly to take flight and watched it until the insect disappeared into a purple maze of ground ivy.

'They want nothing from you. They don't tell lies and they don't hurt you.'

This man isn't well.

'You can talk to me. After all, we're strangers. We all need someone we can talk to, especially now.'

'What do you mean "now"?'

What's all that about?

'The war. I mean the war. It affects us all, doesn't it?'

The soldier shrugged his shoulders and played with the popper on his knife again. 'Dunno, I suppose it does. What I do know is it's no fun fighting them Italians. After all, they're the same as us, I suppose. They're told to fight, and they do. Even though I volunteered, no one in their right mind wants to be shot at – or kill anyone else when it comes to it.'

There's more to this chap than meets the eye. I've heard Dad talk like that about the Great War.

'So you don't hate the Italians?' asked Anna.

'Hate? That's the wrong word. Sure, when you're looking over a shallow trench at them pointing a rifle at you, then yes, it's kill or be killed, and the army teaches you how to be aggressive. But when the battle is over, and you're sort of safe in your compound or wherever, no, you don't hate them – except for the mad ones. The army's clever with them; they get them to do the really dangerous

187

stuff. I sometimes think they detail them for that stuff, hoping they won't come back. Sort of kills two birds with one bullet, if you know what I mean.'

Bless the man. This is what governments do to people they send to war?

'Then what about the POW camp over there? Do you resent them being here?'

He shrugged his shoulders again. 'I know this much, when I go back to fight in a few weeks' time, their mates will try to shoot me or blow me up, while that lot in the camp are mucking about on our land, the land I left to fight them. Who knows, they might even be messing with our women. Don't expect me to think of them as mates.'

Anna tried to comfort the soldier. Her move toward him resulted in an ugly glare. 'What's your game?'

Careful, Anna.

'Game? There's no game. I want to—'

'Have a go at me like all the rest? My family hate me because I joined up before my time and it meant they had to do more robbing to keep the money coming in. My girlfriend's family hate me because of my family name when all I'm doing is fighting for my country. And then my girlfriend goes and does the dirty on me. Why should I care what happens?'

The private took the knife out of its sheath and looked at the gleaming blade.

It's now or never.

Anna panicked and tried to run.

The man was too quick for her and grabbed the fabric of her jacket sleeve. 'See, you're not interested in me. You're like all the rest. Well, I'm in charge now, see?'

Uh-oh, she's not back yet. Where on earth's she gone?

188

As Eddie walked back down the path from the vicarage front door and opened the garden gate, a familiar voice rang out.

'Stood you up, has she? All the same, young women, even a vicar's daughter.' Village gossip Beatrice Flowers stood before the American in a black skull-type hat more suited to the 1920s, a heavy brown calf-length coat and a black patent leather handbag, which she swung furiously back and forth.

'Good afternoon, ma'am. I'm not sure if I get your meaning?'

Beatrice eyed the American up and down. 'That Anna Grix girl. Always was a bit flighty. Too independent if you ask me. Nothing good will come of it, you mark my words.'

With that, the spinster walked towards the village centre shops with a spring in her step.

I really don't understand some of these folks.

As Eddie sat on the low front wall of the vicarage, he mulled over what options he had to find Anna.

I can't report her missing to the inspector; he'll send me packing for wasting his time. Her parents aren't around. I guess the only thing for it is to see Tom Bradshaw. That's if he doesn't punch me for getting him in trouble.

About to fire up the Jeep, he suddenly remembered Vinny, who'd need picking up from his first day of school. He slipped the clutch and drove the hundred yards to the thrift shop, hopped out of the vehicle and bounded into the small shop.

'Oh, hello, are we being invaded? Only the way you flung that door open, I imagined you had some of those nasty paratroopers after you,' said Flo Bassett.

'Worse than that, ma'am. I can't find Anna anywhere and if I don't get young Vinny sorted out after school, she'll be after me. I don't suppose you know where she's gone?'

Flo smiled and wagged a playful finger at him. 'In trouble with my boss's daughter, eh? I feel your pain.'

Eddie's smile vanished. 'Well, thought it worth trying.'

'Don't be so daft. Have you not got used to our sense of humour yet? Of course, I'll pick Vinny up from school. As for where the lady has gone, I expect it'll be something to do with her growing tribe of evacuees.'

'I expect you're right, ma'am. Oh, and thank you for looking after little Vinny. I'll see you later.'

As Eddie was about to close the door behind him, Flo's voice rang out. 'Not if you don't stop calling me ma'am you won't. It's Flo or Miss Bassett, except if you call me Miss Bassett, I'll throw something that'll hurt at you.'

Eddie was out the door, leaving Flo with a friendly smile and a wave of his hand.

Thank heavens that's sorted.

The drive to Tom Bradshaw took a few minutes. Noticing the old car was missing, Eddie's heart sank.

He's my last hope.

Having given the front door to Tom's house two sharp knocks with a clenched hand, more in hope than expectation, it amazed him when the door opened.

'Eddie, what are you doing here? Where's Anna?'

The American removed his cap and scratched his forehead. 'That's why I'm here. Anna, I mean.'

Tom stepped forward so they were both now outside the cottage. 'What makes you think she's here?'

Eddie shook his head. 'I didn't, but no one's seen her since last night. Anna's parents told me she went out before they came down, and that she got a phone call late last night.'

'Evacuees?'

If one more person says that…

'Nothing to say that's where she's gone. The woman has simply disappeared.'

'That's not like, Anna,' replied Tom, concern etched across his face. 'Unless she got into one of her independent moods; you know what she can be like. Could it be anything to do with Ruth Cotton's death?'

Tom's logic hit Eddie like a train.

Why did I miss the obvious?

'You're a genius, Tom. Your boss arrested Enzo last night, but there's something he isn't aware of. I know what to do.'

'Hang on, Eddie, what doesn't my boss know?'

The lieutenant was already in his Jeep with the engine started. 'And I've got an idea how you can get in Detective Spillers' good books again. Take another look at that idiot who runs the POW camp. He's nuts and needs stopping.'

'What do you mean?' shouted Tom as Eddie made off.

'Prohibition and rations. Do some digging.'

Chapter 17: An Admission

A journey that, in normal circumstances, ought to have taken forty-five minutes, took less than thirty as Lieutenant Elsner raced back to the home of April Rider.

Please be there.

His urgent thumping of the elegant, black-painted front door at first appeared to confirm Eddie's worst fears.

No one in. Now what do I do?

This time rapping his fingers on one of two matching stained-glass panels depicting Admiral Nelson's victory at Trafalgar, to the side of the door, Eddie became convinced his mission had failed.

About to walk back up the impressive driveway of the substantial property, he glimpsed movement through the opaque glass.

Thank heavens.

After what seemed an age, the wide entrance door revealed a portion of the dwelling's spacious hallway.

'Yes? Can I help?' The elegant woman's voice lacked force as she peered curiously at the caller.

'Ma'am, I'm so sorry to trouble you. My name is Lieutenant Edmund Elsner of the United States Army Airforce. It's your daughter, April,

that I'm looking for. Is she available to speak to me for a few minutes?'
The lieutenant had taken his cap off, stored it tightly under one arm and was bent forward at a slight angle in deference to the householder.

Opening the door a few inches wider, the immaculately dressed and manicured lady offered a tiny smile. 'Americans are so charming. Do come in. However, my daughter isn't here. She works in one of her father's factories several times each week. I'm afraid today is one such occasion.'

She's one classy lady.

'Is it possible for me to visit your daughter's place of work? It's an urgent matter that I call about. Please don't alarm yourself, ma'am, however, it's important I see April today.'

Mrs Rider looked across to an elegant granddaughter clock standing at the foot of an impressive dark oak staircase that hugged two walls of the entrance hall. 'Let's see. It's 4.00 pm now. I'm afraid my daughter won't be back for at least two hours. As for visiting, no, I don't think that would be a good idea. Her father won't take kindly to a strange man, let alone a serviceman, talking to his daughter.'

'I don't understand, ma'am?'

Mrs Rider beckoned Eddie further into the hall and closed the front door.

Why did she look down the road like that?

'Oh, dear, this is awkward. Well, you see… certain people place the highest importance on social status. How one is perceived by others, that sort of thing. Particularly those of one's own social rank.' The elegant lady gave Eddie an awkward smile before dropping her gaze to the oak herringbone-patterned floor.

Eddie fiddled with a button on his army jacket, unsure how to respond without offending his host. 'You know, ma'am, us Americans don't have any kings or lords nor suchlike. We like to think we're a, well, I guess we say we're—'

'A classless society… in the best sense of the word?'

'Yes, ma'am, I'd like to think we are, except money talks wherever you are, so we're not all exactly the same, are we? I suppose a man need not be a king to lord it over others, especially in the land of George Washington.'

Mrs Rider returned Eddie's smile. 'My husband is a proud man, Lieutenant. He's worked hard to pay for all this.' She raised her arms and modestly gestured to her surroundings. 'But that pride comes at a significant cost. He won't allow anything to jeopardise his standing in Norfolk. To him, appearance is everything.'

What a woman.

'Might it help if I had a word with Mr Rider?'

'Oh no, I don't think that would do at all. I'm assuming you are the American he had a run-in with at Wells-next-the-sea recently? Although my husband is in London on business and won't be back for some days, I'm sure your visit would get back to him and it's simply not worth the ramifications that it will cause here at home.'

At least that's one complication out of the way.

At that moment, the front door opened. 'My darling, what are you doing home so early?'

April looked at Eddie as she gave her mother a peck on the cheek. 'I forgot some papers that I need for a board meeting in an hour. Is something wrong, Mum?'

'Forgive me, Miss Rider, I—'

'I think Lieutenant Elsner and you met a few days ago, my dear. It's you whose company he seeks, not mine, so I shall leave you to it. Why not show the lieutenant into the morning room? You'll be more comfortable there, I'm sure. Good afternoon, Edmund, so nice to speak with you.'

That woman is lonely.

April gave her mother a second peck and led their visitor into a spacious room that looked as though it had been lifted from a 1920s edition of *Country Life*.

'I hope you don't think me impertinent, Miss Rider, but your mother is a—'

'Remarkable woman, Lieutenant? Yes, she is, and I love her even more for her loyalty and stoicism. Do you know, I've never heard my mother say a bad word about anyone... and I mean anyone, Lieutenant.'

I'll take that as a warning not to mention her father.

'Now, you've driven quite a distance, so it must be important. Any news of Enzo?' She lowered her voice and looked at the closed door of the morning room as she spoke.

Her mother's in the dark about Enzo. If she doesn't know, the father must also be ignorant of the facts.

Eddie rubbed his chin between finger and thumb. 'Miss Rider, Enzo's confessed to the murder of Ruth Cotton, and if nothing changes, they'll execute him. We need your help.'

'But what can I do?' replied April as tears began to flow. 'Who'd believe me anyway? I told Anna, to them he's the enemy, he doesn't count.'

The lieutenant moved closer to April. His body language demanded she pay attention. 'All he'd say to us was something about how talking would cause too much hurt. It makes no sense to either me or Anna. Talking of whom, you'll have noticed she isn't here with me.'

April appeared lost in her own thoughts. 'They can't hang him. They can't.'

This is getting us nowhere.

'April?' The lieutenant's raised voice shook his host out of her stupor. 'I'm sorry if I startled you, but time is short. You see, Anna

195

has gone missing. No one has seen her since late last night, though we know she took a telephone call at the vicarage. You are my last hope, Miss Rider. Have you seen Anna?'

April frowned. 'Of course I have. It was I who rang Anna last night.'

'You?… Why?' replied Eddie, his voice urgent.

I'm missing something here.

April got to her feet. 'In Witton Wood. I wanted to show Anna where Enzo and I met. It's a hide, but we didn't build it. I thought it might help… you know, with Enzo, but all it seems to have done is convince Anna that Enzo committed that murder. He didn't, Lieutenant.'

What on earth has happened?

If April left Anna at around one-thirty, what the heck has happened to her?

As Eddie raced back to Witton Wood, he glanced at his watch.

Five o'clock. This doesn't look good.

After bringing the Jeep to a stop in a cloud of dust as he pulled off the road, Eddie rushed into the dense woodland, hoping he understood April's directions on where the hide stood.

I'm sure it's the same one we came across the other day. Where is it?

Ten minutes of fruitless searching left Eddie at the end of his tether on where to look next. Suddenly, he saw something move.

'Anna, is that you? Where on earth have you been all afternoon?'

He waited for her response. Instead, the call of Arctic skuas just above the tree canopy, beginning their migration, seemed to mock the lieutenant's efforts.

Eddie noticed bushes moving for a second time. Not wanting to waste breath calling out, he rushed forward, only to see the outline of a man vanishing into the distance.

What's a soldier doing in this place?

Pursuing the stranger had its rewards as Eddie stumbled on the hide.

Ignoring the running figure, he rushed to throw back its camouflage net, fully expecting to find Anna within its snug interior.

She's not here. Where is the woman?

After spending a short time checking the interior of the hide, Eddie completed a full reconnoitre of the immediate surroundings.

At least there's no blood.

Fifteen minutes passed as the lieutenant tried in vain to find any evidence at all that Anna had ever been in the hide.

Nothing for it; I must tell Anna's parents.

Wishing he might avoid being the bearer of bad news, Eddie drove the Jeep back to Lipton St Faith at a sedate pace. As the familiar sight of the church's Norman tower came into sight, he steeled himself for what was to come.

What will I say?

The sight that met him as he opened the kitchen door to the vicarage answered his question.

'Fried SPAM again, but's it's boss,' said a cheery Vinny as he tucked into his tea.

At the AGA stood Anna in one of her mother's old pinnies, looking hot as she toiled over the hobs.

'Anna, I—'

Vinny ignored Eddie's strangled cry as Anna turned to look at him. A tense glance soon turned to mutual relief. Both looked to the young Scouser, as if mentally agreeing not to say or do more while the boy remained in the room.

The lieutenant sat down next to Vinny and made as if to steal the last of his SPAM.

'Don't think so,' said Vinny as he stabbed the American's hand with his fork.

'Ow, that hurt.'

'Not half as much as the next one will if you try to nick me scran again.'

Deciding that retreat made for the better form of valour, Eddie smiled at Vinny and held his hands up in surrender. 'I'll leave you to it.'

The boy returned to his food without giving Eddie a second glance as the lieutenant joined Anna in a cup of tea by the AGA.

'Look at that,' said Eddie as he showed Anna four neat puncture marks to the back of his right hand, each capped with a tiny dot of blood.

'Serves you right. Anyway, I suppose you'll want to know what I've been up to?' she whispered.

Both looked across to Vinny, who had finished his meal. 'Can't be doing with all this whispering stuff. Me ma says people who talk quiet have either been on the rob or telling porkies. Anyway, I'm off into the back garden to plant me veg.'

Within two seconds, the young boy had vanished from the kitchen.

'He hasn't yet quite got the idea of asking permission to leave the dining table, but we're getting there… slowly.'

Eddie laughed as he took Vinny's place. 'Right, you. What's been going on? You've no idea how difficult it was to track you.'

'Track me? What do you mean?'

Eddie explained events leading up to his rush to Witton Wood.

'Flo said you looked a bit flustered when you asked her to pick Vinny up from school.'

Eddie shook his head. 'Flustered? Instead of coming across an empty hide and a soldier who looked in need of a bath, I might have found a body instead – yours. Don't you understand?'

His declaration brought Anna up with a start. 'A soldier? What did he look like?'

'Look like? What do you expect a British soldier to look like? He wore an ill-fitting wool uniform two sizes too big for him and the largest boots I've ever seen – and he stank. Does that help?'

Anna frowned at her companion. 'No need to be sarky. It sounds like the one who found me in the hide – his hide, I think.'

Eddie looked astonished. 'You mean to tell me you may have been within feet of Ruth Cotton's boyfriend?'

'I don't think there was any "might have been" about it. And he had a whopping great knife.'

Anna's admission shocked her companion. 'You think he's our man rather than Enzo?'

Anna refilled her cup from the teapot warming on one of the AGA hotplates. 'Think about it. The knife, prowling about in the woods... and the POWs are clearly playing on his mind. I suspect that if Robert Sedwell had the slightest inkling, true or false, that Ruth was messing around, his temper – or whatever effect fighting at close quarters has had on him – might lead the man to do anything. If that's the case, the safest place for Enzo is his police cell. But you know what, I saw both sides of him when he surprised me in the hideout. Yes, he went from quiet, almost placid, to angry like a light switch being turned on and off. But the funny thing was that after he threatened me with the knife, his anger soon subsided. It was as if he knew what he was doing was wrong – and you know, when I told him I was leaving, he didn't try to stop me. In fact, he didn't move a muscle; he just sat there like a little boy. In different circumstances, I might have put my arms around him to give him some comfort. But in those circumstances, I decided to run as fast as I could, once I got out of the hide.'

Eddie held out his cup for a refill. 'You've no idea what a close shave you've had, Anna. Honestly, you're not safe to be let out on your own.'

'Don't start that protective stuff again. I'm a big girl. Anyway, it's Enzo we need to be worried about.'

'Proving Enzo is innocent isn't going to be an easy matter at all,' said Eddie. 'If he is, we must get to him and make him see sense before he's invited to stand on a trapdoor at Norwich prison with a rope around his neck. This time he must tell us everything he knows, or he's done for.'

Anna attempted to hide her anxiety as an excited Vinny re-entered the kitchen. 'Look what I got.' The boy proudly held up two snails he'd retrieved from his veg patch.

'And what are you going to do with them?' asked Anna, not sure she wanted to hear his answer.

'As long as they leave my SPAM alone, I'll leave them alone.' Vinny gave Eddie a piercing look before dashing out of the kitchen again.

Eddie laughed as he made his way to the kitchen door. 'I'll take that as a warning, shall I? Listen, I'll see if I can persuade the inspector to let us see Enzo again tomorrow morning. In the meantime, I think you could do with a good rest after the day you've had.'

Feeling suddenly tired, Anna did little to resist Eddie's suggestion. 'I'll walk you down to the gate. I need to put my bike away anyway.'

Waving Eddie off, Anna picked up her heavy iron-framed bicycle and wheeled it into the old stable yard. A sudden noise caught her attention. 'Vinny, is that you?'

I must be hearing things.

'I thought it was Vinny playing a trick on me, but when I checked around the back, he had his head between a row of cabbages. A bit odd, don't you think?'

Eddie paused for a moment to give way to one of the few vehicles that passed up and down the village high street on an average day in Lipton St Faith. 'Not really, Vinny is becoming quite a gardener.'

Is he taking the rise out of me?

'Eddie, I'm being serious. I definitely heard someone. Oh, I don't know, but there was something there.'

'Who was?'

'Oh, I give up.'

Things were, as usual, orderly in the Victorian village police station. The desk sergeant, Dick Ilford, busied himself with pinning a notice of the latest missing cat on a noticeboard as the pair strode purposefully into the tiny reception area.

'May we—'

'Inspector Spillers thought you might drop in. He's left instructions that you can have five minutes with Conti. He also said to tell you the prisoner's being transferred to Norwich prison later this evening, ready for his trial next Monday.'

The sergeant led the way to a short corridor, along which a pair of austere cell doors stood opposite one another. After unlocking cell number one with a huge iron key, the police officer stood to one side. 'Five minutes and that's your lot. I'll be listening from my desk, so no funny business.'

Inside the cell sat Enzo, unshaven and unwashed. A white enamelled bucket sealed with a tight-fitting lid stood in one corner of the tiny space, whose brown and cream walls made it appear all the smaller.

The prisoner sat on his bed, his eyes cast down as they had been on their previous visit.

'I saw April yesterday, Enzo.' Anna's revelation seemed to strike Enzo like a bolt of lightning. It was as if he'd suddenly discovered the elixir of life.

'My April, she OK?'

Eddie stepped forward. 'April's worried about you. She doesn't understand why you confessed to a murder she says you didn't commit.'

Enzo's smile faded as he shrugged his shoulders. 'No one can help me now. Too late to do things.'

I want to shake you, man, thought Anna.

'You know, Enzo. I want you to think back a few seconds to how excited you were when I mentioned April's name. That felt good, yes? You need to understand that if you don't help us, you'll never see April again. And think about her. Yes, you'll be dead, but she will have to live the rest of her life thinking about you, mourning your loss. Perhaps even living with the guilt?'

'Guilt? My April do nothing wrong. It is other people. Bad people. I protect her.'

Anna sat on the inadequate bed beside Enzo. 'April will always blame herself for not being able to help you. Whether that blame's deserved is beside the point. She will think she should have done something, anything, to help you. After you're gone it will be too late. Do you want April to have to live like that?'

A sharp bang on the cell door told Anna and Eddie their time was almost up.

'Enzo, listen to me,' said the lieutenant. 'We're running out of time. You're going to Norwich later today and will face a judge and jury next week. If you can't help yourself, give us something that will help April.'

The prisoner shot to his feet and kicked the iron frame of his bed. 'If I tell them about April, her father will know she friends with enemy and will throw her out. I not allow this. She must live happy life. Not matter what happen to me.'

Silence fell, which Anna knew couldn't continue. 'Did April ever tell you that? Did she?' Her words were urgent and staccato. 'You *must* understand, Enzo.'

The Italian slowly shook his head. 'No, she not say that, but April tell me about that terrible man.'

Anna felt her frustration intensifying. 'Whether you say anything about April or not, at your trial, details about your relationship are bound to come out. That's the way these things go, so whatever happens, her father will find out.'

Eddie covered the few steps it took to reach Enzo and put a firm hand on each of the Italian's shoulders. 'I also spoke with April today, and with her mother. Yes, we know how the man treats his wife, but she says he loves April so much and, like any father, wants to protect her. From what I can work out, April hasn't said anything about you to them. But I'm certain it won't affect their love for her. You must believe me, Enzo.' Eddie's eyes burned into Enzo, making it impossible for the Italian not to maintain eye contact.

A second thump on the heavy steel door came accompanied by the key turning in the lock.

Enzo looked desperate as he varied his gaze from Eddie to Anna. 'It still better I confess. All this will be over, and April can get on with life and meet nice boy. I have enough of being prisoner and will make this stop now.'

Chapter 18: Seeing Double

For the last day of September, the sun's warmth disguised the inevitable onset of autumn. For now, Anna and Eddie contented themselves with enjoying a break in the weather to feast on homemade sandwiches and a flask of tea within the open sides of the village butter cross.

'I wonder how Enzo is getting on at Norwich prison?'

'If it's anything like ours in the States, it'll be grim.'

Anna bit into her freshly baked bread, coated in the merest skim of butter and finished off with her mother's egg and cress filling. 'Dad's been in there several times over the years. He reckons when you first go through the small hatch-type door cut into the main security gates, you might think you're about to enter a Victorian school. Dad doesn't say much else except you can't help but look at the right-hand end of the front range of buildings.'

'Why?'

'Well, that's where they, you know… do it.'

Eddie took a sip of tea from a small tumbler. 'The drop?'

'That's one way of putting it, I suppose. Apparently, there are two or three cells that all lead off a short, narrow corridor, and one of them is fitted with double doors. I asked Dad once why one cell had double doors. He—'

'For a prisoner with a guard on each arm, I guess?'

'How did you know?'

Eddie frowned. 'Deduction. I don't suppose anyone steps into that sort of room without persuasion.'

Anna placed her sandwich back into its greaseproof paper wrap and brushed some breadcrumbs from her trousers. 'Apparently, Albert Pierrepoint is excellent at his job, which I take comfort in. The last thing you want is someone bodging that sort of thing.'

Eddie poured a tumbler of tea from the flask for Anna. 'What on earth has gotten into you? The sun's out, the village green is looking superb and all you can talk about is the expertise of your country's chief executioner. Here, get this down you.'

Anna sighed as she accepted her drink. 'It's Enzo I'm thinking of, or… Oh, never mind.'

For a full five minutes, silence prevailed as the two companions ate the rest of the snack and finished their tea.

'Right, back to work,' said Eddie as he waved to Flo Bassett, who parked her bicycle on the kerb and disappeared into the haberdashery. 'Enzo told us about "a man" in Witton Wood, who the POWs see when they "escape" for a drink at night.'

'Yes, a bit odd, though, when he said the chap resembled the ghost of a soldier who appears then disappears in front of your eyes.'

'Is it, though?' responded Eddie. 'What if Private Robert Sedwell is that soldier? After all, we know he's an expert outdoorsman. We've both seen the hide he constructed. Perhaps he has more?'

'Maybe,' replied Anna as she finished packing their things back into the rucksack. 'But what if there's a second man?'

'You mean two men working as a team? It seems a bit far-fetched.'

Anna tightened the drawstring and slung the canvas bag over her shoulders. 'We have to lure Robert Sedwell and his accomplice, if he has one, back into Witton Wood to expose their crime.'

'I agree.'

Strolling back towards the vicarage, Eddie called out, 'Nice day, Tom,' as the suspended constable stepped quickly through the old stable entrance of the police station. 'Please yourself,' muttered the lieutenant.

Anna saw her old friend, too. 'That's the second time in a few days he's come out of, or entered, the station via the stables. Perhaps he's barred from using the main entrance while on suspension, poor chap.'

Soon, they reached the vicarage gate. Instead of joining Anna, Eddie turned to the Jeep parked adjacent. 'I'm off to Ely to meet a colleague. He's passing through on his way by train from York to London. Will you be OK baiting the trap for Sedwell?'

She nodded. 'I'll be fine, but what are you keeping from me that takes you to Oliver Cromwell's hometown?'

Eddie smiled. 'You'll see. Just make sure you're careful out in Witton Wood. Remember what happened last time you came across Sedwell.'

'Oh, and I intend on giving Geoffrey Lenox a poke to see how he reacts.' Anna's words vanished in the engine roar of the Jeep as Eddie turned the ignition key before vanishing in a cloud of exhaust fumes, leaving Anna catching her breath.

Filthy thing.

Thank goodness that drive is over. I wonder where all those army convoys are going?

Eddie's journey to Ely along the A47, which took him through Dereham, Swaffham and Downham Market, took over two hours.

I hope I'm not late for Mike's train.

Parking outside the train station, Eddie looked to the near distance and took in the magnificent sight of Ely Cathedral with its majestic main entrance in the Great West Tower.

I bet that place could tell some tales.

Looking urgently at the station clock, which hung above the entrance, Eddie realised he'd made it as the toot of a steam whistle announced his friend's train.

'Look who's a captain now,' laughed Eddie as he clasped the hand of his long-time army buddy, Mike Kowalski.

'And when did you make lieutenant?'

Swapping tales of their recent career progression and past adventures, the two officers exited the station with a spring in their steps as they headed for the nearest pub.

'Have you gotten used to the warm beer yet, Mikey?'

'Not a chance. I stick to whisky if I can get it. Otherwise, I stick to… well, anything they have except that brown stuff, what do they call it, "stout"?'

Walking side by side to the mahogany bar of a pub that Eddie didn't think had changed in five hundred years, both men appeared to lose concentration as they neared the young barmaid.

'Hello, boys, welcome to the Roundhead Tavern. It's rare we see two handsome Americans in here.'

Eddie felt himself blushing and assumed Mike shared his predicament, but was too embarrassed to look. 'Well thank you, ma'am. We're passing through and thought we'd take advantage of your hospitality.'

The auburn-haired young woman's eyes sparkled as she offered a broad smile. 'You Americans are cheeky chappies. What's a girl supposed to say to that?'

What did I say?

'Oh, no, ma'am, no offence intended. I meant… err.'

'You are a daft pair. I'm joking. You're so naive for soldiers, but I like that.' The barmaid winked at both customers.

The two men exchanged awkward smiles and distracted themselves by concentrating on the list of drinks available, which hung haphazardly from a nail in an ancient oak beam.

'Don't take any notice of that, love,' she said to Eddie. 'I've got mild, bitter and bottled stout.'

Eddie watched Mike wince at the mention of stout.

'Oh, and some nice fresh cider from Jack Hilliard's orchard around the corner.

'I'll have the cider,' shouted Mike as if his life depended on it.

'Been a while since you've had a drink is it, soldier?' she said, startled by his abruptness.

'I'm sorry, ma'am, I—'

'Got you again. Crikey O'Reilly, this is too easy.'

Eddie patted his friend's back with an open palm. 'Always getting himself in trouble, this one. I'll have a cider with him, if you don't mind, err… what's your name?'

The barmaid gave Eddie a cheeky grin. 'You can call me Vy. Go on, get yourselves sat down and I'll bring your drinks over.'

Settled into a corner of the old pub, the men discarded caps and undid their army jackets.

'I guess from the things you asked me to check out you're settling in with locals pretty well?'

'You might say that,' replied Eddie. 'Don't ask me how, but I've got myself involved in helping a vicar's daughter as she attempts to solve every crime within ten miles of where she lives.'

'Here you are, boys, two pints of freshly brewed cider. Be careful, now, it's stronger than you might think.'

Eddie retrieved a handful of silver coins from his pocket and offered a pleading look in Vy's direction.

'That'll be two bob. That one there's the one I need.' She pointed to a silver coin in Eddie's palm. 'That's lovely. Enjoy your cider, lads.'

Mike leant into the small round table that separated him from his friend. 'Still not got used to the money?'

Eddie winked. 'Does no harm to play the hapless American. It works wonders.'

Mike examined the golden liquid in front of him and took a long drink from the pint glass. 'Ah, like being back on the range back home. Right. Come on, spill the beans. What have you been up to that brings me here today?'

'You're right, great stuff, isn't it?' Eddie licked his lips as he downed the first gulp of his pint. 'Are you ready for the gory details?'

'Every bit,' replied Mike, and Eddie went on to explain Ruth Cotton's tragic death.

'...So, you can see, the murder could be down to one of several people. But a couple stick out from the rest.'

'Fancy a cheese and onion pie, either of you?' shouted Vy from behind the bar.

Eddie's face lit up. 'I'm in. You too, Mike? That'll be two pies, Vy, we're starving.'

'OK, let's get down to business,' said Mike. 'The knife you asked me to investigate is something special. Fairbairn-Sykes Commando knives are issued to Commando special operations, and Churchill's Auxiliary Units.'

'Auxiliary? I've never heard of them.'

Mike looked around as if checking for spies. 'And there's a good reason for that. The British prime minister ordered the formation of small, secret local units to fight a rear-guard action in the event of invasion.'

Eddie looked astonished. 'I guess it brings home to you what the British are up against.'

'It gets better, Eddie. The units are independent of each other and defend their local patch. Here's the thing. They're not enlisted servicemen but are embedded into their nearest Home Guard platoon. Each Auxiliary Unit is made up of between four and eight men with the skills and courage needed to operate alone to slow an invasion. You know, fight to the last bullet and all that.'

'Here you go, boys. That'll be a shilling.'

This time, Mike paid. 'They look fine, Vy, thank you.'

Waiting for the barmaid to withdraw, the two friends bit into their pies, before simultaneously reaching for their cider to quench their scorched pallets.

'Gee, that's hot,' said Eddie, wafting his open mouth with a hand for added effect.

'You're telling me.'

After several seconds' recuperation, Eddie urged his friend to press on. 'But you're saying regular troops aren't involved?'

'Not according to the briefing notes I've seen, but who knows what a local commander might need for something really special. These units operate in the shadows, Eddie. They're trained commandos and other specialists in their field, handling and planting explosives, to say nothing about the range of weapons they can use. Do you know, their hideouts are even equipped with truncheons for hand-to-hand combat, for which they also use the knife you asked me about. It's a fearsome thing that's deadly in the right, or wrong, hands, depending on who's using it for what purpose.'

Truncheons. I wonder…

'Has my area got an operational unit?'

Mike took a gulp of his cider before returning his glass to the table. 'There's only so much I can tell you. More for your own protection than anything else. But I can say this without giving too much away. If the Nazis dropped anywhere near the wood you mentioned, they'd get a nasty surprise.'

I can't believe this. It's surreal.

'One last thing, Mike, did you—'

'You don't half push your luck. I guess you want to know about that Private Sedwell guy? Well, it turns out he is AWOL.'

Eddie smiled. 'I knew it.'

Emptying the last of his cider, Mike shook his head. 'Don't be too hasty. From what you've told me, that fella has some useful knowledge and skills. If Churchill wanted him for something special, he'd vanish from his unit and not even his commander would be told the reason. As far as his mates and superiors were aware, he'd have gone AWOL.'

This is getting too complicated.

Finishing his drink, Eddie got to his feet. Mike was seconds behind. 'What time's your London connection?'

Mike looked at his wristwatch. 'Heck, I've got seven minutes. Better get a move on.'

'Thanks, Vy, great to meet you,' said Eddie as both men rushed through the entrance and half-walked, half-ran to the station. Neither heard the barmaid's farewell.

'Be sure to keep in touch,' said Mike as he leant out of the train carriage window.

'You too, Mikey, and keep safe.'

As the train began to move, Mike called out, 'I slipped something into your jacket pocket in the pub. Don't take it out until you're back home. That's an order!'

211

Eddie smiled and gave a final wave as the train vanished into a tunnel, causing a thick plume of smoke and steam to coat the already grimy brickwork.

I didn't think he was so sentimental.

'Do you think Sedwell will take the bait?' asked Eddie as he led Anna back into Witton Wood.

'I left the note in his hide and said we'd be here at ten. We're a few minutes early by my watch, so we'll know one way or the other in a couple of minutes.'

The lieutenant used the time by going over his meeting with Mike again. 'I think we've got Private Robert Sedwell, how do you British put it, "bang to rights".'

Anna stifled a giggle as they continued to make their way through dense undergrowth, which made any sort of silent progress impossible.

'I'm still not sure about Sedwell, you know. Anyway, I've been busy doing what I said I'd do. I've been seeing to Geoffrey Lenox.'

'You've what?'

'I knew you didn't hear me this afternoon. You were so keen to get to Ely, which reminds me, you owe me four shillings for specialist laundering to get those filthy exhaust fumes out of my clothes.'

Eddie looked around and shook his head at Anna. 'What are you on about? And what's that got to do with Lenox?'

'Nothing at all. Anyway, as I was saying, Lenox saved me the trouble of calling on him, because he came to me.' Anna smiled, watching Eddie's growing confusion.

'Sorry, you've lost me. Watch out for the brambles, by the way, they'll… oh dear.'

Anna almost cursed as she tripped on several winding leader shoots that lay across the narrow trail. 'Thanks for the warning, even if it was too late, which I suspect you knew.'

'Me?'

'Yes, you, Lieutenant.'

Eddie adopted his little-boy-lost look. 'You were saying?'

Anna finally freed herself from the pernicious undergrowth and cleared the tricky patch. 'I was saying Lenox called at the vicarage, or to be more precise, he lurked.'

Eddie threw his arms in the air. 'Called, lurked. Which is it?'

'Don't be like that; you'll frighten our soldier away. I'd say creeping up on a woman getting her bicycle out of an old stable block is best described as lurking, wouldn't you? Anyway, he came one step too close, so I walloped him one.'

The lieutenant stopped walking. 'As in, hit the man?'

Anna smiled. 'No, as in, walloped him. I grabbed my dad's old shepherd crook and swung it at him. I caught his ear with the end and could have pulled him along like a children's toy if I'd wanted. He didn't half yelp before he passed out.'

'Passed out? Did you kill him?'

'Don't be daft. Dr Brabham says he'll be fine after his stay in the cottage hospital, by which time I imagine the police will want a word with him about stalking. I reckon that's what he was doing to Ruth.'

A sudden noise cut short further conversation.

'Shush, we're at the hide. It must be Sedwell. Well done, your little ruse seems to be working.'

Anna attempted to look over the lieutenant's shoulder to see what was going on. 'It's got to be him.'

'He's running for it, come on.'

Anna sped after Eddie as best she could in the ground conditions and caught sight of an army uniform dashing through some bushes. 'Over there.'

'No, he's gone this way. Look, there he is.' Eddie pointed to a figure lurking in the darkness.

'But he's there. Look. By that tree.' Anna pointed.

In a split second, all sign of Sedwell vanished.

Taking a few seconds to catch their breath, both scanned the area for signs of movement. All remained still.

'Something isn't right here,' said Eddie. 'It's not possible to appear in two places at the same time.'

Anna picked a small collection of vegetation from her jacket sleeve and dropped it on the soft ground. 'Perhaps a trick of the light?'

Eddie put a hand on each hip and gave the area a last glance. 'Either that, Anna, or we have not one, but two killers on our hands.'

Chapter 19: Old Injuries

Apart from the cross-shaped tape on all the windows, it sometimes feels as though there isn't a war on at all.

Anna sauntered down the village high street, not thinking about anything of consequence as she took in the sights and sounds of a tranquil Lipton St Faith. Although approaching mid-morning, the village seemed empty considering it was half-day closing.

Perhaps they all have what they need.

The exception that proved the rule appeared as village gossip Beatrice Flowers almost tumbled onto the cobbled pavement on her way back from what looked to Anna like a successful visit to the milliners and butchers.

'Good morning to you, Beatrice. Someone has been on a busy shopping expedition?'

The flustered spinster at first attempted to ignore the call until it became clear escape was impossible. 'Err… Good morning to you too, Miss Grix. Having saved my ration coupons for many months, I have invested in a new hat.' Beatrice lifted the large semi-circular brown box, its lid secured with narrow turquoise ribbon tied off with a neat bow.

'And all that meat? How will you eat all that before it goes off?'

It's the first time I've known her stumped for words.

Several seconds passed as the spinster, dressed from head to toe in a dark brown tweed jacket and matching calf-length pencil skirt, looked first one way then the other. 'Again, a product of my frugal use of ration stamps. What I can't eat I shall preserve in salt. I have a small store of such items to prepare for invasion.'

I know Mum puts extra tinned stuff aside, but salted meat? Ugh.

Unable to take her eyes off the heavily loaded string bag full of fresh meat within greaseproof wrappings, Anna wondered how Beatrice had saved up her coupons.

There's saving and there's the impossible. Something doesn't add up.

'Anyway, Miss Grix, I must be off. I have one or two other shops to visit before they close at lunchtime. Good day to you.'

More shopping?

The spinster moved off at a pace for her advanced years before disappearing into the village shoe shop.

More ration coupons? thought Anna before giving the milliner window one last lingering look and turning to stroll down to Vinny's school to check on how he was settling in.

As Anna neared the small Victorian building with the school bell sitting proudly in its cradle above the roofline, she remembered the happy times she'd had there, proud she could still remember the names of her teachers.

Who'd have thought scatty Miss Shellbrook would end up as headteacher?

'Thank you for popping in, Anna. It's always nice to see you.'

You always were my favourite teacher.

Anna smiled as she glanced around the compact place of learning and followed the headteacher into her small, neat office, which doubled up as the school library.

'I have such fond memories of this place, Grace. Do you recall when that farmer gave us a talk on his goats and the two he brought ran riot?'

Grace let out a genteel laugh as she pointed for her guest to take a seat. 'I do. We still have the evidence of that dreadful day.'

'Evidence?'

'Yes, when those goats got into the school hall and made straight for the dinner ladies preparing to dish up, one goat butted Lilly... sorry, forgot her surname. Anyway, the goat hit Lilly so hard that it sent her flying backwards, and the jug of gravy she was carrying. You've no idea how many times we've tried over the years to clean behind the radiator, yet still some remains.'

Anna covered her mouth with a hand in a gesture of amused surprise. 'I've heard everything now.'

The headteacher lifted a finger as if about to uncover some great mystery. 'Not quite. Come and have a look at this.'

'Look at what?'

Grace giggled as she walked the few paces to a window. 'The children have gone out for their lunch play. I want you to see something.'

Intrigued, Anna joined her old teacher and glanced out of the small window, which overlooked the playground. 'Noisy children running around like there's no tomorrow. It seems normal to me.'

'Over there. In the far corner.'

Anna strained to see what Grace had pointed to. She noticed a group of boys and girls gathered around another boy.

'Guess who?'

'Vinny!' Anna gave the headteacher a wistful look. 'I should have guessed. But how did you know he'd be holding court without looking out of the window first?'

'Because it's the same each day,' replied Grace. 'Your Liverpool

217

lad has quite a following. As far as the local children are concerned, he's like something from another planet. Do you know, one little girl told me that Vinny knew everything in the world? I ask you; how do you compete with that?'

Anna wiped a tear from her eye. 'If only those children knew what he's been through, Grace.'

The headteacher placed a comforting hand on Anna's shoulder. 'He never lets on. Vinny seems more concerned about watching over the others and stepping in if he thinks trouble's brewing. I suppose that's why the other evacuees have gravitated toward him.' Grace gave her visitor a hug. 'Anna Grix, you're doing a wonderful thing for those displaced little ones. No one will say it to your face, but the village is so proud of you.'

Come on, Anna, pull yourself together.

'That's so kind of you to say, Grace. I'm just doing my bit, like you are, and all the other women, to keep the young ones going… It's such a shame there wasn't anyone there for Ruth Cotton when she needed help.'

The two women shared a concerned look as Anna made her way to the office door.

'I knew Ruth, you know,' said Grace. 'As a teacher new to the area, I taught in the village school she attended. A lovely girl. No trouble to anyone and always had a lovely smile. Who'd have thought she'd end up going out with a Sedwell?'

'Well, it doesn't surprise me in the least that young Vincent is turning out to be quite Churchillian. He has spirit, that's for sure. He's commandeering ever more of my back garden for his growing vegetable empire.' The vicar chuckled as he helped his daughter dish up lunch.

'I love bubble and squeak almost as much as I know you do, Dad. It's a shame Mum's busy at the thrift shop. Still, I suppose that means more for us two.'

Both chuckled as they finished plating up and sat at the pine kitchen table. Lunch took all of ten minutes to eat as father and daughter chatted about things and, as was their custom, little about the war.

'Now, my dear, enough of this chit-chat. I sense there's something troubling you?'

Anna's smile faded as she thought about something she'd tried to banish to the back of her brain. 'It's something Grace said. She seemed to imply that people don't change. Their character, I mean.'

The vicar took a long look at his daughter. 'Has this anything to do with that unfortunate lady in Witton Wood?'

Anna took a sip of water from a glass tumbler to the right of her empty dinner plate. 'If I take Grace's logic to the extreme, that Robert Sedwell comes from a family with, how should I put it, dubious ways of making a living, then I could suppose that he, too, lives by the same rules. But I don't believe that, Dad.'

The vicar reached over, collected Anna's plate and put it on top of his own before taking both and placing them in the sizeable Belfast sink. 'Nature versus nurture, that old chestnut, eh? Well, if it counts for anything, I agree with you. Prejudice can take many forms, even amongst those who might consider themselves too educated to concern themselves with what others say and do. And I see the turmoil such matters are causing you.'

Anna turned so she faced her father. 'Not sure what you mean, Dad. All I'm saying is—'

'You're conflicted, child.' The vicar returned to the dining table, this time sitting on the corner nearest his daughter. 'Over the last week or so as you have tried your best to get justice for Ruth Cotton, I've listened to you as you vacillate between believing Ruth's boyfriend committed the murder, and that Italian fellow.

'Now, unless they're in cahoots, and I come to no conclusions on such a thing, only one is guilty of murder. I say this only from what you tell me and that which I observe. I accuse no one of what is, in the eyes of God, an abomination.'

Anna toyed with the glass tumbler, now empty of water. 'I still don't understand. What is it you're saying to me?'

Getting to his feet, the vicar walked behind his daughter, leant forward and planted a gentle kiss on the top of her head. 'I'm saying you must decide. You must free yourself from a prison of your own making. Let go of all emotion; consider the facts and decide. Do you believe Robert Sedwell killed Ruth Cotton, or Enzo Conti?

'Once you conclude this process, you must do all you can to bring the guilty to justice and protect the innocent. Remember this, my darling, as we speak, a man reaches up as he attempts to glimpse God's beautiful skies out of a high barred window in a bleak cell at Norwich prison. From what you tell me, that man may not escape his dreadful confinement alive. This is no time for the faint-hearted.'

Tears raced down Anna's cheeks as all pretence of being an adult evaporated.

'Be calm, my child. You have it within you to be strong. Believe, Anna, not in something that I, or anyone else, postulates as the correct way. Rather, believe in your own goodness and what you seek to do for others. That way you'll find the right way.'

Anna grasped for her father's comforting touch. 'I hate what's happening. Why can't it be like it was before?'

The vicar's calm words gently filled the air. 'Before what, my darling, the war? If so, which war? For there have always been such horrors to pour turmoil over ordinary people's lives.'

Pressing into her father, Anna tried to stifle her tears. 'Help me, Dad.'

He stroked his daughter's hair as he had when she fell as a child and needed the comfort only a parent can provide. 'Whether a person suffers pain because they are, no matter how hard they try to prove otherwise, tarred with the same brush as their family, or injured in war and wish to be treated as normal despite how those around view them, the result is the same. Isolation, a feeling of helplessness and, if not dealt with, anger that may eventually over-whelm them. At such times, we know all too well what a person is capable of. Don't you think they want things to go back to how they were?'

Anna's tears subsided as she attempted to understand what her father meant. 'I'm sorry, Dad. I forgot about people like Jack Skidmore in his wheelchair.'

The vicar exhaled a gentle sigh. 'Sadly, child, physical injuries are all too easy to spot, even if people assume the disabled person has somehow also lost their ability to think and speak. Injuries of the mind are much more difficult to discover, let alone treat. Remember I mentioned that poor chap I came across in church the other day? He suffers from an injury he received in 1916, yet no one sees his scars. To them, he looks, sounds and, mostly, behaves as society expects. However, deep inside he's as damaged as Jack Skidmore, perhaps more so.'

I still don't understand.

'You look awful.'

'Thanks a bunch. Is that your idea of American sweet-talk?'

Anna rummaged for a bright green Bakelite compact in her small leather handbag, opened the lid and inspected her complexion.

Being dragged through a hedge backwards springs to mind.

'Let's say it's been an interesting afternoon, and that's why I'm taking you to Tom's,' she said. 'I must get something off my chest. His suspension is my fault and I have to let him know how much I care for him.'

Eddie looked over from the driver's seat of the Jeep. 'Wow, where did that come from?'

'I guess sometimes things need saying instead of thinking. Let's leave it at that for now.'

'If you say so. Well, let's hope he's at home this time, shall we?'

Anna replaced her compact. 'It's seven now,' she said, looking at her watch.

'No reason for him to be out,' said Eddie.

The passing of ten minutes saw them a few hundred yards from the house where Tom lived with his widowed father.

'I don't believe it.'

'What?'

'He's going out again. Look, he's gotten into his dad's car.'

Anna clipped her handbag shut and leant forward. 'Can't this thing go any faster? We'll miss him.'

'It's a Jeep, not a Cadillac, Anna. Too late, he's off.'

Eddie pulled the Jeep off the road and turned off the engine before hitting the steering wheel with his open palms.

Anna shook her head. 'He's like the Scarlet Pimpernel – first you see him, then you don't. For a man suspended from the job he loves, he's not sitting about moping, that's for sure.'

Both sat in silence as they pondered what to do next. Overhead, a congregation of starlings danced as they readied themselves for roosting. 'Look at the shapes they create. Isn't it fascinating?'

Eddie didn't reply. Instead, he mirrored his companion's amazement at the complex ever-changing patterns painted across the reddening sky by a thousand pairs of wings.

'You know what, Eddie, all we need now is chocolate, especially after the day I've had.' Anna gave the lieutenant one of her best coquettish looks.

He smiled, shook his head and rummaged in his left jacket pocket. 'Will this do?' As he retrieved a half-bar of Hershey's, a piece of paper fell into Anna's lap.

'You know what men say about never digging into a girl's handbag?' Eddie frowned. 'Eh?'

'You know, what lurks in a woman's handbag and all that. Well, does the same go for anything that comes out of a man's pocket?' She held up the scrap of paper before unfolding it and reading the contents.

'What, you mean except chocolate, I suppose. Anyway, it'll only be rubbish, I… Wait a minute, I think Mike gave me that in Ely; let's have a look.'

Anna held it out of Eddie's reach.

Ring York 2563. When answered, tell them the name of the dog you got for your eleventh birthday.

Eddie gently tapped his forehead with the palm of his hand. 'I thought he meant don't read it until I got *home*, as in America. He meant *this* home.'

Anna handed her companion the note. 'You're talking in riddles; this home, that home?'

The lieutenant read the note again. 'Never mind that now. We need a telephone box.'

After a frantic fifteen-minute search, one of the familiar red boxes came into view. Eddie leapt from the stationary Jeep, bounded to the kiosk, threw back the heavy door and picked up the receiver.

Re-emerging two minutes later, this time change in hand after pushing button "B", the American ran back to the Jeep, wearing the broadest of smiles.

'Well?'

'I know how he did it.'

Chapter 20: If Only

'Good luck with this one, Grace; he's so excited. What's all this about a field trip to discover creepy-crawlies?'

The headteacher rolled her eyes at Anna as she greeted a lively Vinny along with the other children who passed through the village school gates for the start of another busy day of learning. 'I'm regretting promising his class our brief trip. I'll get no sense out of any of them until we're on our way.'

Anna put her hands together as if praying. 'I'll say one for you; I suspect you'll need it.'

Grace gave a hapless smile as she turned to engage a mother eager for her attention.

So glad I didn't go into teaching.

Back at the vicarage, Eddie tucked into a thick slice of toast coated with raspberry jam. Beside his plate rested a sizeable mug of strong tea.

'Nice to see you making yourself at home, Lieutenant.'

'You dropped him off all right?'

Anna lifted a small circular lid from the brown and cream clay teapot and peered inside. 'So nice of you to leave me some.'

About to take another bite from his toast, Eddie held his breakfast halfway between plate and mouth. 'OK, what have I done?'

'Oh, nothing. I'm wondering when you're going to get around to telling me what you found in Witton Wood last night after you dropped me off?'

He's doing this on purpose.

Eddie offered his host a bite of his toast as a peace offering. 'Oh, you mean after I made the call and told them about the dog I got as a kid?'

'No, I don't want any of your soggy toast and yes, the call. If you don't stop being awkward, you'll be wearing that mug of tea. Get it, cowboy?'

'Not just any cowboy, though. I think of myself as the Lone Ranger. Did you know he's apparently based on a real-life Lone Star Ranger?'

Anna shook her head as she sipped her hot drink. 'You're as daft as a brush when you want to be. Now tell me what happened, or else...' Anna held up her cup to reinforce the earlier threat of a drenching.

The lieutenant made Anna wait a few seconds longer as, on eating the last of his toast, he licked his fingers, pulled his handkerchief from a pocket and delicately dried each finger. Only the nearing cup of tea persuaded him it was time to talk. 'Instead of going back to Witton Wood last night, I left it until after sunup, if that's what you can call a drizzly Thursday morning in Norfolk. Anyway, the information from the woman I spoke to last night from the telephone box was on the money. It's making sense now.'

'No, it isn't. What do you mean by "on the money"?'

'Ah, sorry, I guess I should back up a little. What I mean is that she told me the exact position of where the Royal Engineers built a secret hideout in Witton Wood, and—'

'Hang on, Eddie. Royal Engineers? What are you talking about?'

The lieutenant took a moment to gather his thoughts. 'For the local Auxiliary Unit. The Royal Engineers have built a network of

226

them on or near the coasts, mainly in the southeast of England, for these units to use to slow down any invasion. The thing is, I don't know who murdered Ruth, at least not yet, but if my logic is right, then whoever killed her used the one in Witton Wood to strike from.'

'But how does that help us?'

The American sauntered over to the kitchen window, leant over the Belfast sink and scanned the vicar's healthy-looking vegetable patch. 'You know I've always thought Enzo killed Ruth. Well, part of me still hangs on to that thought. The problem is, the hideout I found early this morning counts against that theory because it's not something that's been thrown together for shelter; it's a complex piece of engineering.'

Anna wandered over to the table, sat on one edge with both legs gently swinging back and forth in unison. 'I'm sorry, Eddie, you've lost me again. Are you saying the den we came across, you know, the one Ruth's boyfriend caught me in, well… that *isn't* the hideout you're talking about?'

Eddie shook his head. 'They're as different as chalk and cheese, Anna. The one I discovered this morning is built like a tank and kitted out like a bunker; food rations for at least two weeks, I reckon, and an armoury that would put a local militia to shame. Guns, truncheons, kniv—'

'What's up with you?'

'Why does everything keep coming back to truncheons?' exclaimed Eddie.

'I didn't know it did.'

'Think back to when we found the body. I said the headwound hadn't been caused by anything with a sharp edge or more than a couple of inches wide. Well, a truncheon fits the bill perfectly, doesn't it?'

Anna suddenly understood. 'You're saying whoever killed Ruth used—'

'Yes, which means whoever was in that hide that night is our murderer. If one of the truncheons has traces of her hair or... well, you get the idea, then we have our murder weapon.'

Wow, Eddie's on top form.

'The question is, who uses the hide?' said Anna.

The Lieutenant thought for a moment, then smiled. 'From what Mike told me, it'll be one or more members of the local Home Guard. The problem we have is that the platoon commander won't know who they are, and they're hardly going to identify themselves, even if we get the military bigwigs to allow us to question them, which they won't.'

At that moment, Anna's father appeared. 'Good morning to both of you.' The vicar offered a cheery wave as he passed the open kitchen door that gave access to the vestibule.

'Morning, Dad. Off on your calls already?'

A pause occurred as the vicar put on his grey mackintosh raincoat and picked out an umbrella from an ancient wooden stand his mother had left to him years before.

'The lord's work cannot wait, my darling, except in this case it's more of joining the queue at the fishmongers to appease the lord and master that is your mother.'

The lieutenant and Anna giggled as they exchanged funny faces, playing out an imaginary domestic dispute between husband and wife.

'However, once I have accomplished my domestic task, I want to track down that fellow I've mentioned to you. Now, what was his name? Ah yes, Burt. He's a troubled soul and I'm worried about him. Anyway, bye-bye for now, darling. See you later, Lieutenant.'

The levity between Eddie and Anna evaporated.

'What's all that about?' said Eddie.

'To be honest, I don't know, unless he's referring to the chap he came across praying alone in church the other day. From what Dad said, I think the man's ill, but he didn't really explain why he'd come to that conclusion, except to say wars have always happened and that people don't always show the injuries they sustained fighting.'

What's up with Eddie? thought Anna as she glanced at her friend.

'You look like you've seen a ghost.'

'Do you know, I think I have. What was it Enzo said about seeing an old man appearing and vanishing into thin air? Well, what if it wasn't just any elderly person, but an old soldier? You're a genius. Get your coat. We need to see the inspector and ask for his help. I think Ruth's murderer may appear as if a spirit tonight.'

'I think Norfolk has finally got to you, Lieutenant. Anyway, before you make a fool of yourself in front of Spillers, I'll ask you the obvious thing he will want to know. Why tonight? Why not wait until Saturday, because that's the day the old man seems to be seen most often?'

Now I've thrown him, but it's for his own good.

'Not always. Enzo mentioned he'd seen an old man on a Thursday, too. So why not tonight? Now, I need you to find someone, no, a man, who can speak German. Second, you must get Ruth's boyfriend back into the wood for 11.00 pm.'

'And?'

'And get a list of the local Home Guard. I bet the caretaker at the memorial hall will have one, since he organises the hire of the place and the platoon use it for drill practice or whatever it is they get up to.'

'Is that all?'

'Who's being sarky now?' replied Eddie.

'I'll give you sarky. Right, let's get going. It seems there's a lot to do.'

'This had better work, Lieutenant Elsner. Have you any idea how difficult it's been to get so many men here, never mind the dummy

229

grenades? I've called in several favours and if this goes wrong, I'll probably end up directing traffic in Great Yarmouth.'

Anna watched on as Inspector Spillers grilled Eddie for the umpteenth time about his plan.

I hope his hunch is correct or we'll all be for it.

Turning to her father as the assembly of police officers and specialist army personnel huddled together in a concealed clearing two miles from Witton Wood, Anna asked, 'Are you sure you're OK doing this, Dad?'

The vicar looked pensive yet gave his daughter a smile of encouragement. 'The inspector has promised me no live ammunition will be used, to prevent serious injury or death. On the positive side, it's been some time since I've spoken German, so that bit will be fun.'

'Have you got the piece of paper Eddie left for you?'

'Don't fuss, my darling. It's only half a dozen words, which I've committed to memory. If I can deliver an hour's sermon from memory each Sunday, I'm sure I can accomplish the task to the lieutenant's satisfaction.'

As the time neared for each group to move into position, the atmosphere changed. Gone was the light-hearted banter whispered between colleagues. Everyone now focussed on their allotted role.

'Remember,' said Eddie in a low voice, 'Don't vary from the route I've given you to take up your position. Get it wrong and we'll have wasted our time. Also, a murderer will escape justice, so make sure you await my order when the time comes.'

Anna marvelled at the attention Eddie commanded.

Wow, every inch the leader. He's very impressive.

For a reason Anna couldn't fathom, all eyes turned to her father.

'Ah,' said the vicar, 'yes, I see, a prayer.'

Each member of the clandestine group straightened up and lowered their head.

'Almighty God, we ask for your guidance in helping each of us to do our duty this night. That all will remain safe. That the innocent receive justice. That the guilty repent their sins and receive your forgiveness. In your name, Lord, amen, amen.'

'Amen,' repeated each person quietly.

After allowing a few seconds for individual reflection, Eddie took control. 'My watch says 22:40 hours…'

An uncomfortable murmur filled the still air.

Eddie looked to Anna. 'What?'

She pointed to her watch. 'I thought you'd reset your watch from Lipton St Faith time. 23:40 hours. You know, 11.40 pm?'

Eddie closed his eyes before lowering his head. 'I apologise. OK, check watches. On my mark, 23:41 hours… Mark.'

Time confirmed, each team broke away to mount their transport and left the clearing.

'Won't Robert Sedwell hear them?' said Anna.

'No, we'll each park up around half a mile from our allocated positions and walk in. If we do this right, Sedwell won't hear a thing until it's too late.'

By 11.00 pm, all were in place. Eddie, Anna and the vicar occupied one position. Detective Inspector Spillers and six uniformed constables took up a second, while a unit of twelve army personnel positioned themselves in a secure ring, according to Eddie's instructions.

'Time to go, Anna. Remember, do nothing sudden, keep your eyes on him and don't panic; we'll be able to see you at all times.'

About to move towards Private Robert Sedwell's hide, she noticed movement to her right and gave the lieutenant a startled look. 'What's he doing here?'

Although he was obscured by the dense forest, she recognised the clumsy and untidy frame of Major Leonard-White. By his side stood four military policemen and a fifth shape she couldn't identify.

Eddie reacted instantly. 'Shush, don't worry about him. You'll get the picture soon. Go on, or he'll think you're not coming.'

I hate secrets.

Moving off from the vicar and Eddie, Anna stepped cautiously as she neared the hide. Fifty yards further on, she caught sight of the tell-tale signs of a camouflage net.

Easy to spot when you know what you're looking for.

The late evening remained quiet except for the occasional owl calling out and rustle of leaves in the canopy as a light breeze kissed each surface. Less pleasant was the dampness of the forest floor vegetation from the day's drizzle.

Eddie owes me a fresh pair of trousers.

Nearing the hide, Anna slowed to a snail's pace, instinctively ducking to make her frame appear as small as possible.

I hope he took the bait, or do I?

Tentatively, Anna lifted back the camouflage net. Before she knew what was happening, a uniformed hand shot out of the hide, caught her by the leg and pulled Anna in with a force that caused her to fall backward. She let out a short scream.

Keep back, Eddie. Not yet.

'What's your game? Why do you want to see me again? I thought you understood. I thought I could trust you. Are you on your own?'

Anna remembered Eddie's words:

Keep calm and make sure you maintain eye contact with him.

'It's OK, Robert, I'm alone and yes, you can trust me.'

Relieved that the private had released his vice-like grip on her lower leg, she shuffled into a seated position on the dry, crisp bedding within the hide. 'I wanted to see you again because—'

232

The soldier reacted to a noise outside the hide by undoing his knife from its sheath. 'If you've—'

'I haven't, honest,' she replied while keeping her gaze firmly on the fearsome knife.

'Stay there,' he barked, as he bundled himself out of the small space.

What's he doing?

After what seemed like an age and still with no word from Sedwell, Anna hesitantly got to her knees and popped her head out of the hide.

Where is he?

Anna got to her feet. Within a second, a familiar voice whispered its menacing message. 'Don't move.'

Immediately, she heard a much louder voice.

'Verstecken Sie Ihre Fallschirme. Das Lager ist da drüben.'

'Germans. Get back into the hide. When I see them I'll lure them away.'

Anna fell back into the hide as Robert Sedwell rapidly brought the camouflage net down and shielded her from the hide entrance.

'My German isn't that good, but I think he's ordering his men to hide their parachutes and telling them where the POW camp is.'

Seconds later, a cacophony of noise erupted as ammunition exploded and rifle shot filled the shaken night air.

'Stay down. Don't move. You're OK, I'll keep them off you. If it's a special operations group, there won't be many of them and the camp is in the opposite direction. Best to lay low here.'

Witton Wood once more fell silent as if the violence of the previous few minutes had never taken place.

A minute later, a quiet English voice sounded from outside the hide. 'You can come out now, both of you.'

Sedwell turned on Anna.

'It's OK,' she said, working hard to reassure the confused and frightened squaddie.

The soldier cautiously lifted the camouflage net and peered up to see a man dressed from head to foot in black, save for a white band around his neck. 'Blimey, a vicar?'

'It's my father, but you're correct, he's also a vicar.'

Scrambling to her feet, Anna hugged her father. 'Did it work?'

'Yes, it did, my darling. Everyone's safe now.'

'I've had enough. I'm out of here,' said the soldier as he turned.

'Private Robert Sedwell, I think it best you stay. There are some gentlemen who are rather keen to speak to you and no, it's not the police, at least not the ones with a blue uniform.'

Sedwell had stopped in his tracks to hear the vicar out. Turning to Anna, his shoulders slumped as he looked to the floor. 'I never thought I'd say it but I'm glad they've caught me. Time to face up to what I've done. All I wanted was to see my girlfriend for a few days. Is that too much to ask? Anyway, it doesn't matter anymore, does it?… I mean now that Ruth's…'

Anna walked over to the sullen man and put her arms around him. Stepping back, she put a finger under his chin so he had to look at her. 'Robert Sedwell, don't let anyone tar you with the same brush as your family again. You did the right thing tonight. You're a brave and honourable man. Always remember that.'

Robert slowly smiled at Anna, his shoulders now high, his torso straight. 'No one has ever said anything like that to me before, except for Ruth. Do you know who did it now?'

Anna looked at her father, who was nodding. 'Come with me, both of you.'

As they walked back to the position Anna had started from, all was quiet except for the murmuring of several men.

She watched as Eddie comforted an elderly man in uniform who had curled himself into the foetal position on the ground. Eyes closed, the old man was shaking uncontrollably.

That's what all the shouting and bangs were about from Leonard-White's men; tricking whoever was in the secret hide to show himself.

Robert Sedwell bent down to comfort a comrade in distress before giving Eddie an angry glance. 'What have you done to him?'

Anna's father placed a healing hand on his shoulder. 'Robert, please stand up and look at me.'

After a few seconds, the soldier complied with the vicar's request.

'This man is Sergeant Bertram Brownlow, Burt to his friends. This hero suffered terribly during the First World War. Oh, you can't see his injuries because he has—'

'Shellshock. I've seen it in Italy, vicar. I had a mate who got it. No one took him seriously until he walked straight into the enemy lines one day and copped it. They took notice then… but I don't understand.' Robert looked back down at the stricken veteran, who still shook violently and whose eyes were now fully open, looking at something no one else could see.

Eddie took over. 'I'll be honest with you, Private Sedwell; at first we thought you had killed Ruth.' Sedwell got agitated. 'Calm down, soldier.' Eddie's command took effect immediately. 'But something didn't add up, even though that jealous streak of yours will get you in real trouble if you don't do something about it.'

The soldier relaxed. 'What are you saying?'

'I'm saying we needed to find out if you would run tonight once the action started. That would've told us you probably had something to do with your girlfriend's death.'

Robert shook his head.

'But you didn't, Robert,' said Anna. 'In fact, you did the reverse.

235

When you thought trouble had broken out, your first thought was for my safety. That's not the action of a murderer, Robert.'

Sedwell once more lowered his gaze.

'Don't do that, Private. Remember what I told you back at the hide. Never be cowed again because of your name or upbringing.'

The vicar rubbed Robert's back with a calming hand.

'Lieutenant Elsner found a specialist knife near Ruth's body. No, it wasn't the murder weapon,' said Inspector Spillers, 'but it set several hares running as to how such a knife might end up in Witton Wood.'

'You mean the commando knife?'

'You knew?' said Eddie.

'When I saw it, I assumed the army had a special unit looking for me. I thought if I disturbed it, they would know I was near and set a trap. I know how they operate.'

Eddie looked at the inspector, who shrugged his shoulders. 'News to me.'

'That knife,' continued Eddie, 'led me to discover, via a friend I met in Ely the other day, there's an Auxiliary Unit operating in the vicinity. I don't know who its members are, and I don't want to, but I found out they often recruit local landowners, individuals with specialist military skills, gamekeepers… even poachers. What—'

'Poachers?' exclaimed Spillers.

'Clever, eh? Who better to recruit for a rear-guard operation than people with a detailed knowledge of the local landscape, those who know the lay of the land blindfolded… like a poacher, for example? And as for specialist military skills, who better than an old soldier who's experienced combat close up?' The lieutenant looked down at Burt Brownlow. 'It's likely more than one member of the local Home Guard belongs to the same Auxiliary Unit as this chap, but they'll have kept it such a secret that not even their commanding officer will know who they are, as per the orders from Mr Churchill. Nor will they admit their involvement now, even after this tragedy, so it's no use us trying to find out. In times of invasion, the Auxiliary Units are expected to fight wearing a Home Guard uniform but not be subject to the constraints of normal warfare. I suppose you might call it guerrilla fighting.'

The vicar patted Robert on the back again before turning his attention to Eddie. 'That's all very interesting, I'm sure, but how did you guess this poor fellow was a member, or had anything to do with Ruth's death?'

Eddie smiled. 'The long answer is it had to be a local with something special to offer the Scallywags. So—'

'That's no way to talk about—'

'Charles, that's what members of the Auxiliary Units call themselves. In fact, when they're on active duty it's known as Scallywagging. A bit of gallows humour, I suppose, for men whose life expectancy under attack is, I'm told, a maximum of twelve days. They have to be a special breed, because they're expected to shoot each other, or themselves, if all's lost and they're about to be overrun by the enemy.'

'Good gracious, how awful,' responded the vicar. 'And the short answer?… To my question, I mean.'

'You told Anna.'

'I did no such thing,' replied the vicar, his voice tinged with indignation. 'I've never seen this… Wait a minute.' Charles crossed to the old soldier, who was now sitting up on the floor and being comforted by a police constable. 'Yes, it's him. Oh, you poor man.'

'Let's not forget he caused the death of a young woman, Vicar.'

'No, Detective Inspector. War caused this to happen, except not the current one. The seeds of what happened to poor Ruth were sown in 1916 on the Somme.'

'Shellshock,' Sedwell cried out.

Anna comforted the broken soldier. 'Come here, Robert. You see, there's nothing you could have done to save Ruth.'

Eddie crouched beside the old man and held his hand. 'Remember, Charles, when the Home Guard was carrying out an exercise the other Sunday, you know, when you complained about the noise? Well, as Anna and I watched, we saw one soldier cowering when the dummy grenades went off. I knew whoever it was suffered from shellshock. I thought nothing of it at the time, but then I made the connection between Ruth's injury and what Mike told me about the weaponry Axillary Units have access to in their hideouts – including truncheons. Then, I rang the number Mike gave me and discovered the existence of an Auxiliary Unit in Lipton St Faith and the presence of a hide, which turned out to be equipped with truncheons, in Witton Wood. And when Anna explained what you meant when you said this morning that you needed to find a troubled soul… well, I put it all together and hoped I'd come to the right conclusion. Luckily, Inspector Spillers believed me, or at least enough to back my plan. I couldn't be certain who our man was, but I had a good idea by then.'

Eddie pointed to the secret hideout. 'If you look at the access chamber, you'll see a truncheon laying on the floor. I expect the police will find Burt's fingerprints on it, and if it's the same one he picked from the rack last week, it will also have traces of Ruth on it.'

Spillers walked over to the open hatch. 'You're right, Lieutenant, there is one lying on the floor. I guess he dropped it when all hell broke out.'

A reflective quiet fell as attention turned back to Burt's sad frame until Leonard-White sprang to life.

'How the blazes did you know whoever it was would be in his hide tonight?' This was the first intervention of Major Leonard-White, who the inspector had asked to attend, ostensibly to lend his expertise to the proceedings, not least should there be a need to apply military law.

'Because we learned that an old soldier was often to be seen a couple of nights a week in Witton Wood. Someone who was paranoid that German paratroopers were about to invade. That someone turned out to be a member of the Auxiliary Unit responsible for the local area in case of a general invasion.'

Inspector Spillers took centre stage. 'And that was the bit I didn't like at all. The lieutenant became convinced that our man would be on duty, and that he'd react instantly to hearing German voices as he hid in his secret hideout. When he came to me this morning with his madcap plan, I was far from convinced. However, as he reminded me, we all have a duty to find the truth for Miss Cotton, even if that truth is uncomfortable. A woman who came to the woods to see her boyfriend met her death at the hands of an ill man who did his duty twenty-five years ago, and thought he was doing it again when he hit Ruth so hard with a truncheon that the blow killed her. Once Anna got the list of Home Guard members from the memorial hall and we saw it contained his name, we expected to find Burt here tonight. However, we couldn't be sure, which is why my officers didn't pick him up earlier today. We had to catch him coming out of the hideout. I believe that because it was dark and the clothes Ruth wore the evening she died resembled army fatigues, dressed as she was to go camping, Burt thought she was the enemy and did what he'd been trained to do in defending his country.'

Private Sedwell put his head in his hands and broke down again. 'I thought she had stood me up because she was seeing someone else. How could I have…'

Anna took hold of Robert and led him a few yards away from the sad scene.

'Thank heavens your intuition paid off and this poor fellow went into shock when he heard my poor imitation of German, came out of the hide to attack but dropped his weapon and collapsed in a heap when you ordered the dummy grenades and rifle blanks fired. Do you know, it occurred to me that if you had been wrong, one or more of us might have been dead by now.'

The vicar felt for the crucifix hanging from a delicate chain around his neck.

Quiet fell as two constables helped the old soldier to his feet who, although conscious, seemed not to be aware of his surroundings.

'So, a tragic accident then,' said Anna. 'Burt thought he was under attack, grabbed a truncheon and came out expecting to engage a German paratrooper in hand-to-hand combat. Instead, he hit Ruth.' She turned to face the old soldier. 'Looking at him now, I doubt he even remembers doing it.'

'Not so, my darling,' responded the vicar. 'Let's not forget he came to church, so he must have remembered, yet he didn't submit himself to the police. Consequences must follow actions. Is that not the case, Inspector?'

Spillers frowned. 'To be truthful, I doubt there's a jury in the land that will convict the old man of murder, but he won't walk away scot-free.'

'A load of old codswallop if you ask me,' interrupted Leonard-White. 'There's no such thing as shellshock. It's just an excuse for cowards to leave the frontline. If you ask me, I'd—'

'But I'm not,' interrupted Eddie. 'However, there is a matter that concerns me.' Lieutenant Elsner turned to single out Sergeant Hatcher, the most senior member of the Corps of Military Police present. 'Please detain Major Leonard-White and charge him with sedition, corruption and fraud in that order.'

'What… what are you doing?' shouted Leonard-White. 'Have you gone mad? You asked me here this evening for my help and expertise. These are my men, and you have no jurisdiction over me. Wait a minute, who are you?' The major hissed at one of the men restraining him.

Spillers smiled. 'That's a word you like to bandy about, isn't it? Jurisdiction. Let me tell you, Major, you have no jurisdiction to take over the civilian population and subject them to military rule. Yes, the lieutenant told me about your exchanges. As for your ration book scam and plan to intimidate local pub owners into paying you protection money, well, I have newly promoted Sergeant Tom Bradshaw to thank for his outstanding undercover work.'

'You?' spat the major as he offered futile resistance to being handcuffed and held by two burly military policemen.

Tom stepped out from the shadows, causing both Anna and Eddie to gasp.

'It was remiss of you, Major, to believe that Sergeant Bradshaw had gone rouge,' continued Spillers. 'Still, the fact you did played into our hands. If you insist on employing greedy small-holders to do your dirty work in selling the stolen ration books to even greedier, gossiping villagers like Beatrice Flowers, you get what you deserve.'

Major Leonard-White smirked. 'As I said, you have no jurisdiction over military matters and personnel. Sergeant, let loose these handcuffs at once before you find yourself on a charge of treason.'

The military police held firm.

'You're quite correct, Major. I have absolutely no authority over you.' Leonard-White's smiled broadened. 'But your commanding officer does.' Spillers reached into his coat pocket to retrieve a one-page document. 'This gives me full authority to direct Sergeant Hatcher, you know, the man you didn't recognise a few seconds ago. You may wish to know he's attached to the Corps of Military Police Special Investigation Branch, and he's here to have you detained. I have to say, an army charge sheet is rather different to the one His Majesty's constabulary uses, but I imagine the effect is much the same. Perhaps more significant since you'll be detained in solitary confinement in a place the gentlemen holding you won't identify to me. You see, they have their orders, too.'

Epilogue

'You're a dark horse, Tom Bradshaw, or need I now address you as Sergeant?'

Laughter bounced around the tiled walls of the vicarage kitchen as Eddie and Anna, her parents, Tom Bradshaw and the inspector crowded around the kitchen table while tucking into a tall pile of thick-cut toast made from a wheatmeal loaf, served with dripping and a selection of homemade jam spreads.

'That's down to me and I must apologise,' said Inspector Spillers as he reached for his second round of toast. 'I thought it too dangerous to get others involved with the mad major to discover exactly what he was up to, even though these two put me onto him.' Spillers pointed at the lieutenant and Anna.

'You suspended him!' said Anna.

Spillers blushed. 'Again, I should apologise, but what better way to throw you two off his scent? After all, you had your hands full.'

'Tom Bradshaw, I shall never believe a word you say to me again. When we were at school, you were always such a good boy.' Anna playfully wagged a finger at her long-time friend.

'It wasn't easy, especially after you saw me driving out of the police station then came to Dad's house.'

'Quite the Inspector Hornleigh now, aren't we?' said Anna playfully.

'Er, I think you mean his assistant, Sergeant Bingham,' said Inspector Spillers with a smile.

'Now, what was that film called that came out a couple of years ago? Yes, I have it… *Inspector Hornleigh on Holiday*. Excellent film,' said the vicar.

'Will you charge Burt Brownlow, Inspector?' Eddie's question immediately changed the previously light-hearted atmosphere.

'If he had been of sound mind the charge might have been murder, or at the very least, manslaughter. The man is damaged. Of course, it will depend on the psychologist's report; however, my own view is that Ruth Cotton paid a dreadful price for being in the wrong place at the wrong time.'

'I guess it means the old fellow will still be incarcerated?' asked Eddie.

'I'm afraid so. An assault leading to death has occurred. My gut feeling is he'll be committed to a secure asylum for the rest of his life.'

The vicar sighed. 'What a tragedy, on all counts.'

Heads nodded in mutual agreement.

'And what about Enzo, Inspector?' asked Anna.

'We've already put a call in to the Governor at Norwich Prison. The trial will no longer go ahead and all charges have been dropped. He'll be back at the POW camp later today, when I think he can expect a visit from April on compassionate grounds, courtesy of the new commander.'

'That's a relief. April must be out of her mind. I'll give her a ring shortly.'

Eddie sighed. 'That's if her father allows it. However, from what April's mother told me, and the girl herself, perhaps this may be a turning point for the whole family. You see, the father has agreed to

244

give up his – err, let's call it his "other life" – and try to make a go of things. I guess all we can do is wish them good luck.'

Vinny came barrelling into the kitchen and caught sight of the inspector. 'The cops, I'm off.'

'Come here, young man,' shouted the vicar as Vinny was about to disappear through the doorway. 'You said you had toothache, which is why you aren't at school.'

Vinny suddenly remembered and put a hand to his left cheek. 'Err... yes, it hurts horrible.'

'That's strange,' said Anna's mum. When I got you up for school, you said it was on the opposite side.'

Vinny thought for a moment and grimaced before placing his free hand on his right cheek. 'It was. It's spread.'

The more earnest Vinny tried to look, the more laughter he generated.

'Are you lot laughing at me?'

'That doesn't work anymore, Vinny,' said the vicar. 'We know your little tricks now.'

Eddie felt in his pocket and pulled out a new bar of Hershey's chocolate. 'It's a shame you have toothache. I guess the grownups will have to share this before it melts.'

Vinny spotted his opportunity. 'Look at that, it's gone.' He removed his hands from his cheeks, displaying a look of astonishment. In one swift movement, he relieved Eddie of the chocolate and made his escape.

A roar of laughter broke out. 'You have one hour before Helen takes you to school. Did you hear me, young man?' The vicar listened for a response, smiled and shook his head. 'He's a rum one.'

Anna stood up to clear away the plates when her father held his hand up. 'I have one further piece of information for you all. I called a meeting of the church parochial committee at seven-thirty this morning, something the members did not appreciate, I can tell you, but I thought it vital we discussed a particular matter.

'Let me guess,' said Anna. 'You've told them to put your silly church clock forward one hour to match British Double Summertime again?'

'You have it in one, my darling. It seems our short experiment in establishing Lipton St Faith time had the potential to be more dangerous than any threat of invasion from the enemy!'

English (UK) to US Glossary

AGA: A type of combined oven and hob. The larger models can also provide hot water and heating. They were traditionally found in British farmhouses and commercial kitchens. In modern times they are also used in larger domestic homes. AGA stands for Aktiebolaget Gas Accumulator, the Swedish industrial gas company that invented the product.

Axis Powers: Germany and its allies during WWII.

(the) Balloon will go up: Service slang for when an attack or action begins.

Belfast sink: Derived from the 'Butler sink'. Sometimes known as the Butler Belfast sink and used in the butler's pantry of medieval castles etc. for preparing food and cleaning afterwards.

Blert: Liverpudlian slang for a stupid person, 'You are a blert'.

Bobby's hat: The reinforced helmet traditionally worn by British police officers.

Boss: Liverpudlian slang for excellence, 'That meal was boss'.

Bubble and squeak: Traditionally made from potatoes, meat and cabbage, especially in WWII when the meat was often missing because of rationing. Often made from leftovers of a previous meal to save waste.

Buttercross or butter cross: A type of market **cross** associated with English market towns and dating from medieval times. They were located in the town or village marketplace, where people from neigh-bouring villages would gather to buy locally produced **butter,** milk and eggs.

Butty: Short form of the term 'a buttered sandwich'.

Brylcreem: An emulsion of water and mineral oil stabilised with beeswax, invented in Britain in 1928 as a men's hairstyling product.

Carrot-cruncher: Liverpudlian slang for a person who lives or works on a farm, or in an agricultural setting.

Chunter: To mumble.

Commercial traveller: A person representing one or more vendors who wish to sell their wares to retail outlets.

Div or divvy: Liverpudlian slang for a stupid or silly person.

Getting bladdered: Getting drunk.

Inglenook: A recess on either side of an open fireplace for sitting to keep warm.

Judy: Liverpudlian slang for girlfriend or wife.

La': Pronounced 'L-A-R'. Liverpudlian slang for person, 'Come here, la', I want to speak to you'.

Lav: Shortened British form of the word lavatory.

Lorry: British word for a truck.

Lychgate: Also known as a Resurrection Gate. Used at the entrance to churchyards to rest the coffin before it's carried into the church for a funeral service.

Nomark: Liverpudlian slang for a person of no importance.

On the rob: Liverpudlian slang for stealing.

Newsagent: A retail outlet that specialises in selling newspapers, tobacco and candy.

Rum one: Term used by older British people to mean cheeky or mischievous.

Sag Off: Liverpudlian slang for leaving or not going somewhere, without permission, 'I sagged off school today.'

Sarky: Shortened form of sarcastic.

Sausage roll: Sausage meat contained within a flaky pastry.

Scoff: British slang for eating.

Scran: Liverpudlian slang word for food, 'I'm going home for some scran'.

Shilling: A UK coin used until 1971, worth approximately four US cents today, the cost of a pint of beer during WWII.

Sixpence: A UK coin used until 1971 and worth about two US cents today.

Soft lad: Liverpudlian slang for a stupid person often used as a 'friendly insult'.

Squaddie: A private in the British army.

Snug: A small private room or area in a traditional British pub with access to the bar and a frosted glass window, set above head height. Modern pubs tend to be 'single room' establishments.

Sweets: Candy.

Tally man: A person who calls door-to-door, collecting debts.

Thrupenny bit: A British coin used until 1971.

Telling porkies: London 'cockney' rhyming slang for a lie. Porky pie = lie.

Toque: A traditional tall hat worn by chefs.

Two-shilling piece or Two bob: A British coin used until 1971, worth ten per cent of one British pound sterling.

Ten bob: Ten shillings, fifty per cent of a pound in British pre-decimal currency.

Waste of space: British slang for a person not worth wasting the time of day with.

Wellington boots: Latex knee-high waterproof boots with a name derived from the Duke of Wellington, a famous nineteenth-century

British army commander and later, prime minister.

Woolly back: Liverpool slang for someone living in a rural area.

WVS: Acronym for the Women's Voluntary Service. Founded in 1938, members carried out a wide range of services to keep the 'home front' going, from assisting with the evacuation of children from British cities to the countryside to operating 'tea wagons' after air raids.

Wherry: A traditional sailboat used for carrying goods and passengers on the Norfolk & Suffolk Broads.

Your Old Man: A wife's husband.

About the Author

Keith Finney grew up in the North West of England listening to two distinct sounds: Brass band music and a loud hooter calling employees to work at the town's cable making company.

Discovering construction sites involved working in foul weather, which he hated, so Keith opened a joinery business soon after completing his apprenticeship, and ran this until entering teaching in his early thirties.

Over the following twenty years, Keith steadily rose through the ranks, ending up as an Assistant Principal at a large college of further & higher education in Norfolk, England.

Now retired, he divides his time between writing mystery stories and helping mind his two youngest grandchildren. However, his wife calls into question Keith's definition of 'helping'.

Keith Finney is the author of the successful self-published Norfolk Cozy Mystery series, together with Lume Books, Lipton St Faith Mysteries.

Keith loves hearing from his readers and you can email him at keith@keithjfinney.com.

9 781839 012235